IRRESISTIBLE

R.C. STEPHENS

Copyright © 2020 by R.C. Stephens (Irene Cohen)

All rights reserved.

No part of this book may be reproduced in any form or by any electronic or mechanical means, including information storage and retrieval systems, without written permission from the author, except for the use of brief quotations in a book review.

Resemblance to actual persons and things living or dead, locales, or events is entirely coincidental.

Cover Designer: Sara Eirew

Photographer: Sara Eirew

Editor: Lauren McKellar

Proofread: Christina Gwin

LETTER TO THE READER

Dear Reader,

I am so excited to bring two worlds together. The character's from Irresistible are a combination from my best selling military romance, Halo and Corinne Michaels best-selling Salvation Series. Avery Montgomery is a single mother from my novel Halo who lost her husband in an IED explosion. By coincidence her deceased husband's name is Liam. The reason I bring this up here is that I do refer to Liam Dempsey from Corinne Michaels Salvation Series in my new book and I wanted to prevent any confusion from the start.

A little about Irresistible...

It's crazy but I feel like this book wrote itself. I kid you not. I haven't written a book this fast, like ever. It was just fate that Avery's love was meant to be Bennett Sheridan, a SEAL who was injured. I don't want to give too much away here, but this book is about true love, fate and new beginnings. If this is your first time reading one of my novels then I thank you from the bottom of my heart for choosing this story. I hope you will fall in love right along with Avery and Bennett.

XOXO

RC

CHAPTER ONE

Avery

After a long shift at the hospital I come home tired and hungry. I open the door to Jessy's room. She's sitting at her desk doing homework. That's usually where I find my daughter this time of night.

She lifts her head. "Hey, Mom." Her smile is sweet. Her long blond hair falls over her left shoulder. She's such a good kid. Grounded, smart, beautiful.

"Hey hon." I smile back but it's tired and lacking enthusiasm.

"You look exhausted." Her lips turn down.

"I am." I frown too. Every bone in my body hurts.

"What are you working on?" I ask.

"Pre-calc. It's a pain in my ass," she says, rolling her eyes.

"We all got to do what we got to do." I shrug.

"I know," she answers, exasperation lacing her voice. I ignore it. As long as she's getting good grades and working toward her future, all is good. "By the way . . . I passed the driving test."

"Wow! Why didn't you text me? You said you would try to go with Rory. I thought her mom wasn't available," I say.

"Sorry. I wanted to surprise you. Now you can take me driving," she says, since there is graduated licensing in Jersey.

"I'd love to. Maybe tomorrow after work?" I ask.

"Sounds good," she says.

"I'm going to shower. I'm beat. I need my bed. Congrats again, honey." I walk over to her and kiss the top of her head. My daughter can now drive a car. *Wow.*

"Good night," she says as she picks up her pencil and continues her homework.

"Good night, sweet pea," I say softly.

My feet are cramping as I head to my bedroom. I turn the knob on my door.

"Avery, is that you?" Aunt Bee calls from her room.

"Yes," I say softly. Dammit. I was hoping to go to sleep undetected.

"Dear, would you mind making me and Uncle Jim a tea?" Her voice rises on the word 'tea' as if she feels bad for asking.

"Sure." I turn on my heel.

"Oh, and dear?" she calls out, her voice scratchy and high-pitched.

"Yes?" I answer, trying to hold back my nerves.

"Would you mind making a sandwich? Your shepherd's pie was a little dry today and we're hungry," she says, her voice saccharine. I don't know why she asks me to cook for them when they complain about my meals all the time. If she can do better, she should do it herself.

"Sure thing, Aunt Bee. Any suggestions for the type of sandwiches you want?" I answer, trying to appease the woman. I've almost saved enough money to move out. Jessy and I have stayed here twelve years too long.

"Uncle Jim will take a grilled cheese—he loves the way you fry them up—and I'll have an egg sandwich," she says.

I roll my eyes. Freaking hell. I knew she would ask for something complicated when I am dead on my feet.

"No problem." I grit my teeth together.

As I walk downstairs, the door to Jessy's room creaks open

and the pads of her soft footfalls come up behind me. "What's up, kiddo?"

"Nothing. I'll make it for them. You look exhausted." She sighs.

I exhale too. She's the one thing I got right. "Thanks, but I'd rather you do your homework," I answer. *You know, so you don't end up like your mom, having to depend on people who take advantage of you.*

"I'm almost done." She smiles sadly. "You go sit at the kitchen table. I'll make you a tea," she says in a sweet, commanding albeit quiet voice.

"What did I do to deserve you?" I ask.

"You're a great mom. I wish you would just use the money Dad left behind so we could have our own life already. You're sure not staying here when I leave for college," she says as I take a seat at the kitchen table. My legs are so tired they feel like two logs and my back is a little sore.

"We have time to worry about that," I remind her, rubbing my neck. I feel like an old thirty-three-year-old.

"It'll be here faster than we realize." She's right, but I don't have to admit it. I scoff instead.

Jessy presses the button to start the kettle and pulls a pan out of the drawer. I'm just so proud of her. If only Liam could see what a fine girl we created together.

She places the cup of tea in front of me. I pick it up and inhale the steam. Jessy gets to work on the sandwiches.

"There's a party tomorrow night at Justin's house. Is it okay if I go?" she asks.

"It's a school night," I remind her.

"It's a Thursday, and everyone is going." She looks down at the pan and flips the bread. Her hunched shoulders and pensive brows tell me there is something else going on.

"What is it?" I ask.

She blows out a harsh breath. "Are you some kind of mind reader?" she asks, her tone carries a hint of exasperation.

"Only because I made you, gave birth to you and raised you," I remind her.

She nods like she's heard that one before. Her lips quirk on the right side. "Dylan asked me to go with him," she blurts in a nearly incoherent mumble.

"Who's Dylan?" I ask. I know all her friends pretty well. They've been hanging out together since middle school.

"Dylan Anderson. He's new. His family just moved here from Australia," she says with nonchalance. My mind draws a picture of a young Chris Hemsworth holding a surfboard. In my vision, a lot of young women flock around him adoringly. Plus, the kid has an exotic accent. What teenage girl wouldn't become stupid over that?

I take a slow breath. *Jessy is not you,* I remind myself. I was a wild child, grasping for love and affection anywhere I could find it. Turned out it wasn't love I was getting, and it only made me feel emptier. I got pregnant one night at a party and while I don't regret having Jessy so young, I do wish I had followed a more traditional life route of grow up, go to college, get married and finally, have a kid.

"Mom!" Jessy whisper-shouts, snapping me from my thoughts. "Can I go or not?" She holds the plate with the grilled cheese sandwich in one hand and the egg sandwich in the other. She is responsible, smart and beautiful. *She is not me.*

"Yes, you can go. Will I get to meet this Dylan?" I ask.

"Yeah. Tomorrow."

I take my tea and follow her up the stairs.

"You're going in there. It can't be me. I may dump the sandwiches on their heads or maybe smash them in their faces," she warns playfully but there is a hint of truth to her words.

She follows me into my room so I can place my tea on the side table next to my bed. I walk back out to the hallway, take both plates from her and place a peck on her cheek.

"Thanks, kiddo."

"You're welcome, Mom. Love you. Good night."

"Love you too."

Jessy heads into her room and closes her door. I head to my aunt and uncle's room. They glance at the plates, judgement painted on their raised eyebrows.

Damn it.

I forgot the tea.

"Here are the sandwiches. I'll run down and bring your teas," I say, knowing exactly how they like it.

I turn on my heel. It's not like I'll get a thank you out of them.

My legs are barely carrying me as I prepare the tea using the already boiled water. Aunt Bee will probably complain it isn't hot enough.

I head back upstairs my body and mind exhausted. I place each of their teas beside them. "Good night," I force a smile.

Uncle Jim nods with his mouth full of grilled cheese while Aunt Bee doesn't even acknowledge me.

So be it.

I saunter back to my room, open my closet door and take down the old brown shoebox sitting on the top shelf. I pull out his letter and read it—a nightly ritual I can't seem to stop.

Dearest Avery,
It's funny how life turns out, isn't it?
We didn't have some full-blown love affair. I know I didn't sweep you off your feet or make your heart skip a beat but when push came to shove, we were family. We stood by one another and that meant something to me.
I love you. I loved you, and Lord knows I know I did a bad job of showing it. For that, I'm truly sorry. Maybe it was my messed-up childhood—maybe it was how much my feelings for you scared me. Leaving you and Jessy each deployment tore me up. I wanted to open up to you and share my feelings each time I left. I tried, believe me, I tried, but there was this concrete wall inside me, tall and strong, a fortress of sorts that prevented me from showing both of you.
I know I erected that wall to protect myself as a kid. That wall kept me

from feeling, and that's what saved me from my brutal childhood. I thought it would continue to save me, but it only divided me from the only family I ever knew. The pain of feeling distant from you and Jessy was like a blade cutting me open slowly, deeply.

I pause, reminding myself to take deep breaths. My chest feels so tight, air is begging to pass through. I fear gripping the letter too tight and it ripping. I would have nothing left of Liam then. Nothing at all.

I try to drag some air into my lungs to release the tension I feel and continue reading.

The sad part is that I know if you're reading this letter, I'm gone. I never had a chance to make amends. I never had a chance to show you how much you both meant to me. How much I love you. Don't ever doubt it. I'm a selfish man, Avery. I never claimed to be anything else, but you, dear wife, hold my heart.

I clutch the worn paper to my chest. His words are piercing and cathartic all at once. Why couldn't you tell me this when you were alive? How many nights did I cry myself to sleep feeling alone and unloved?

As a glutton for punishment, I continue to read.

I have one last request. I don't want you to be scared to fall in love. To give your heart. Not every man will be like me. I didn't hold you dear and it's my biggest regret. Your heart is so full of love. And Jessy? She is the best of both of us. She deserves a father and you deserve a husband who will cherish the ground you walk on. There is a man out there— believe me. Don't be scared. If I had a second chance to be a better husband, it would have been me.

Tears flow down my cheeks like a river run wild. His words gut me every time and bring me peace all in one messed up wave of emotion. Gosh, Liam. I didn't know how to break your walls down. My heart wasn't warm enough to take a sledgehammer to them. I read on.

My last wish, Avery, is that you give your heart. I need to know that I didn't completely shatter your trust in men, in love. I will be smiling down on you and Jessy from heaven knowing you are well taken care of. Knowing that another man could give you what I couldn't.
Love you always and forever,
Liam

I fold the paper and slide it back into its original envelope. It's been fourteen years since he died, and I still haven't found love. Sometimes I just think I may be broken.

Liam was right; we didn't have some whirlwind love affair. We basically went to the same high school and attended a party one Friday night where we both got drunk and had sex. Sad part is, he wasn't even my first. I had given my virginity to Tony Fantino three months prior. We had dated for a couple months and things just felt right. He made me feel wanted and I confused the intimacy we shared for something more. So I gave him something I could never get back and then he broke up with me a week later.

I finally place the envelope in the brown box and place it back on the top shelf of my closet.

Breathe, Avery. Breathe.

I take a change of clothes and head across the hall to the shower. After going all these years without a man, loneliness has become my best friend. I don't even believe in love. Sure, I love my daughter, but I've never felt heart-pumping excitement over a man—not even Liam. We were too young. Too naïve. Too in too deep.

I try to push my loneliness away to a place that doesn't make me feel so empty. I finish my shower and slip into my pajamas. Then, like I do on many other nights, I lie alone in bed, staring at the ceiling. Fantasizing about a life where I found love. Where Jessy has a loving father like Liam mentions in his letter.

I take another deep breath. Tomorrow will be better. It's a lie, but hey, I've become good at lying to myself.

CHAPTER TWO

Bennett

"Maybe we should leave," Quinn whispers quietly.

"No, man, we should wait. Look at him. He has no one," Jackson says. "He needs us."

My eyes are closed but I'm awake. I hear every pitiful word. I'd rather pretend I'm asleep than talk to either of them. I don't need to see the pity in their eyes. I don't want to fucking see it. I'm drowning in a boatload of it right now without their help. Problem is, my back is screaming from pain. Flipping to my other side is impossible on my own but it's what I need to relieve the pressure. Pathetic asshole that I am.

"Things are messed up, man. Ashton is still not trusting me," Quinn says.

"She'll come around," Jackson answers.

Their voices seem more distant now, like maybe they're on the other side of the room. Maybe I can press the call button for the nurse to come without them noticing. Then, when she comes into the room, she can kick them out. I have nothing to say to either of them. Luckily, the call button is by my hand and I squeeze it. The pain is too much. I need more meds.

It only takes a minute for the door to swing open. My eyes remain shut.

"You buzzed, Mr. Sheridan?" a woman's voice asks. I have no choice but to open them.

It's Nurse Peterson today. She turns to look at the two large men standing in the corner of my hospital room, raising her brows. "Gentlemen, I'm going to need to ask you to wait outside," she says, matter-of-factly.

"Of course," Quinn says, looking pensive. Jackson nods and follows him outside. What is Jackson doing on this side of the country anyway?

She turns back to me and walks up to my bed. "What can I help you with, Mr. Sheridan?"

"I need to turn on my other side. My back is killing me," I groan. I don't know what's going on, but the pain is getting worse, not better.

Her lips turn down. This is my routine a few times a day. I'm a helpless fuck who has a piss bag by his bed because he can't make it to the bathroom.

The nurse maneuvers the sheets under me, and grabs hold of my arm, leaning herself over my body. She pulls the sheet beneath me so that my body will shift.

"Shit!" I scream as my back goes into spasm. The pain sucks the air from my lungs. I've shouted worse expletives in this poor woman's face, but I can't help it. The agony sucks me under like nothing I've ever felt before.

"Sorry, Mr. Sheridan. Doctor ordered we lower your morphine dose. He doesn't want you becoming addicted."

"Give me something else. Anything. I can't live like this," I croak, my throat feeling dry from the stagnant air in this room. Now that she has me on my other side, the strain on my back lessens but the pain in my knee still pulses angrily. I can't catch a breath.

"You're about two weeks post-op on your back. Only a week out on your knee. A couple of weeks and you'll be able to start physical therapy. You have a long hard road ahead of you, sailor, but I can tell you're tough and it will only get better as time passes."

"Time does not feel like my fucking friend," I snap, not meaning to. The fucking pain has me by the nuts. What kind of life is this? A shitty one. I should've fucking died in that explosion.

"You have some fellas outside waiting to see you. Are they friends?" she asks with a smile that isn't contagious.

"Yes," I splutter.

"Well, then I won't keep them from their visit with you," she says. "If you don't need anything else . . ."

"Can you make sure the piss bag is covered? I don't need them seeing that shit," I say my cheeks flaming.

She frowns again and walks over to a cabinet that sits above a sink. She pulls out a sheet and tucks it to the side of the bed, arranging it so the folds drape over the embarrassing round bag.

"There you go. If you need anything else just buzz," she says sweetly, which makes me feel bad for being such a sourpuss.

"Thanks," I mutter. "Talk to the doc about the meds. I'm losing it here," I say, sweat beading at my forehead.

"Okay," she answers, but I know it's going to be moot.

The two fuckers I call friends walk back into the room. "You shouldn't have come," I say.

"I'm living in Jersey now. I plan to be here a lot," Quinn says.

"I'm here on a short visit because of a job Cole was hired to do. I'm glad I had the chance to come see you," Jackson says, his tone filled with emotion.

"I can't talk. Too much pain," I say, clenching my jaw. "Fuck, this is crazy. Weeks ago, we were fighting terrorists; now, I can't go to the bathroom myself." I try to shift my body and scream from the pain. "Just go," I say to them.

Quinn takes a few steps toward me. "Look, man, it'll be hard for you to be in here a few months, but you got to do what you got to do, right? I mean, you need to get better. They say you can start PT in a couple weeks," he says, sounding so fucking hopeful.

"Then what? Huh? Fucking look at me. I have a metal rod in my back. There is no way the navy is taking me back. What the fuck am I supposed to do? I probably won't even walk right. I'm a fucking nothing. You should leave," I boom, as pain and anger consume me. "Just fucking go," I say, reaching for the cup of water on my bedside table. I pick it up and it slips through my hands and falls to the floor, causing a splash.

Jackson picks up the cup and looks to me sympathetically. Quinn opens his mouth and takes a step toward me but Jackson taps his shoulder and whispers something I can't hear.

Quinn shakes him off. "I was there too. I lived through the same explosion that day. King is gone, but Trevor, me and you? We made it out. We get to live." His lips quiver while his eyes gloss over but he won't a shed tear because that is the type of men we are. We don't cry; we take care of shit. Only I can't because I'm a fucking useless mess.

"Quinn, do me a favor and take your grateful ass out of here. I don't want to see you guys. I have nothing to say. You getting the message?" Again, I'm shouting and I don't know why.

Jackson knocks Quinn in the shoulder. "Let's just go, man."

Quinn turns to look at me like he doesn't know me. That's okay because I don't know this version of myself either.

They walk out the door. I punch the side rails of my bed as hard as I can.

"Mr. Sheridan, Mr. Sheridan. . ." There is more than one voice screaming my name.

"Bennett!" someone shouts.

I open my eyes. Two nurses and an orderly are in my room. I stare at them in shock.

"Mr. Sheridan, just take a deep breath," Nurse Peterson says in her calming southern accent. I do as she says but then the pain takes over and I groan.

"It hurts," I croak.

"I know, Mr. Peterson. Your injuries involved nerve damage and were close to your spine. There are so many nerves that can trigger and hurt. I know it's hard. It does get better, please believe that, but if you make abrupt movements like you just did you can reinjure yourself and make matters worse. I'm going to call the doc in just to make sure no damage has been done," she says softly.

"Meds please," I beg, because right now, nothing feels beneath me.

"Let me see what I can do. Maybe I can grab you some Naproxen," she says.

"Thanks," I sigh and try to close my eyes, but it feels like time is standing still. The nurse is wrong. Time isn't making things better. Time isn't on my side because it isn't moving, and I can't live like this.

CHAPTER THREE

Avery

After I change into my scrubs in the locker room, I head over to the rehabilitation office to check in.

"You look energized," my boss and good friend Kathy beams.

"Nope, I'm totally exhausted. I think my cheeks may still be rosy from the spin class I just did." I laugh.

"Well, good for you. I don't know how you do it. There's nothing on this planet that would entice me to wake up at five thirty a.m. to get on a bike or anything else." She smiles.

For me, it's a big stress reliever. But I don't say that out loud. People tend to draw conclusions when you've been single for, like, ever.

"I love it." I shrug.

"I know you do. Good for you, sweets."

"So, what's on the agenda today?" I ask.

"You got a new patient. Injured SEAL. Fractured vertebrae with a metal rod and nerve damage in the knee. They are weaning him off morphine. Doctor Simmons thought that some laser and ultrasound therapy may help reduce the inflammation faster so we can get him into PT," she explains.

"Is he able to come down to the gym area? Or should I treat

him in his room?" I ask, since on rare occasions we do conduct therapy in a patient's room.

"He's still confined to his hospital bed, so you'll have to bring the machines to him," she explains.

"No problem," I say. We go over the progress of some of my other patients and I head to the supply room to collect the ultrasound and laser machines.

With one device perched on my shoulder while pushing the other device in front of me, I head into the elevator and up to the fourth floor.

"Hey there, Avery," Sutton says, wheeling his way over to me.

"How you feeling today? Been doing any of those arm reps we practiced last week?" I ask him. He's only about twenty-four years old and he'll be in a wheelchair for life.

"Yes, my arms are killing me, but I'm not complaining. Could be worse, right?" he asks me back. His optimism is endearing. He was wounded during a training exercise.

His family lives in Alabama. They were here when he first got injured but they had to get back to their jobs.

"You're an inspiration. Honestly. Most guys that come through here don't share your positive outlook," I say, smiling to him.

"This is the life that the Lord gave me. I might as well do the best I can," he answers.

"Amen to that," I say. I've never really been overly religious, but Sutton's faith is truly inspiring. Even though I'm not a psychologist, I still deal with the mental wellbeing of my patients. Sometimes recommending some religion can help. I've seen it with my own eyes.

"Do you think you can help me with my technique on the arm pull up? I think I have it wrong."

"I'm starting with a new patient today. I have to check in at the nurse's station, but I can stop by your room later to see you," I explain.

"Sure, no problem. Maybe if you have time after your shift, we can watch something on Netflix together," he suggests.

"That sounds perfect. We'll need to find a new show to watch—maybe something a little more chill. I swear I started biting my nails from *The Blacklist*," I say. He laughs.

"I was thinking of *The Irishman*. It's like three hours long though," he says.

"Let's aim for Thursday night. Jessy isn't home then," I say.

"I'll keep that day open since, you know, my social calendar is so full and all." He chuckles, clearly joking.

"Is your family scheduled for a visit soon?" I ask.

"My sister is planning to drive over from Alabama for Thanksgiving. Mom and Pops said they would try to make it too, but we'll see. Not getting my hopes up," he says, and my heart cracks for him.

"Hopefully they can make it." I smile. I always have the biggest urges to cook a massive meal on Thanksgiving and bring all the patients with no family home.

"Oh, Avery, wait up. I hope your new patient isn't the dude in 4B," he says, whispering.

"Why's that?" I lean down a little so we are eye to eye.

"The man is mean and angry. Been giving everyone around here a real hard time," he says.

"I'm used to all kinds of patients. Don't worry about me. I've got thick skin." I wink. "You have yourself a good day and stay out of trouble."

"Yes, ma'am." He salutes me.

I smile and head off to the nursing station.

"Hey Cindy," I say, reaching the counter with my equipment.

"There you are. I've been calling you since last night," she whispers.

"Sorry, I got home late from work and crashed," I say.

"Clearly." She rolls her eyes playfully.

"What's up? Did something happen?" I ask because she looks like she has something important to tell me.

"I wanted to know if you were coming to Blackhead tonight. A bunch of us are going for beer. I want you to come; it will be so much fun," she whines quietly.

I shake my head, smiling. "No can do. Jessy is home early tonight."

"Jessy is going to go off to college soon, leaving you. What will you do then?"

Great—another reminder. "She's only two months into junior year. I've got plenty of time before my girl leaves me," I say. Truth is, time is passing so quickly. It feels like she just started high school yesterday and she's already a junior.

"Fine, say you'll come out Thursday night then." Cindy places each of her fists on each of her hips and waits. Both of her brows are raised as she waits expectantly for me to answer.

"I can't." I wince my voice raising an octave.

"If you tell me because Jessy is home then I'm taking you to the mental health department. You need to let that girl breathe," she says. She's being overdramatic. I give my daughter space. I just work a lot so on the nights we are both home, I like to spend time with her. Shoot me for being a caring parent.

"Actually . . ." My tongue clucks accidentally. "I'm staying here after work to watch a movie with Sutton."

She frowns. She isn't necessarily disappointed in me. She thinks I'm a good person for spending time with the veterans. She is worried about me.

"Woman," she whispers getting close to my face. She picks up her hand to cover her mouth and brings her lips to my ear. "You need to get laid, and fast. Your vag may have already closed up. This isn't natural. How many times do I have to explain it to you?" she says. I hold back my laughter because she takes my lack of sex life too seriously. "Did you at least use the dildo I gave you?" She pulls back and looks me in the eyes.

I bite my lower lip. "Not exactly."

She blows out an exasperated breath.

"Cindy, you know I love you, but love like that isn't in the cards for me. Maybe I'll start trying when Jessy leaves for college. I don't see the point of bringing a man into our lives right now. She's been raised well without a daddy," I say.

"I won't accept that you're a lost cause. I'll keep trying to get through. One way or another," she says with an evil tone, tapping the tips of her fingers together. "You're beautiful and such a good person. You have so much to offer."

"Thank you." I smile sadly. "I love you too." She's been my best friend since I started working here seven years ago.

"Now go off to 4B," she says.

"How do you know I've been assigned to 4B?" I ask, my brows dipping.

"He's been here a few weeks already. He's my patient. I'm the one who recommended to Doc Simmons that a little therapy might help. He's good-looking and built. A woman could do worse than spending time with him." She wiggles her brows.

"You're incorrigible, you know that?" I laugh, shaking my head, and with that I head into 4B.

CHAPTER FOUR

Bennett

There's a light knock on my door. I don't answer. It's probably Quinn and Jackson again, trying to convince me that life is worthwhile.

"Hi." A woman peeks her head into the room. "I'm Avery Malone, your physical therapist."

"I can't move, Sherlock. What kind of therapy do you think you can give me?" I snap.

"Okay then." She straightens her shoulders and pushes a machine into the room. What is she, deaf or something?

"I can't start therapy. Not for a couple weeks. You've made a mistake," I say, my voice gruff. I've spent the last few days without any morphine and the Naproxen does shit.

"No mistake, Mr. Sheridan. I'm just here to give you some ultrasound and laser therapy," she says in a singsong voice.

"Look, lady, I'm on edge right now. This isn't a good time," I bite out. I begin to try and turn to my other side since the pain in my back is getting to the point of unbearable. I wince and a string of expletives leave my mouth.

"Let me help you," she says, walking briskly to my bedside.

"I don't want your help," I snap.

She flinches, taking a step back.

"Let me just show you a better way," she says. "You need to move with your body. Try to use your abdominal muscles to pull yourself up, then twist. The way you're twisting now is just aggravating your injury."

"Okay, yeah," I mutter. She sounds like she knows what she's talking about and I'll do anything to make the pain stop.

She places her hand on my abdomen. "Is this okay?" she asks. "You look muscular and strong, but I want to feel you activating these muscles here. Right beneath my hand."

As she speaks, I take in her features. Silky long blond hair tied back in a ponytail that swings with her movement. Almond-shaped brown eyes, high cheekbones and full, pouty lips that call to me on a frequency I've never heard before. Fuck me. Where did this woman come from? I don't want to feel the attraction simmering under my skin. It tells me I am alive, and I was happy feeling dead inside.

"Mr. Sheridan, is it okay if I touch your abdomen here?" she repeats her question because I've apparently zoned out.

"Fine," I snap, pushing away whatever feelings were threatening to erupt. I don't want to feel. I don't want anything at all. I just want to be left alone.

"Good, now use your abdominal muscles and be sure to keep your spine straight. No twisting. Once you've reached an almost seated position, you will need to use your arms to shift your body sideways. Does that make sense?" she asks, watching me.

"I think so." My voice comes out gravelly.

I pull up like she says and I don't feel the knife cutting pain I usually do.

"Good, I can feel you have a lot of strength in your abdomen. We will need to make sure you have a strong core too to help with your recovery but not yet. Now, pull a little higher then use each hand to plant just behind your glutes here." With her free hand, she takes my hand and places it where she wants. She's close enough that I can smell her and it's heavenly, like a mix of lavender and vanilla. It's intoxicating.

"Okay, now use your gluteus maximus to shift yourself to the side. Use your arms for support. I can see you have a strong upper body. Use it to your advantage," she says, and I hold back a laugh. What the hell did she just call my ass?

I follow her orders because what she's saying eases my pain and I haven't sat upright on my own for weeks. Every muscle in my body feels tense from lack of movement.

I flip to the side.

"Excellent, now lower yourself down slowly. If you like, I can lift the head of the bed a little. You don't have to lie so flat. On my end, it would be fine for you to be upright as long as your entire spine remains straight."

"Raising the bed would be good," I say.

She presses a button and my head raises. She's right; I feel the blood flowing through my body. I take another easy breath.

"I wanted to start ultrasound and laser therapy today. It doesn't involve much. The ultrasound is basically using sound waves to ease the inflammation and the laser does the same thing for the same purpose. The ultrasound machine requires a gel and may feel warm on your skin. If you feel any discomfort, please let me know right away and we can stop," she explains.

I nod. If it will help with the pain, it's worth a try.

"I'm going to put a sheet on your lower end to keep you covered. I need to have the back of your hospital gown open so I can access the injured area," she says.

"Okay."

She places a sheet on my ass and opens my hospital gown. I can't see her, but I hear her pushing buttons on a machine because it makes a beeping noise.

"Okay, I hope the gel isn't too cold. It takes a few minutes to warm," she explains as she puts the machine to my back. "How does that feel?"

"Tender. Still painful." *But also good because I really like your hands on me.* Geez. I've turned into a slime bucket.

"It should be getting warm now. It will increase blood flow and reduce inflammation," she says.

Yup, blood flow is definitely increasing, but inflammation is not reduced. It's the first time in weeks I've thought of something other than my pain.

The machine warms, like she says, and it feels good. I close my eyes and enjoy her touch as she moves the machine along the aching muscles in my back. Twenty minutes or so passes.

"Okay, now we can move on to your knee. Is it okay if I wipe the lubricant from your back?" she asks. My eyes move to her lips and my thoughts run away with me. Damn, I need to stop this now.

"Yes, thank you," I say politely, realizing I've been acting like an ass to everyone around me. They don't deserve it and I know better, but I am tired of the pain. I'm tired from not sleeping and feeling so damn useless all the time. Most of all, I'm scared of what my life will be like now as an injured, jobless vet.

"Of course. Did you find it helped with the pain?" she asks, pulling me from my thoughts.

"A little, yes," I say. My body isn't so tense and it doesn't hurt to breathe.

"Now for your knee. I can just lift the blanket and press the laser on your knee from an angle. I don't want to ask you to move again. I know it takes a lot of energy. Pain can get really tiring but honestly, once we get you moving, you're going to feel so much better," she says.

"What's the point of trying? My life is meaningless now," I say quietly.

She pauses and watches me like she truly hears me. It's unsettling.

"Ignore me. I don't know what I'm saying. I want morphine. I want to feel like I'm floating. I don't want to feel at all."

"Your feelings are common around here. I see a lot of patients that have been through some terrible things. With effort and perseverance you'd be surprised with how far you can come," she says.

"The navy sure isn't taking a guy with a metal rod in his back and a leg that doesn't work. I'm out of a job. I've been yanked out of the only life I know," I answer, rubbing my head. I feel a headache coming on.

"Let me grab you a cool cloth," she says.

She walks over to the sink in my room and opens the cabinet above it, taking out a face cloth. She wets it and returns to me, placing it on my forehead.

"Thank you," I sigh, my eyes pinched shut.

"You're welcome. I know the Naproxen isn't as helpful as morphine but getting addicted to the morphine will lead to a lot of other problems. The hospital likes to remain cautious," she says.

"This sucks. Everything just sucks right now," I say.

"If there is anything I can do to help you let me know. I'm around quite a bit." She smiles sadly. I see the pity party floating in her gaze. Fucking great. "Are you up for some laser therapy on your knee? You can say no."

"If it will take away any pain, then I'll try it."

She cleans off the wand she was using and covers my back then moves to the other side of my bed and lifts the blanket up to my thigh. My knee has a crisscross of scars all over it but at least the stitches are out. "Make sure to tell me if I'm pressing too hard. I need to apply some pressure to reach the inflamed tissue behind the kneecap," she explains.

I nod. I can't be affected by this woman. Even though I would let her touch me any way she wanted.

She applies a little too much pressure, but I don't say a word. It's crazy but I just want her in here a little longer.

There's a knock at the door. I want to scream to whoever it is to fuck off and not come back, but I have to tame the beast that's taken residence inside me since the accident. There's another knock.

"Yeah," I shout. A nurse wouldn't knock twice.

"Hey man." Quinn sticks his head in the door. "Nurse said you were getting PT; that's great news. Said I could probably come in because you're about done."

"Yup. We're all done." Avery stands from the stool she was sitting on and I give Quinn the stink eye. Talk about bad timing. "I'll check on you in a couple hours to see how you're feeling and then we can decide together if you would like more ultrasound therapy tomorrow. Have yourself a good rest of the day, Mr. Sheridan." She gives me a curt nod, collects her machines, gives Quinn a clipped smile and walks out of the room.

Quinn stands off to the side until she leaves and then a shit-eating grin takes over his face faster than I can tell him to fuck off.

"Nice-looking PT you got there, bud." He winks and takes a seat by my bed.

"Fuck. Who told you to come back?" I mutter.

He laughs and shakes his head, giving me an I-know-you look.

"What the fuck is wrong with you? Do you have something in your eye?" I ask giving him a wry smile.

"No, but something definitely caught yours. I know you better than the back of my hand," he says.

That part is true. We were on the same team for years. You learn a lot about a person when serving side by side and facing death together.

"She's a hot woman. So what? She's my PT and I'm . . ." My voice cracks. *I'm broken.*

"You're what? A SEAL who got injured. That's all. You're still the same man, Bennett, honorable and loyal. Your injuries and that accident didn't change who you are. You're a stand-up guy that jumped into the line of fire before any of us saw it coming and for that, I am grateful," he says.

"I just wish I wouldn't have survived. I have nothing. No job. No family," I say. Did I really say those words out loud? Fuck me.

For some reason my head feels clearer now than it has in weeks. The pain is easing a bit.

"You've got family. I'm your family. Jackson, Trev, Liam, Mark—we are all your family," he says adamantly.

"The other guys are part of Cole Security. I barely see them, and Trev isn't doing well, and you're going back in. I can never do that. I've been given a medical discharge. I'm a fucking invalid," I splutter.

"Stop talking shit. You're not. I'm not going back either. I got my discharge papers. Ashton is pregnant, man," he says and his lower lip quivers.

Emotions I haven't felt in a long time hit me hard right in the center of my chest. "Fuck, man, I'm happy for you, bro." I extend my hand to him but I lift it too high and my back spasms. I scream out from pain and Quinn flinches.

I try to laugh it off. "I'm a fucking mess."

"You'll get there," he says. I want to believe him but it's too damn hard to picture.

"Anyways, I've taken a job at Cole Security. I wanted you to know. I'll be staying here in Jersey so expect to see my face," he says with a bastard smile.

"If I don't have a choice then fine," I say sarcastically.

"And Bennett, the guys at Cole are good men. I know we haven't spent a lot of time around them but now that I am a part of the team, they've taken me in. It's been good for me," he says.

The guys at Cole are all ex-SEALS. Some of them were active duty at the same time as me but on different teams so we have come across each other quite a bit over the years, but I don't share the same bond with them that I do with Quinn.

"I'll see you soon," he says. He doesn't try to shake my hand, considering my reaction last time.

"See you."

He walks out of my room and I'm alone again.

CHAPTER FIVE

Avery

I can't get out of the room fast enough. It was important that I do my job right. That I help this man with his pain—that isn't a question. So why the hell is my heart beating so fast? It feels like it will pump right out of my chest. My hands are shaking. What is wrong with me?

You know what's wrong with you. You thought that man was hot.

No, it was more than that. Something in the depth of his molten eyes called to me. His beauty is hidden behind a wild beard growing all over his face, but it's there, nonetheless. His sculpted cheekbones and full lips are still visible. Damn, his lips make me think about kissing them.

Geez! What in the hell is wrong with me? This is not me. I don't melt over a man. I see a handsome man and move on. Getting affected by good looks is not how I operate, that's for damn sure. That was something teenage Avery did.

The problem is the man in there was more than good looks. His dark eyes were filled with despair. He's broken. He's hurting. He's lonely, and I can relate.

I can hear him talking to his friend through the door. I should not be eavesdropping on a patient, but I can't seem to move either. He just looked so lonely. I know that feeling all too well. Even though Liam my deceased husband and I weren't in love, he was there for me. We became family. He had my back. Well, at least he did when he was around. When he was deployed it was me and Jessy. I learned how to become a mom the hard way—by making mistakes. I was lucky to have other SEAL wives around who offered advice and cooked meals. It was nice to be a part of a community in that sense.

Cindy stops in front of me, her head tilted to the side. "Avery, darling, are you okay?"

I jump like I've been caught with my hand in the cookie jar. Getting seriously attracted to a patient is seriously against hospital rules.

"Me? Yeah, totally. Why do you . . . uh . . . ask?" I stutter. I fucking stutter. Shit, Avery, get a grip. It's like I've digressed into a teenage girl version of myself.

Cindy's brows draw together, and she taps her chin with her pointer finger. "You've met Mr. Tall, Dark and Handsome," she says. "Huh! I knew it. Not even you're immune to him," she says, sounding proud of herself.

I take a deep breath and straighten my shoulders. "You're seriously nuts. There's nothing wrong with me." I attach the wand to the side of the ultrasound machine and put the laser pen back in the pack. "I need to get going. I have another patient in the gym in five minutes."

It's a lie. My next patient isn't for about a quarter of an hour but there is no way I will stand here and let her grill me. I need to figure myself out first. This isn't me. I'm just having an off day.

I begin to push the ultrasound cart toward the elevator without another word. Why is my heart still beating fast? Dammit.

"Yeah, sure, right. You keep telling yourself that Avery Malone," Cindy shouts behind my back.

I wave goodbye. I take a right and press the elevator button. When I'm in the elevator, my phone vibrates. Since I'm not with a patient, I take a quick peek. It's Jessy.

Jessy: Is it okay if I go over to Rory's house tonight? We are going to study together.

I sigh. My baby is growing up and she is out of the house more and more lately.

Me: Sure, have fun.

I send Cindy a quick text.

Me: I can do drinks tonight. Looks like I'm flying solo.

Cindy: Yay! We're gonna have so much fun.

After a long day I head home and prepare some roasted chicken and potatoes for dinner. I leave the cooked food on the counter and head upstairs to take a shower. Aunt Bee and Uncle Jim are probably on their daily evening walk. They walk rain or shine, which suits me fine because I get the house to myself.

After my shower I put on a pair of skinny jegging jeans and a simple heather grey cotton shirt. I brush my hair and let it air-dry despite the dropping temperatures outside. I don't go out very often, so I've never invested in going out clothes. There isn't a sexy thing in my closet. Most of my paycheck goes into savings every month except of course for any necessities Jessy and I need, and the food I buy for the household.

I look in the mirror feeling very plain. I head into Jessy's room and borrow a new pink lip gloss she just bought. I pucker my lips and look in the mirror. I'm still not excited about what I see.

The drive to the bar isn't far. I figure it's better I take my car because I don't plan on drinking more than one beer and this way I can leave whenever I want. Cindy is at a table with some of our co-workers. I spot Kathy, my boss, a nurse named Beth, another named Tina and a couple of the doctors. Whoa! I'm not the social type. This is going to take a lot of effort from my end.

I walk up to the table with nerves in my stomach. Everyone looks laidback, happy, and maybe a little tipsy. The women look sexy and the men look *GQ* chic.

"Avery girl, I'm so happy you made it." Cindy stands to give me a hug. Everyone at the long table stops their conversation and they all focus on me. They say hi and I answer them individually. Doctor Rudgers smiles and waves. "Nice to see you, Avery. Glad you could make it."

"Thanks," I answer with a smile.

"What kind of beer do you want?" Cindy asks.

It takes me a moment to answer. I look at the table to see what everyone else is drinking. Dr. Rudgers stands. "You ladies have a seat. I can go over to the bar and get you what you like," he says to me with a wide smile. He's a handsome young doctor. He can't be older than thirty-two.

"That's okay, Dr. Rudgers. I can go get the drink myself," I answer, fixing my shirt.

He smiles and raises a brow. "Avery. May I call you Avery?"

"Yes," I say hesitantly. Gosh, why did I hesitate? I am so awkward. He motions for me to follow him away from the table. I figure he wants me to walk with him to the bar.

"Please call me Colin. We aren't at work and truth is, I've wanted to get to know you outside of the hospital for some time," he admits and his cheeks flush. *Whoa. Is he hitting on me?*

"Oh."

I feel Cindy's gaze burning a hole into my cheek. I side eye the table because we haven't gotten too far away. As I suspected her smile is so wide it stretches from cheek to cheek. Her reaction causes a flush to crawl up my skin.

"What did you say you wanted to drink?" he asks me again furrowing his brows. My stomach sinks.

"I didn't," I say. Damn now I sound like a bitch. "I can buy my own drink." It comes out all wrong. I'm so bad at adulting. He frowns.

When it comes to men I'm weird and difficult. After getting knocked up at the age of sixteen because of a one-night stand, I became cautious.

"I know you can buy your own drink." Colin smiles like he thinks I'm cute and not testy. "But I would like to buy it for you."

Cindy walks over and elbows me in the ribs. Okay, fine. "Sure, that would be nice. Let me come with you. I want to see what they have on tap," I say. As I walk off, Cindy pinches my butt and says, "that a girl."

Colin looks over to me and laughs. It's friendly and relatively calming.

I lean on the bar and the bartender walks over. After he gives me a rundown of what's on tap, I choose the Guinness. Colin clinks his glass with mine. We both drink.

"So what do you do for fun?" he asks cheerfully.

"Not much." I wince. "I'm boring," I roll my eyes and try for a more playful approach.

He smiles flashing his perfect white teeth. "I'd love to take you to dinner sometime," he says.

I don't have a good comeback. He is a handsome doctor. I'm sure he can get any woman he wants. Why would he want a single mom? Why would he want me? Besides, I think he's handsome, but he doesn't get my heart pumping fast.

As soon as I think those words I startle and remember the debacle I became this afternoon inside Mr. Sheridan's room. It was like someone slipped a crazy pill inside my coffee this morning.

"Say something. I'm guessing your silence means that you're not interested," he says, and takes a sip of his beer.

"I'm just . . ." So awkward. "I just . . . I don't really date. I have a teenage daughter."

"I know, Avery. I've met her. Remember? She does drop by the hospital on occasion. You've introduced us," he says.

"Right. I have." I didn't remember that.

"So, what do you say? A friendly meal? We can get to know each other better," he says with a grin.

"I don't date," I blurt out. Gosh, this is just getting worse and worse by the minute.

He chuckles. "I can kind of tell," he says with a wince. "You seem to spend all your free time with your patients."

"And my daughter but when she isn't home, I spend time with my patients."

"I figured as much," he says thoughtfully. "But why so much time with the patients? When my shift is done, I can't wait to get home and relax."

"My patients are lonely. Some of them don't have families or friends close by who can visit. Me spending time with them makes them happy. Gives them something to look forward to," I explain. It gives me something meaningful to do so that I don't have to go home and hang out with my aunt and uncle who will just pile on my chores. Of course I leave the last part out.

"You're very sweet." He grins. "And totally beautiful." He leans a little closer his cheeks tinged pink. He's cute and charming and yet I don't feel a thing.

"Thank you," I say, because he did compliment me.

"So is it a yes to dinner?" he asks, sounding hopeful.

"If it's a friendly dinner, then sure, I'd love to," I say. I'm not one for fake smiles but it happens almost subconsciously.

"Great," he pauses and waits.

Does he want my number? I don't offer it.

"So we can make a plan at the hospital then," he suggests.

"Yes," I smile.

We head back over to the main table and get into the conversation with everyone else. He lingers a little close to me. He gives me looks and small smiles, and I tell myself he's a good man and yet I feel nothing. Like I'm dead. Cindy sees it and she frowns. Maybe she's starting to believe me when I say I truly am broken.

CHAPTER SIX

Bennett

The door to my hospital room begins to open. I take a deep breath. Who the hell is here to poke and prod at me now? Or maybe it'll be Quinn, reminding me to get my shit together. I can't even walk on my own so that's a definite no.

"Mr. Sheridan, hi, good afternoon. I wanted to see if you were up for some PT." Avery is back. She's been in here the last couple days giving me treatment. I want to talk to her, but I don't have it in me. I told myself that today I would try more.

"Yes, thank you," I say. She looks like a breath of sunshine.

She smiles and it's warm and friendly. "Just a reminder . . . you can tell me if anything we do feels uncomfortable or painful," she says, pushing the machine toward my bed. She doesn't look me in the eyes when she talks to me today and it completely sucks. She has warm brown eyes, soothing and calm. I want her to look at me. "I spoke with Doctor Simmons and he said you should be ready for your initial assessment on your knee. We can conduct the assessment here or I can call a transporter and we can do it in the gym just for a change of scenery."

I want to tell her the gym because I wouldn't mind leaving this room, but I am guessing the gym might be busy and I want my time with her all for myself.

"Here is fine," I answer.

"Sure. So if we can get you on your side, we can start the ultrasound treatment on your back," she says. She begins to lean over me to help me.

"I can do it myself. I've been doing it the way you showed me," I say.

"That's great." Her tone is cheerful. She beams, showcasing white teeth and cute dimples.

My heart skips a beat and then I get to work turning on my side. There is some pain, but I keep it to myself.

She walks over to the same cabinet she always goes to and pulls out a sheet. I really need to make a point of ordering some clothes online. It sucks having my butt exposed all the time. She leans over to place the sheet on me and I take in her familiar lavender and vanilla scent. I hear her pressing a few buttons and then the gel is on my back and she is using the machine.

Say something to her. Anything.

"So, have you been working with veterans' a long time?" I ask. I seriously could do better but I'm not on my A-game, that's for sure.

"Seven years," she says with a sing-song voice. "Were you a SEAL for a long time?" she asks. "If you don't want to answer you don't have to."

I like that she gives me an out. "A heck of a long time. I enlisted in the navy at eighteen straight out of foster care. Joined the SEALS a couple years after that."

"Did you grow up in Jersey?" she asks.

I like that she doesn't throw me a pity party over the mention of foster care. "I was in and out of foster care around New York City mainly Brooklyn and Queens," I explain. "Are you from Jersey?"

"Born and raised," she says. I wish I could see her face right now because I heard hesitation or possibly disappointment in her tone.

"Is that a bad thing?" I ask.

She laughs. "I don't know. It's boring. I grew up here, went to Seton Hall and raised my daughter here," she explains. "Sometimes I think it would be nice to live somewhere else."

"How old is your daughter?" I ask. I'm pretty sure I didn't see her wearing a wedding band but a woman like her is probably already spoken for.

"She's sixteen. A junior in high school. She'll be seventeen soon," she explains.

"Cool. I seriously thought you were under thirty. I guess I had that wrong," I say, knowing there is a fine line with mentioning a woman's age. She may hate me after that statement.

"Well, thank you." She giggles. "I'm thirty-three. Almost thirty-four," she says, and I think it's cool that she doesn't feel the need to hide her age.

"And do you have a husband or boyfriend?" I ask. Shit! Did I just really go there? *Not smart, Sheridan. The woman needs to fix you.*

She laughs. "I'm not sure I should answer that question. You are my patient."

"Aw! Come on. I bet you looked in my chart and know everything about me. Fair is fair," I say, playing hard ball.

"Alright. I'm single by choice," she says.

I want to say *tell me more, sweetheart*, but I don't want to push. We have time. *What the fuck? Damn*, her relationship status is none of my business. I. Have. Nothing. To. Offer.

"By the way, I didn't look at your personal details. I just reviewed your injury. How does the ultrasound feel today?" she asks.

"Nice. Good," I answer. *Your touch is magical.*

"Good. Okay." She removes the wand from my back. She takes some paper towels and wipes the gel off me. "If it's okay with you, I need to conduct an assessment of your knee."

"Okay," I say, and then I feel a pulsing headache starting. I use my thumb and pointer finger to rub my temples.

"Do you have a headache?" she asks.

"I have an everything ache. I can't sleep. The pain meds they give me don't take the edge off," I say.

"I'm sorry you're having such a hard time but as time passes you will get better," she says.

"That's what they keep telling me. I'm waiting to see results."

She takes hold of my foot with one hand and places her other hand behind my knee. "Let's take a look at your knee and get things moving. I'm going to go slow. I need you to tell me if I'm hurting you."

"Okay."

She begins to move my leg slowly, engaging my knee joint. I bite my lip.

"This hurts?" she asks.

"Yes," I answer.

She moves in another direction and then another and then she places my leg flat on the bed. "I'll be able to get a better sense when we can get you on your back. You'll have more movement then."

"Okay."

She takes some notes in a folder.

"I think we should have our next session in the gym. I know you have to be in bed another week, but we can transport the whole bed there," she explains.

"Whatever you think is necessary," I say. Our eyes lock. Our gazes hold.

She exhales. "Do you have any guests coming in this week to visit?"

"I'm not sure. My friend Quinn lives in town, but he's been MIA," I say because I tried calling him these past few days and he hasn't answered. I figure he must be on duty with Cole Security now.

"Okay. Do you have a spouse or girlfriend?" she asks.

My eyebrows raise and I smile. "Now you ask me? Why didn't you ask me when I asked you?"

"I'm not asking out of personal interest, Mr. Sheridan. It's just this place can be a bit of a bore at night. Sometimes I watch TV with some of the patients here," she explains, her cheeks resembling a Red Delicious apple.

I frown. "It does get boring and to answer your question, I'm on my own. Given my previous employment I was married to the job. At least that's what some of my exes complained about."

"Okay. Well, I'll be Netflix binging with another patient tonight. We'll be watching a movie tonight if you want to join—you're welcome. Hopefully it will tire you out and you will sleep better," she says.

I don't like that I've been invited along with another patient but hey, I'll take what I can get.

"Sure, yeah," I say.

"See you later, Mr. Sheridan," she says with a sing-song voice again and she pushes the equipment out of the room.

"Please, call me Bennett," I answer.

"See you later, Bennett," she says with a hurried smile as she walks out the door faster than usual. Maybe she's late for another patient.

"See you, Avery," I say to her back, watching her leave. She has this way of making my days seem better and right now, I'll take anything not to feel like death.

CHAPTER SEVEN

Avery

What did I just do? My insides are shaking. This has to stop. I have a crush on my patient. On Bennett. My mind races a mile a minute. I need to go to Kathy. What will I say to her? I've gone and developed feelings for a patient? That will sound completely unprofessional. I could lose my job. Anyway, nothing has happened so no need.

"Avery, there you are?" Cindy says, pulling me from my thoughts. Her smile falls when she takes me in. "Are you okay?"

I force a smile. "Me, yeah . . . w-why?" Sweat breaks out on my forehead. I can't even share this with my best friend. I love Cindy with all my heart, but she's terrible at keeping secrets and my job is on the line.

"I don't know. You seem off. Are you feeling well?" she asks.

"I-I'm I . . . feel a headache coming on. That's all. I'm still overtired from going out Tuesday night," I explain.

"I heard you and Colin have a date. I'm really happy for you," she says.

"Date? It's not a date. He said we'd go out for dinner as friends," I clarify, whispering just in case he's on-call.

"Oh dear." Cindy's lips squeeze together like she's getting ready to kiss someone and her eyes turn round.

"I was super straight with him," I say with a wince. "He was pressing, and I didn't want to seem unfriendly. I told him a dinner as friends would be nice. I'm hoping to put it off though."

Cindy smiles to someone behind me and then does a weird thing with her eyes.

"Nurse Connor. Ms. Malone." I hear his voice before I see him. I spin around to a smiling Colin, walking up to us.

"Hey, Dr. Rudgers. I'm off to check the patient in 4A," Cindy says quickly, then walks off, leaving us alone. I'm going to strangle her.

"I'm glad I ran into you, Ms. Malone. Are you free for dinner tonight?" he asks.

Shit. Shit. Shit. If Cindy heard it's a date, then he thinks it's a date.

I make my lips tilt up unnaturally at the corners. When did I become so fake? Gah. "I'm actually staying at the hospital late tonight."

His lips turn down and it doesn't look forced at all. He looks completely disappointed. "Don't tell me you're staying to hang out with patients," he says, like he just had a taste of something sour.

"Um . . .yes, that was my plan. I'm sorry. Rain check?" I ask, raising my brows. *Oh dear, why did I say rain check? I will never get out of this now.*

"Are you sure I can't convince you? We can go wherever you like. We can drive into the city," he offers, sounding hopeful.

"Colin, that is super sweet. I appreciate the offer, I really do. I've just got plans tonight," I say.

"Okay," he sighs. "I'll see you around. Have yourself a good day." He walks off.

Good, that's done with. I will need to go home after my shift and then come back since I want to meet this guy that Jessy is taking to the party.

I head down to the gym were my sessions have been scheduled for the afternoon.

I catch Cindy in the locker room at the end of the day.

"Dr. Rudgers has it bad for you, huh?" she says, changing out of her scrubs.

"Quiet, will you?" I whisper. Even though it's only us in the locker room, you never know who could walk in, or maybe there's someone in the washroom and we don't know. I don't want to be featured in the hospital gossip.

"Fine. Then should we talk about your reaction to Mr. Tall, Dark and Handsome?" she asks with all seriousness. I appreciate that she didn't mention a name or room number.

"No," I snap in a friendly way. "Please drop it." I push out my lower lip.

"Fine, I get it, but I'm calling you later. We need to talk," she says, giving me a pointed look.

"Call me later," I say, slipping on a pair of leggings.

"Are you going to work out?" she asks, looking confused.

"I want to try a class at that new Pilates place that opened on Seventh and Carlton. You interested in coming?" I ask.

"I told Carla I'd help her with a job application but let me know how it is. If you like it, I'd be willing to try." She smiles.

"Okay I'll let you know how it goes. Wish your sister luck on the job hunt for me." I grab my jacket, then my backpack, which I slip onto my shoulders.

"Thanks, I'll tell her. See you, babe," Cindy says, stuffing her scrubs into her backpack.

"Talk later."

The fall air is brisk as I walk to my Civic. I take a shaky breath. Cindy saw me after I left Bennett's room today. I was so shaky, and I had felt like I had this jolt of electricity running through my body from being close to him. This is really, really bad.

I begin to drive, and my mind is still filled with thoughts of Bennett. His dark hair. His wild and unruly beard. His molten eyes.

I don't know what my type is. In high school I went for the guys who wanted me. To my dismay, there were many. Liam had light eyes and his hair was a light shade of brown. He looked nothing like Bennett other than they are both tall, very muscular men.

Stop thinking about him in that way. Scolding myself doesn't help. My chest feels weird when I think about him. It's a stupid crush.

I head into the new Pilates place and take a class. I hope it will distract me from my thoughts. As I hold my plank, I'm giddy about going back to the hospital to see Bennett tonight. This can't be happening. How do I turn off a crush? Thank goodness Sutton will be there tonight too.

After class, I head home in my sweaty gym clothes. Walking in the front door, I see evidence that Jess is home. Her schoolbag is on the floor and her jacket is hanging on a hook.

"Jess, I'm home," I call out.

"In the family room, Maw," she shouts. "Can you take me driving soon? I need to practice," she says. It's only been a short time since she got her license but I still feel guilty that I haven't taken her to practice. She's only had time driving with her instructor.

"'Kay, let me just take a quick shower," I shout back.

Aunt Bee and Uncle Jim aren't home, which is a relief. I run upstairs and take a super-fast shower. I want time with my daughter before I start making dinner. After my shower, I towel-dry my hair, run a brush through it quickly, slip on panties and yoga pants and then a bra and long-sleeve T-shirt. I head back downstairs to the family room.

Jess turns her head from her laptop to look at me when I walk in. Her smile is knowing. "I don't know how you can shower and dress so quickly," she says. She knows I have my routine down pat. Aunt Bee has mentioned on more than one occasion that I should be careful not to use too much hot water and with Jess taking longer showers, I figure mine should be short and sweet.

"You know me." I shrug it off. "What are you watching?" I ask since she has her laptop propped on the side of the couch.

"Disney plus. *Wizards of Waverly Place.* I'm reliving my childhood." She blinks twice.

"Cute. I'm glad you're liking it," I say. I got a subscription for her as part of her Christmas gift. "How was school?"

"Same old," she answers, fixated on her screen.

"Any tests coming up?" I ask and take a grape from the bowl she has perched beside her on the couch.

"Pre-calc and Shakespeare, *Macbeth*," she answers. She pauses her show and looks up at me. "You know I have the party tonight. Right?"

"Yeah, I came home to meet your date. What was his name again?" I tap my chin.

"Stop being weird, Mom. His name is Dylan. Don't give him the third degree," she says, eyeing me in warning.

"Is he your boyfriend?" I ask because from what I know she hasn't had a boyfriend yet. I've been bracing myself for it for some time now.

"No," she says quickly, then pauses. "But I'm hoping that he will be," she says hesitantly.

I take a seat beside her on the couch. "Is he nice?" I ask.

"Super nice, Mom. He's different than the other boys. I can have a real conversation with him, and get this. He's seen *The Notebook,* and he liked it. He said he felt like crying when he watched it. How cute is that?" She looks up to me with puppy-dog eyes filled with young hopefulness and love.

"He said that, did he?" I say, hoping not to sound too untrusting. The kid sounds like a real charmer. I just hope he's genuine and doesn't want to just get in her pants. That comment about *The Notebook* puts me on high alert. "Well, I hope he's a nice guy and I look forward to meeting him. What time are you leaving?" I ask, just to plan my return to the hospital.

"Seven," she says. "Can we go driving now? Before you start dinner. I really need to practice."

I can't say no even though I feel slightly terrified at the thought of my daughter behind the wheel.

"Okay, let's go, but just around the block," I say, in case I feel like I will have a panic attack. It's better to keep it short.

We head to the front door. We both put on jackets and boots and I put a hat on my head since my hair is still damp and I don't need to get sick.

I pass Jess the keys and we head outside to the car. She starts the car and it all feels very surreal. She backs out of the driveway and stops abruptly when we reach the driveway's end.

"Good," I say.

"Are there cars coming?" she asks me.

"I don't see any," I say.

"Me either," she says.

She proceeds to back out but she hits the gas a little too hard and we fly back. Then she slams the brakes right before we are about to hit the curb. My stomach falls. What did I just get myself into?

"Okay, so where should we go?" she asks.

"Well, for starters let's move to the right side of the road in case a car comes," I say. Our street is quiet and a dead-end, but you never know.

Jess begins to drive toward the stop sign. She slowly comes to a stop.

"Good." I hold onto the handlebar.

"Are you nervous, Mom? You look nervous," she says.

Am I supposed to lie?

"Maybe just a little," I admit. "You're my baby and you're driving."

She merges onto the main street. "Where should we go?"

"You can take a right onto Cullen," I say. We almost reach Cullen and she hasn't signaled. "You need to use your right signal when turning," I remind her.

"Right, I forgot." She signals.

We get to a main street. "Are you going to be comfortable making a left?" I ask.

"Oh Mom." She rolls her eyes at me.

She signals and takes the left, only she cuts across a lane. Sweat pops on my forehead. It reminds me of when Liam taught me how to drive. My parents were too busy to teach me. I got my license when I was pregnant with Jess. Liam was kind and patient. I liked the attention.

"You'll need to get back in the left lane," I say. "Don't forget to check your blind spot."

By the time we get back home I'm completely drained. My body is tense and I feel drained. How will I get into a car with her again? She needs more lessons with an instructor but I don't want to insult her either.

"So, how did I do?" she asks.

"You're getting there. I think you can use more lessons," I say.

"Yeah, but for only a couple in-car lessons I'm really good, right?" she asks, beaming.

"For two lessons, yes but you still have a long way to go," I say.

"You hated driving with me, didn't you?" she says.

I can't lie. "I didn't love it. I'm sorry, honey."

"It's fine." She waves me off. We head back in the house and take off our jackets and boots.

"'Kay. I'll go get started on dinner," I say. I press a kiss to the top of her head and walk to the kitchen. This is the part of being a single parent that isn't so easy. Liam was so good when he took me driving. He was calm and cool. Teaching your daughter to drive is something a father should do. And now I feel even worse for not trying to find myself a partner earlier.

At ten to seven, Jess comes down with her hair blown out wearing a black body suit and a pair of loose jeans and converse. I take a breath. At least she knows she doesn't have to dress half-naked to get a boy's attention.

"You look amazing." I grin.

"Do you think I look too simple?" she asks, turning herself around. Her golden hair shines and sways as she moves.

"You look perfect," I answer.

"You're my mom; you have to say that," she says.

"Dude, I love you, but I tell you when I don't like something, and I'm telling you, you look beautiful." I nod.

"He's going to be here in like ten minutes. I'll go up to my room. Call me when he comes. I really hope Aunt Bee and Uncle Jim won't come home soon. Did they tell you where they are?" she asks, and I don't blame her. They aren't very friendly.

"No." I frown. They don't tell me where they are, which sucks, because sometimes I make dinner and they are a no show. If I serve it the next day, they'll complain about eating leftovers.

"Hopefully they'll stay out," I agree with my daughter.

"I feel like I'm burning up," Jess says waving her hands in front of her face.

"Aw! You're just excited sweetheart. I'm happy for you," I say.

I give her a kiss and she gives me a wide-eyed look with her doe eyes, and then she turns and charges up the stairs. I was thinking of slipping on a pair of scrubs for heading back to the hospital just so people know I work there and to make that divide between me and Bennett more transparent. He did ask for my relationship status and sometimes it feels like he's flirting with me but maybe he's just bored out of his mind and needs a friend. I'm sure that's all that's going on. I really need to get out of my head. Maybe a date with Colin would do me good. He is cute even if he doesn't cause a chemical reaction to go off inside my body.

The doorbell rings and I head to open the door. A six-foot-two teenager wearing a leather jacket with long floppy brown hair and dark eyes smiles at me at the door. "I'm here for Jess," he says.

"Yes, hi. I'm Avery, her mom." I shake his hand. He looks a little surprised and gives me a once-over. Given that I had her so young some people mistake us for sisters.

"Pleasure to meet you." His Aussie accent is thick. I can see what my daughter sees in this boy. I just worry that he has heartbreak written all over him. *Let her live her life.* She has a good head on her shoulders. *She isn't you. She will be fine.* I can't exactly leave her locked up in her room for eternity.

"Come in please." I take a step back and let him in. Then I walk over to the staircase. "Jess, your friend is here." *Is that what I am supposed to call him? Maybe using his name would have been better.*

The door to her room creaks open and then she walks toward the stairs, taking the steps slowly. I suddenly feel like I'm living out every teenage movie I've seen when a girl gets picked up for a date.

Jess's blond hair sways as she walks calmly, a light smile brightening her face. She reaches the front door and says, "Hi Dylan."

She isn't flushing or awkward. Not that I would expect her to be. I really don't know what I was expecting.

"You ready to head out?" he asks.

"Yeah," she answers, grabbing a coat from the closet. "Bye Mom." She kisses my cheek and she walks out the door.

Emotions crash through me like a wave threatening my balance. My baby is growing up. When I was her age, my parents didn't care to learn where I went or who I went out with. They had me late in life. I'm pretty sure I was a mistake, and then they died. I didn't have boys come to our door. I didn't kiss my mom goodbye. I'm overwhelmed to feel this way now—to have with Jess what I never had before. Tears slip down my cheeks, cold and bittersweet.

I grab my coat and scoot out the door before my aunt and uncle arrive home and ask me to serve their dinner. I head out to my car and drive back to the hospital. The drive is short, and I head up to the fourth floor, going to Sutton's room first. The lights are dimmed this time of night. Everything is quiet except for the night-shift staff making their rounds.

"Oh hey there, Avery." Monica, one of the night nurses stops me just as I am about to enter Suttons room. "You here for Sutton?"

"Yeah, we're going to watch a movie in the media room," I say, just in case she looks for him. "Mr. Sheridan will also be joining us too."

Her brows knit together and her head tilts to the side. "Really? Mr. Sheridan? I didn't peg him as the social type."

Her words irk me. Bennett has been in a lot of pain. It isn't fair to judge his character under the circumstances. "He's my patient."

"Nice." She tilts her head a little more to the side. I don't know what she means by the word *nice*. She sounds condescending but I am not going to call her out.

I usually get along with most of my co-workers. Monica does the night shift, so I don't see her all that much. I know she has a little boy at home. She lives with her mom, who watches him at night while Monica works.

"Okay, well you have a good night," I say.

"You too." She presses her lips together and gives me an odd smirk. Then she walks away.

I knock on Sutton's door.

"Yeah?" he calls out.

"Hey there." I smile, walking into his room. He's sitting in his chair, playing a video game on the TV.

"Hi Avery, just give me a minute. I'm winning," he says. He's playing some sort of NBA game.

"Sure take your time. I was going to suggest we watch the movie in the media room. I've asked the patient in 4B to join us and he is still bedridden." I explain why we need more space.

My comment gets Sutton's attention and he snaps his gaze to

mine. His lower lip is dropped, and his eyes are round. "You got to be kidding me. He sounds so mean. Seriously, nurses go running out of that room like it's on fire."

Hmm. I definitely don't feel that way. "He's been through a lot. When people are in pain, they aren't the best version of themselves," I say. I don't feel comfortable divulging any information about Bennett to another patient, but I add, "He doesn't have many visitors'."

Sutton's lips press together and he frowns. "Okay. Do you think he'll want to watch *The Irishman?*"

"Can't we watch something easy for once? Like something that will make us laugh?" I ask playfully.

Sutton considers my words looking pensive for a brief moment. "What does it feel like to laugh?" he asks, jokingly.

"Funny. I don't know about you but I'm tense tonight. Jess is out with a guy that wears a leather jacket and looks like a heartbreaker. I'm freaking out and need a distraction," I say.

"Good for Jess. She needs to get out more and enjoy life," Sutton says. He knows my daughter spends a lot of time studying in her room.

"I know. I'm trying to be cool about it," I say, rolling my eyes.

Sutton says he will head to the media room while I get Bennett.

I knock on Bennett's door before entering.

"Come in," he says.

I open the door and walk in. The lights are dimmed, "Sorry to bother you," I say taking him in. His dark hair looks like it's at that between stage when someone grows out their hair and it isn't long enough to form a style or short enough to look neat. His beard is wild but his sculpted cheekbones aren't fully covered and his lips are full and pouty. He's a beautiful disheveled mess. My heart stutters.

"You're never a bother, Avery," he says, his timbre deep and smooth. His voice does something to my insides.

"Did you still want to join me and Sutton for a movie? I just convinced him we need comedy," I say.

Bennett dark eyes are rimmed in darkness. What would he look like without the beard? "I can do comedy," he says. He isn't very talkative, but I get that he may be feeling solemn sitting here all alone in this room for hours on end.

"Great. I'll wheel you out there. We're going to watch in the media room," I explain. "It's kind of a central social area for patients but it isn't really in use this time of night."

"It's good to be able to leave the room. Thanks for doing this," he says. I don't know why everyone seems to think he's a villain. He's been polite to me.

We get settled into the room. Sutton stays in his wheelchair. Bennett is facing the large-screen TV from his bed and I take a seat on one of the La-Z-Boy chairs with my back leaned back and my feet resting on the footrest.

I yawn. I access my Netflix account. "What are we watching?" I scroll through the list.

"She always has chick stuff on her list," Sutton says to Bennett.

"I can see," he says dryly. He doesn't sound necessarily rude, just indifferent.

Sutton eyes me. I shrug slightly. He blinks and I blink back. There is an understanding between us. Many of the injured veterans feel low about life and themselves. Bennett's situation is familiar to Sutton who experienced it himself and to me since I work with the veterans.

"I was injured during a training exercise. Jumped off a plane and the chute didn't deploy properly. I'll never be able to walk again. I'm confined to this chair for life," Sutton says, looking at Bennett.

My heart lurches Sutton's words freeze me in my spot. I know the story but his bravery in sharing it with a complete stranger has me floored. He is truly an inspiration.

"I'm sorry. That's really rough," Bennett sighs and looks Sutton in the eyes.

"Yeah, it's rough. I don't think I'll ever get married. What kind of woman would want a man that can't walk?" Sutton says.

My heart clenches some more. It squeezes so tight I feel like I don't have air.

"I'm sorry, man. That's really awful and messed up." He takes a large gulp of air. "I was in the Middle East. I was a SEAL. My jeep was hit by an IED. Lost one of my best friends in the accident. I was injured but . . ." Bennett pauses. I don't know what I was expecting by bringing these two together but not this. I didn't think Bennett would open up to Sutton this way.

"You can say it, man. It's okay you aren't as bad off as I am. That's okay. I'm happy for you. I took the news hard at first, and then I said to myself there is a reason the Lord made me this way. My life isn't over. Just taken a turn I didn't see coming. I leave here in a couple of weeks and then I plan on going back to school. I want to get my degree in social work. I plan on working with injured vets. It's my way of still serving my country," he says. He looks over to me. "Geez, Avery, I didn't mean to get you all teary-eyed," he says in faux complaint.

I giggle. "You really are something special."

Bennett eyes me and eyes Sutton. "That's honorable," he says to Sutton. He doesn't say much else though.

"Let's pick a movie," Sutton says. "I swear she takes forever to decide what she wants to watch."

Bennett smiles. It's subtle and hidden behind his wild beard, but it's there nonetheless.

CHAPTER EIGHT

Bennett

Talking to this kid who must be in his early twenties has me floored. I don't know if Avery's invitation to watch a movie tonight was meant as a therapy session or not but hell, I feel like a fucking idiot. This kid has barely had a chance to live. I've got to at least have a decade or more on him age wise and he has his shit together. He knows what he wants. He's made new goals for himself. I'm just a loser treading water until I figure out which direction the wind will take me.

"How about *6 Underground?*" Sutton asks.

"I told you I need funny tonight," she says. They are clearly close. She must be a special lady to take such care of her patients. She turns to me. "My daughter took me driving tonight for the first time and then went on a date and I'm freaking out," she says with a wince. She picks up her phone to text. "I've been accused of being too overprotective, but Jessy is all I have." My heartbeat stutters. Her openness and caring is getting under my skin. I've never met anyone like her. She's so real it's unsettling.

"That sounds rough. I never thought of having kids," I say. I'm used to keeping things short and superficial with women. It's a habit I suddenly want to break.

She doesn't call me on my comment. I'm not sure if I am

happy about it or not. Eh! Keeping a lid on things is for the best. She's beautiful, sweet and smart, but she isn't going to want a man like me. Why bother even trying?

"Jess is driving," Sutton sounds pleased. "That's awesome. I taught my sister Caroline to drive because Maw was too freaked out."

"Well, since it's only me, I don't have a choice, but between me and you, my heart was in my stomach," she says.

Sutton winces.

"Now, no more talk about driving or dating. I need a movie to clear my head," Avery says, flipping through the Netflix options. "Oh! Oh!" She stops on a movie. It looks like a chick flick.

"I thought you didn't do romantic movies?" Sutton says, giving her a quizzical look.

"I don't," she says, and I want her to say more, to explain herself, but she doesn't.

"Well, it's fine by me. I grew up with three sisters. I've watched enough romantic movies to last me a lifetime, but hey, another one won't kill me," he says.

"Thanks Sutton." She smiles at him and he shrugs. "What about you, Bennett?"

Yeah! Bennett, what about you?

I cough to clear my throat. "We can watch whatever. I'm not picky," I say. *I actually find romance movies to be a bore but if it means spending time with you then I'll take it.* I am clearly developing a crush on my physical therapist, which is problematic on a lot of levels.

She starts the movie. Avery turns on her side and curls into a ball. I wonder what it would be like if we were a couple and we were at home watching a movie together, snuggled on the couch. The thought comes way out of left field. I've never thought about settling down or quiet nights in.

I watch Avery and her reactions more than I watch the movie. I think she said it was called *The Holiday*.

Sutton crosses his arms in front of him. "They are so going to hook up."

Apparently, the actors in the movie are well-known. I don't have a clue who they are. When I was home, I worked out and went out to bars. I didn't sit home and watch movies.

"That's the point of the movie," Avery says.

The male character shows up to his sister's house but it turns out his sister isn't there and he's too drunk to drive. Instead, he finds this hot woman. When the actors begin to kiss, Avery's cheek flush. I wonder what type of relationships she's had. Where the father of her kid is and why a beautiful woman like herself chooses to spend her free time at a veterans hospital instead of going out and living it up.

After an hour, the couple separates, and Avery's looks crestfallen. Her brown eyes are filled with tears that don't fall. *What is it about you, lady, that gets under my skin?*

Sutton catches me watching her and I turn away. The kid smiles to himself like he's happy he caught me. I wonder how much he knows about her. If I want to know more, I'll need to ask her more questions. Problem is I don't know if she will be interested in sharing answers with me.

The movie ends and Avery lets out a big yawn, stretching on her chair like a cat. Her body curves deliciously, pressing out her chest.

"Well, I'm beat. I'll head back to my room," Sutton says. I wonder if the kid is a mind reader too.

"I can walk you back," Avery offers.

"I'm good. The movie was cute. Thanks for coming in," he says. I wonder how he is getting himself into bed with only use of his arms. My heart aches for him—for all the special forces that serve our country and get hurt in the line of duty.

"I'm glad I did," Avery says. "You have yourself a good night. I'll see you in the gym tomorrow."

"Have a good night. See you tomorrow. And you too, Bennett. Have a good night." He winks at me.

"You too, Sutton," I say with a smile. The kid is pretty cool. He leaves.

"I can take you back to your room now," Avery says, standing and stretching again. She makes me want to do anything she tells me to do . . .

"Thanks." I want to say more but I don't know what.

She wheels me back to my room and locks the wheels on my bed. "You have a good night."

I reach out and place my hand on her arm. "Will you stay a little longer?"

She looks back to the door and then to me. "You want me to stay?" she asks, raising her brows.

"Yes."

CHAPTER NINE

Avery

His touch does something to my insides. *Everything I have been feeling is real. I want this man.* This beautiful, broken man with his wild hair and beard and kind eyes.

I should leave. I shouldn't stay. Being his therapist at this point is wrong. I've developed feelings for him. I don't even know how it's possible yet something is happening. When I'm not with him I am thinking about him and when I am with him my heart flutters. Staying is wrong. His touch causes a trail to blaze from my arm down to my core and it feels so very right that I can't resist.

"Okay. I can stay for a bit," I agree, moving out of his grasp because I can't seem to think straight when he's touching me. I pull up a chair by his bed and take a seat. "What's going on?"

"Nothing, I just like your company. When you come around something inside me eases. When I'm alone with these walls, my mind is constantly thinking what I will do with myself, or I focus on the pain and just spiral out on this self-loathing path that feels like a one-way street to hell. But with you here, it eases. It all just melts away," he says somberly.

His words surprise and soothe me. It doesn't mean he feels

the way I do. I'm attracted to him but he just views me as his healer. I think.

He chuckles. "I've scared you silent, haven't I?"

"No." I sit up straight and lean forward. "You haven't. I'm glad I can make you feel better. That is my job. The therapy should at least take the edge off—"

He shakes his head. "Not the therapy. You, Avery. You take the edge off."

My breath hitches. "Me?"

"You're so kind and caring. You're beautiful, and I know I'm way out of line. I'm not thinking straight, and I can't blame the pain meds because I think they have me on Advil's now." He laughs.

I laugh too. "I-I'm your therapist. I-I c-can't." I shake my head, unable to get the words out.

"Tell me that you feel something too. That I haven't gone and lost my mind. There is something here between us, right?" His dark eyes bore into me and something inside my heart cracks and then this overwhelming feeling washes over me like molten lava erupting inside me warming me from the inside out.

I nod and swallow hard. I can't fight this feeling. It's too much. Feels too good. I'm not thinking about my job or what this could mean; I'm suddenly embracing the moment, like Jude Law and Cameron Diaz did in *The Holiday*. There was a reason I didn't usually watch romance—because I didn't want to be reminded of what this feeling was or that it even existed. Yet tonight I wanted that feeling because of Bennett.

"Say something. You're killing me here," he says.

"There is something. I don't know what," I begin to say. He reaches his hand out to me and winces. I stand from the chair and take his hand. He pulls me gently toward him, his gaze never leaving mine. If I don't want this there is plenty of time to pull away. His lips are full and so darn kissable, and as I approach them my heart beats fast and steady. Our lips touch and my eyes close and fireworks erupt in my chest.

His lips are warm and soft, and as we deepen the kiss the spark between us ignites a heat down in my core. He knows how to kiss; his lips scorch mine as they move. His tongue peeks out and mine comes to mingle with his. Sparks fly between our bodies. The electricity between us is alive and magnetic. I want to put my hands in his hair and touch his beard but then I remember where I am and my eyes open. He must sense my hesitation because his eyes open too.

"Wow," he says.

His reaction makes me smile.

"I shouldn't have done that." I pull my hand away from his grasp. Anyone could have walked in. Nurse Monica would probably be all too happy to report me to human resources.

"Yes, you should have. I like you. We are two adults," he says.

"This is my job on the line. I can't lose it. I have a kid. It was irresponsible of me," I say.

"I won't tell anyone. I can promise you that," he says, and those thick lips of his curl into a sexy smile.

It's contagious and warm, and I smile too. "My lips must look swollen," I say, touching them.

"Your lips look like you've been kissed well," he says playfully.

I feel light and airy—happy. *When have I felt this way? Never.*

"Thank you for coming in tonight and making me watch that awful movie," he says, grinning.

"It was a cute movie and you're welcome," I say, and I'm pretty sure my voice sounds flirty. *Where on earth did flirty Avery come from?*

"You have yourself a good night," he says with a nod. For some reason, I picture him standing tall in his fatigues and smiling at me with a curt nod. This man is too hot.

"You too, Bennett," I say, knowing full well I have a smile plastered from cheek to cheek across my face. I turn out of the room, knowing I need to stop smiling and fast. As I am leaving, I see Monica. She gives me a once-over. *Shit! Can she tell what we were doing?* "Have a good night," I say to her.

"You too," she eyes me warily then looks down at her chart.

I can't get out to my car fast enough. When I do, I crank up the heat and my palms come up to my cheeks. I smile wide and laugh giddily. This is bad. Really bad.

CHAPTER TEN

Bennett

There's a knock on my door. I look at the clock; it's ten a.m. Fuck, she sent a transporter again. "Come in," I say.

It's been a week since I had the movie night with Avery and Sutton. A week since my lips touched hers and she rocked my world to its core.

"Hello, sir," the transporter says. "I'm here to take you to your physical therapy session."

Fucking great. I want her but she's sent him again. She hasn't said anything about the kiss. She's kept conversation with me to a minimum outside of what's necessary for therapy. It's driving me crazy. This isn't me. I don't pine for a woman's attention.

The transporter helps me into a wheelchair since I am able to sit upright now. He pushes me out of my room and down the hallway.

"Hey Bennett," Sutton says, wheeling past me.

"Hey man," I say, because it's not like the transporter has time to sit around and let me chat. "Catch you later."

He nods and waves. When I first met the kid, I pitied him. Felt sorry for him and the way he will have to live his life. Now I think he's got bigger balls than anyone I've ever met.

The transporter and I head into the elevator and I get

wheeled into the gym area. Avery is waiting for me holding a clipboard.

"Hello, Mr. Sheridan." She looks at me and gives me a professional smile. It's not what I want to see. I want the warmth in her smile like she gave me the night we kissed.

"Ms. Malone." I nod.

"See you tomorrow, Mr. Sheridan." The transporter says politely before taking off.

"How are you feeling this morning?" Avery asks, sounding too professional.

"Like crap," I scoff. "I'm still not sleeping well. Staying in one spot is making me crazy."

"Okay. Let's head over to the bed. I'd like to check your knee. How is it feeling?" she asks.

"Not great either," I say.

She wheels me over to a bed and then closes the curtain around us. The minute the curtain is closed, I can't take it anymore, I whisper, "Did that kiss mean nothing to you? Because it meant a whole lot to me."

Her eyes, which are more of a cognac-caramel color than brown, turn wide. "Bennett, please keep your voice down. If anyone hears us, I could get fired." She sounds terrified and that isn't my intention.

"I'm sorry. Will you at least stop avoiding me? Can you take me back to my room instead of the transporter?" I ask, unable to hide the hope I feel from my tone.

"We have protocol. I'll stop by your room later to see how the treatment went," she says. Her words ease something inside my chest. I shouldn't be pursuing a woman like her, not when I have nothing to offer, but hell, I'm not thinking straight when it comes to her.

She gives me ultrasound treatment and checks my knee. She gets me to do some strengthening exercises. I like this part of the treatment because it means I have her close to me. The heady scent of lavender and vanilla fills my nostrils.

"I want to take you over to the bars now. They are used to help you stand up. Are you okay with that?" she asks.

"I don't know. Small movements hurt," I answer.

"The pain is from the inflammation. The movement will be good for you. We can take it slow. It's just that we need to get you walking with a walker. Kind of like baby steps," she says.

"I'm back to being a baby?" I push out my lower lip for effect.

Avery frowns. "You're not. Your body has been through a trauma. You need to let it heal properly but you also have to build up strength again. You're a hero, Bennett, to this country and to our people. SEALs take care of some of the most dangerous tasks and ensure our safety overseas so we can be free to walk the streets here at home. That's a pretty big deal. You should feel proud."

"And how many guys have you given that speech to?" I chuckle.

She smiles and shakes her head. "Too many, but that is because they laid their life on the line for us. It's something that can't be overlooked. Not many men or women would do such a thing. Be proud of what you did. Don't let the negative feelings suck you under," she says. Her words resonate inside me. Not many men would lay their life on the line to keep America safe, but I had no one when I joined the navy. They gave me a purpose. They trained me to defend and protect. Now what?

My gaze returns to her and I see her eyes are watery. "What is it?" I ask.

She shakes her head and the tears welling in her eyes don't fall.

"Please, whatever it is," I say.

"Not here, Bennett. Please," she practically begs, and I let it go. If she lost her job 'cause of me, I'd feel worse than terrible.

She takes me over to the bars, but first she passes me some arm weights and guides me through some very slow exercises.

"These have to be done slowly. You need to activate the muscle, but you also don't want to pull something in your back."

"Okay." I do what she says.

After the weights, she shows me how she wants me to lean on the bars and use my upper-body strength to stand.

"You may only be able to take a few steps at first and that's okay," she says.

I slowly lean forward using the bars as support.

Avery stands close beside me. "Good. You're doing good."

"I'm holding my breath," I admit. I'm scared of the spasming pain.

"Breathe. Slow breaths," she says with her soothing voice. She takes slow breaths to show me and I follow. Before I know it, I'm upright. "That's great. You're doing really good. Now, if you can slowly move one foot in front of the other," she says.

"I can't believe I have to learn how to walk again but I guess there will be a lot of things that I'll have to learn from scratch. Like how to live my life outside the navy," I say.

"You'd be surprised at all the opportunities that are available out there for a guy with your skill set. I'm thinking you're going to be just fine, Bennett Sheridan," she sing-songs my name the way she did that first day she came into my room.

"I hope you're right," I say. "I really do,"

CHAPTER ELEVEN

Avery

After I finished my shift, I went up to say hello to Sutton and saw that Monica was on shift tonight. I don't know why but I want to avoid her like the plague. Something about the way she watches me doesn't feel right and her friendliness feels insincere.

I want to check in on Bennett like I told him I would but something about Monica's presence screams trouble and I don't need any. Instead, I head home and go through my usual nightly routine. Aunt Bee is in the kitchen, looking inside the fridge when I arrive.

"Oh, hello there, Avery. Jess is up in her room studying. Such a fine girl she is," she says, and I hate to think it, but the woman reminds me of Cruella.

"Thank you."

"I was thinking we could have some grilled salmon for dinner tonight. We haven't had fish in a while, and you know it's good for Uncle Jim's heart condition," she says, as if she didn't see the ground chicken breast defrosting in the sink.

Jessy likes the burgers I make. They are healthy and low in fat, so I'm still being considerate of Uncle Jim's condition—but Jessy hates salmon.

"I'll go out and grab some." I force a smile.

"That's so nice of you, dear," she says, even though she knows I don't say no to her. That I will do pretty much anything to keep the peace around here.

"Of course, Aunt Bee," I say, my tone even and kind. A part of me wants to scream out that it isn't okay, that she should appreciate my efforts around here, but she's given me and my daughter a roof over our heads. I don't want to seem ungrateful.

I head up to Jess's room. "Hey there. I need to run out to get Aunt Bee something from the supermarket. Do you want anything special?"

"No. Aunt Bee is such a pest. I was hoping we could do some driving practice tonight," she says quietly.

"Sorry, sweetie." Now I feel bad. "I'll see you soon," I say as guilt eats away at me. I need to spend time with my daughter, not wait on Aunt Bee and freakin' Uncle Jim.

"I'm planning to go to Rory's house anyway," she says her tone laced with disappointment.

"And will Dylan be there?" I ask.

"Yes, Mom," she says, fighting a smile. Her cheeks also flush. *My girl has it bad.*

"Okay, well can we at least have dinner together? I was going to make those chicken burgers you like."

"Yeah." She nods like it sounds good to her.

"See you soon," I say.

I head downstairs, grab my jacket and keys, and slip on my runners, then head out the door. The last place I feel like going right now is the supermarket. I usually like to get my weekly shopping done early Saturday morning when everyone's asleep. Now, the place will be packed.

When I arrive at the supermarket it is just as I predicted. Needing to weave around shopping carts stresses me out because I know I have to get home to spend time with Jessy before she leaves. The check-out line turns out to be a nightmare too and by the time I'm driving home, I get a text from Jess saying it's getting late and Rory's mom invited her to eat there. I feel like I am losing all around. Between missing time with Jess and giving in to Aunt Bee's ridiculous requests, I'm at the end of my rope.

I stop the car off to the side of the road and tell Jess to enjoy herself and head on over to Rory's now, since she said Dylan offered her a ride and I prefer that over her walking alone when it's dark outside. I make a note about talking to Jess about us moving out. I've wanted to buy my own house for some time now, and I finally feel like financially and emotionally that time has come.

When I get back home, Aunt Bee and Uncle Jim are watching television in the family room.

"Good you're back. I hear you're making salmon," Uncle Jim says happily.

"I am." I force a smile.

"Will you make that mango salsa that I like so much?" he asks.

"Sure, Uncle Jim," I say. Knowing that request would arise, I'd picked up some mango and cilantro while at the supermarket.

I get to work making dinner. While I prepare the salmon, I make the burgers too, figuring I can take one with me to-go. There's no way I am sitting to eat dinner with those two. I don't want to feel like I'm choking on my food.

I set up the table for them and use one of the ready-toss salads I picked up, and set it on the table with a balsamic vinaigrette. I call them to the table and they both have pleased expressions on their faces.

"Won't you be joining us, Avery?" Aunt Bee asks.

"I'm going to head into the hospital," I say. "You enjoy."

"That means more for us." She giggles, looking at Uncle Jim.

I inwardly roll my eyes. I grab my burger that I wrapped in some paper towel and head out the door. I haven't changed out of my scrubs, but now I just feel like I don't want to be here anymore.

I drive to the hospital. On the way, I call my old friend Halo. She lives in Chicago with her husband, Thomas. Thomas and

Liam served together. He was with Liam when the IED explosion happened. When Liam died.

She answers after two rings. "Hello?"

"Hey there," I say.

"Avery, oh my gosh. I'm so happy you called. I was just thinking of you this week," she says.

"Really?" I ask. "What's going on?"

"Thomas and I were thinking of spending Thanksgiving down in Jersey. We'd love to see you and Jessy," she says.

"Halo, you know I live with Liam's aunt and uncle. I can't really accommodate," I say, feeling kind of stupid.

"We aren't inviting ourselves over." She laughs. "My friend Jenny has an aunt who lives in some crazy mansion in Jersey. They're coming with their kids too. I was thinking you and Jessy could join us."

Getting away from Aunt Bee and Uncle Jim on Thanksgiving would be a dream come true but . . .

"I've kind of been organizing a big Thanksgiving shindig at the hospital. I hate that all the patients have to eat alone in their rooms. I've managed to get a few sponsors and we are holding a huge dinner. I'd love to see you guys though. I haven't seen Brandon and Macy for eons. They must be so big now," I say.

"They are. Brandon is growing literally by the minutes. Twelve-year-old boys are something special and Macy is sweet as sugar. She's taking dance and texting her friends all the time." She laughs. "Do you think we could crash your Thanksgiving meal at the hospital then? It would be really great to see you, and you know how Thomas is. He feels like he hasn't seen Jessy enough over the years and it's starting to eat away at him," she says. "I'd love to contribute to the meal and Jenny would too. Just let us know what we could bring."

Thomas was really good about coming around when Jessy was little. He is the only father figure she's really had in her life. Him and Liam were close. He would come and tell Jessy that her dad was a superhero and when he left, my daughter always felt good about who her daddy was.

"That sounds really great, Halo. I can check in at the hospital and see what we need. I'll text you. I can't wait to see you guys," I say. It isn't a lie. I love Halo and Thomas. They are a great couple, but being around Thomas makes old memories rise and it's painful.

"Me too," she answers.

"See you in a couple of weeks," I say. "Have a good night."

"See you soon."

Jessy is going to be super excited about their visit. I can't wait to tell her. As I close the call, I pull back into the hospital parking lot. I eat my burger quickly in the car and down a bottle of water. On some level I know that I need to get a life even if I am making some patients happy.

I head over to the second floor first. There's a new patient a female medic named Julia who was injured in the line of duty. She has broken bones in her hand, among other injuries, that will take some time to heal.

"Hey there," I say, walking into her room.

"Isn't it late for therapy?" she asks, wincing. Her face and body are black and blue. She has some stitches on her arm and close to her eye, and her right hand is in a brace.

"Just wanted to check in to see how you're doing," I say.

"I guess as good as I can be, considering." She shifts a little and winces.

"Well, we'll work hard on getting you better fast," I say.

"Thank you," she says. "The pain isn't too bad. I'm more upset that my husband and daughter were supposed to fly in tonight, but they couldn't make the flight."

"Where are you from?" I ask.

"Well we live in Cali. I'm originally an Ohio girl though," she explains.

"Hopefully they'll be able to come see you soon," I say.

"Yeah." She sighs with a far-off look on her face. She blinks. "This place is pretty freaking boring."

"I know. I've been working here for seven years. I watch military men and women come and go. There's an entertainment room—they call it a media room—on each floor, but I know that isn't always accessible with certain injuries," I say. "Have you tried Netflix?" I ask. I swear, there is something with soldiers and Netflix. They think TV watching is a waste of their time.

"Hell no," she answers.

I laugh. "I thought you might say that. You've got a choice of audiobooks, which can be cool; you should give 'em a try, or Netflix. You'd be surprised by the quality of programming they offer. I know sitting around and not being able to do anything is against everything your body knows and wants, but for right now, you need to heal."

"Okay, then show me how to turn the dang TV on." She snickers. "It's my right hand that's fried. I'll need to maneuver with my left."

I access Netflix on her television. I show her how to scroll through shows and then I say goodnight.

"Thanks for stopping in." She smiles.

It's these moments with my patients that give me purpose. I didn't think I needed anything more than this and Jessy—until I met Bennett.

I head up to the fourth floor. I shouldn't go to see Bennett, but I did tell him I would stop by, then I chickened out. I figure I will drop by Sutton's room to say hi first—that way Monica won't be on my case. Then I will have to slip into Bennett's room briefly.

I knock on Sutton's door but there's no answer.

"He's in 4B," a voice says from behind me.

I startle and turn around. It's Monica. "Sutton's become good friends with Mr. Sheridan," she says.

Since when? Of course, I don't ask that question out loud.

I walk over to 4B, knock, then push the door open. Sutton is telling Bennett a story about something and he's so animated that neither of them stop to notice my presence.

"Hello there." I smile, looking between these two men. If I didn't know better, I'd say it looked like they were old-time buddies.

Sutton pauses and looks at me. "Avery," he says excitedly. "I wasn't expecting you tonight."

"I had a change of plans and decided to drop by," I say.

"Hi Avery," Bennett says with his deep timbre.

"Hi Bennett," I answer, hoping to hide the shiver his voice sent down my spine.

Sutton looks between us and lets out a big over-exaggerated yawn. "I'm beat. It was nice talking to you," he says to Bennett. He turns his attention to me. "I don't mean to be rude, but I'm exhausted. My physical therapist made me work my ass off today." He grins.

I smile. "You have yourself a good night."

"You too, Avery," he says, and then wheels himself out of the room like he's been doing it all his life.

When the door closes, I turn to Bennett. "Did you say something to him . . . about us?" I can't hide the accusation from my tone.

He shifts up the bed and I can see the pain move across his face. "No, but I swear that kid is super smart—like, I think he's figured out life's secrets and everything." He chuckles, deep and throaty.

"He is special," I admit, exhaling.

"Glad you came in," he says, but his smile falls fast. "Why did you come in? Is your daughter out or something? I was expecting you this afternoon," he says, and my stomach dips.

"I'm sorry. I wanted to come see you but I'm paranoid after what happened . . . I can't lose my job," I explain.

"I'm sorry. I know. I'd never want that. I just wanted you to know that I don't make a habit of hitting on my nurses or therapists. What happened last week . . ." He scratches his beard. I feel like I'm sitting on pins and needles. "I like you. I've never wanted to kiss a woman so bad before."

My heart kicks up a notch. I don't know how to stop this giddy feeling. "Bennett I . . ." I'm not sure what to say. I surely can't admit it was the best kiss of my life.

"Don't worry; I get it. You're my therapist," he says with defeat.

"I like you. It's just, there are rules," I explain.

"I understand, I do. Can I ask for visits whenever you drop by at night? Sutton mentioned you visit often. I'd like you to drop by my room too. Of course, for friendship reasons only." He smirks deviously.

"Of course I'd like that," I say.

"Good. So take a seat," he says.

"Okay." I take a seat by his bed and take off my jacket.

"So, I don't mean to get personal on you, but do you not like where you live or something? Every time your daughter is out you leave," he says. Of course, I shouldn't be surprised that he's perceptive; he was a SEAL, after all.

"Huh . . . well, it's a long story. Jessy and I live with family," I say.

"And that's a bad thing?" he asks. "I don't mean to pry, but I would like to get to know you better," he says.

I don't know why, but I find it easy to talk with him. At least, it's easy when I'm able to keep my gaze leveled at his eyes and not wondering down to his thick lips. "I moved in with them after my husband died," I say. He flinches.

"I'm sorry. I hadn't realized . . ."

"No, don't worry; there's no way you could've known. He was a SEAL. Died when Jessy was two. It's been fourteen years. We are both fine," I say.

"Do you mind me asking if he died on active duty?" he asks, and the question doesn't surprise me. I've spoken to other patients about Liam. Some of them figured it's why I chose to work in a veteran's hospital. Maybe his death played a part in that.

"Yes, Afghanistan back in 2006. IED roadside. Only one man made it out alive," I say.

"Shit," he hisses. "I lost my best friend in the incident that put me in here. It's messed up."

"I'm sorry. I know it's hard, and everything seems dark and bleak to you right now, but it does get better," I say.

"Were you two high school sweethearts or something? You must've been young," he says.

"I became a widow at twenty. No, we weren't high school sweethearts," I say, not adding anything more.

"That's rough. My friend that died wasn't married. Didn't have kids," he says.

"What about you? I ask, and he raises his eyebrows. I manage a laugh. "Not do you have kids. Have you ever wanted them?"

"Nah, not after the way I grew up. Jumping around from foster home to foster home doesn't make for a memorable childhood. I always thought, what's the point?" he pauses and looks at me.

"My childhood wasn't all that great either," I say as I cross my legs. "My parents had me when they were older. I'm pretty sure I was conceived when they got back from a Rolling Stones concert. Spent all the money they had on the tickets and then found out that wasn't the only gift they gave themselves." I laugh.

"Are they still alive?" he asks.

"No, they died in a car accident when I was in high school," I say.

"Shit. I'm sorry," he says. I look at Bennett. He is so easy to talk to.

"It's fine. My life wasn't all that bad. I had good friends. Hung out with their families. Then I got pregnant at sixteen and my friends' parents didn't want their kids around me. Catholic neighborhood and all," I explain.

"I'm sorry Avery. That couldn't have been easy. I know all about living a hard knock life. My mom was a drug addict. I don't remember much. I'm pretty sure I was in school one day when social services came. That was the end of it. Never saw her again. I'm pretty sure she's dead," he says, staring out to the space in front of him.

"I'm sorry. That sounds really hard," I say.

He extends his hand to me. "You too, Avery. It sounds like you had a hard time too and here you are, just . . . amazing," he says. I give him my hand and he gives it a light squeeze and we stare into each other's eyes. I feel like I'm swimming in the depths of his mocha gaze when the door to his room opens. I pull my hand from his and clear my throat.

"Well, I'm glad I got a chance to come in tonight," I say.

Monica walks into the room. "Just wanted to check your vitals, Mr. Sheridan."

"Okay, well, I won't keep you. Have yourself a good night, Mr. Sheridan," I say.

"You too," he mutters, and I grab my jacket to leave.

My heart feels like it may beat out of my chest. That was a close call. I head down the elevator and straight out to my car. A sheen of sweat coats my skin. Even though it's cold outside, I don't wear my jacket, my overheated skin welcoming the cool November air.

When I get to the car, I call Halo. There is no way I can talk with Cindy about this. If she accidentally slips up and says something at work, it would be the end of me at the hospital.

The phone rings once.

"Avery. Are you okay?" Halo answers, sounding worried. We usually talk once a month, not twice in a day, but she is the only one I can talk to about this. I know she won't judge me.

"I'm fine," I exhale. "I just needed someone to talk too."

"What's going on? You know I'm always here for you," she

says. She's truly amazing. Thomas had suffered from severe PTSD from his deployments and Halo was a rock, pregnant and alone. She took care of Brandon by herself. *She'd understand me.*

"I've gotten myself into a bit of a jam. I don't know what to do," I say. Halo knows that my relationship with Liam was dysfunctional. Liam would tell Thomas what a screw-up he felt like.

"Tell me what it is," she says softly. "The kids are asleep in their own beds; you have my attention."

"I've met a man," I say, as if I've contracted a horrible disease.

She laughs. "Congratulations. Finally. Is that so bad?"

"He's my patient." I pause, my tone heavy. "There are strict rules at work about fraternization."

"We have strict rules about that at work too," she says. She's a teacher. "There is this couple at work. They met at school and were dating secretly. They are both teachers and we also have a fraternization policy," she says.

"And what happened to them?" I ask.

"It came to the principal's attention that something may have been going on . . ." she says.

"And . . . ?" I urge her to continue. I bite my nails, and I'm not much of a nail biter.

"They eloped and got married." She laughs.

"Halo. That scenario is so not happening to me. This man . . . he's injured. He's vulnerable. I could lose my job," I say.

"Do you really like him? I mean, you said he is a man, so he is clearly of age. You're both adults. I get why there are fraternization policies in place but when two adults like each other I don't see the problem," she says.

"He's an injured SEAL. He's been given a medical discharge. We . . . I don't know . . . I like talking to him and he listens, and I just feel this bond with him I can't explain," I say.

"I'm happy for you, Avery. It's about freaking time you found someone to be with. You're young and beautiful," she says.

"I can't be with him though," I say.

"He won't be your patient forever," she says.

"I'm guessing he has another four to five weeks of therapy," I say.

"Then wait," Halo says. "That way you don't risk your job."

"I . . . I kissed him at the hospital," I say, my voice shaking, but my insides burning as I remember the kiss and what it felt like.

"And is he a good kisser?" she asks excitedly.

"So good it felt like fireworks. I'm scared, Halo. When I see him, I want to kiss him and . . ."

"You're scared of messing up your job because you can't keep your hands off him," she says knowingly.

"Something like that." I sigh.

"I don't know what to say that would be good advice. This guy must be something special. I mean, you literally refused every blind date I've tried to set up for you. I don't feel right as your friend to tell you to wait or control whatever is happening, because it sounds like it's happening and I'm happy for you, friend," she says.

"Gah, that isn't helping," I groan.

"Sweetie, it should help you. Even if you do lose your job, you have a great profession. You can work in another hospital or clinic," she says.

"It'll be on my references that I messed up," I say.

"Then let's hope you marry the guy—that way, it won't be a messed-up situation, just a completely adorable love story," she says.

"I don't even know what to say." Halo isn't helping. My anxiety is increasing, along with my want for Bennett. "I get you, though. After what you went through with Thomas, I get why this is your advice."

She blows out a breath. "Exactly. I have the man of my dreams, but our road was bumpy as hell. I got my happy ending; I want you to have yours."

"Thank you. I just don't know what headspace Bennett is in. He was injured in an IED explosion and lost a friend; he's in a lot of pain. What if I'm some temporary relief to him? He said he doesn't make a habit of hitting on his caregivers, but he's also never been in a real relationship," I say, pinpointing the source of my worry.

"There's always a chance of heartbreak. It's scary, but if you don't take that leap of faith you'll never know. This is perfect timing, Avery, honestly. Isn't Jessy leaving for college next year?" she asks, and I want to scream.

"It's over a year and a half, thank you very much," I growl. "Why does everyone have to remind me? Sheesh."

She giggles. "Hey, I hear you. I'm not looking forward to my kids moving out either. All I'm saying is I want you to have love, to experience it."

"Thanks, Halo. I'm sorry for calling so late," I say, letting out a yawn and shiver. I start the engine.

"Call me anytime and keep me posted," she says.

"Have a good night. Say hi to Thomas for me and tell the kids I can't wait to see them," I say.

"You too, sweets. See you in a couple weeks," she says, and we end the call.

I slip on my jacket and drive home. The whole way home, I think of Bennett. Is Halo right? Should I take that leap of faith?

CHAPTER TWELVE

Bennett

"You seem close with your therapist," the nurse says as she takes my blood pressure. She's a pretty woman with long brown hair and green eyes but there's something about her that rubs me the wrong way.

"Not really," I say dryly. I don't want to give her ammo to ask more.

"Blood pressure is stable," she says, leaning over me slightly to place the cuff back on the wall. It feels like she presses her chest into my face. I don't like it one bit.

"Good. Thanks." I keep my gaze forward and away from her.

"Can I get you anything, Mr. Sheridan?" she asks with a sweet voice.

"No, thank you," I say curtly.

"You have yourself a good night," she says, smiling wide.

I know women like her. I can tell she's trying to get my attention and it isn't happening.

"Good night," I answer. She leaves. Why did she make that comment about me being close with Avery? I don't think she saw us holding hands. We had pulled away before she came around the door, but why would she ask that question? I know Avery visits a lot of her patients.

I push thoughts of the nurse aside. Maybe it was nothing. I think of Avery. I'd love to take that elastic she uses out of her hair and watch her hair tumble down her back. I wish I could have more time to see her smile. Just to be around her. She's so kind. So caring.

She's had a rough life too. She's a widow. I wanted to ask her a million more questions. She got pregnant at sixteen. Seems like she was alienated. She's so strong, vibrant. She makes me want to be a better man. Problem is, hospital rules. I can't get to know her better and have her risk losing her job. And what do I have to offer her anyway? Nothing.

I fall asleep. The next morning, Nurse Peterson is back. She's nice and professional. I meet up with the doctor and they send me for an MRI. It takes longer than expected and I miss my appointment with Avery.

Sutton stops by my room later in the afternoon. We hang out. He doesn't say anything weird about me and Avery, so I take it as a good sign. Hours pass, and I feel like I could lose my mind in here. I get up and use a walker to go to the bathroom by myself, which is a definite improvement. I take a shower on my own. Finally having privacy is nice. My legs aren't stable enough to stand for long periods of time, but I use a chair.

Back in bed, I wonder when I'll see Avery again. I don't even have her number. If I had it, I could text her and no one would be any the wiser. I fall asleep.

The next morning, the doctor comes in.

"Your healing is on track," he says. "Both the knee and back are looking good, which means we need to up your physical therapy. We need to get you strong," he says assertively.

"Sounds good to me," I answer, because that means I can leave this place soon and more physical therapy means more time with Avery.

"I'm going to recommend that swimming be added to your therapy sessions," the doc says.

"Sure, I'm up for that," I say. "I'm a strong swimmer. Was in the navy."

The doctor's lips turn down. "Mr. Sheridan, you've been through major surgeries; don't expect to be where you were before. It's going to take time, patience and perseverance. You may have to use a cane for walking from here on out. It's hard to tell at this point. I don't mean to sound like a downer; I just find that sometimes, with sailors of your caliber, your mind remembers your body in peak physical shape but after the trauma you've endured there can be setbacks, and the road to recovery isn't always easy," he says.

"That speech doesn't sound too promising," I scoff. *Way to dampen the mood, doc.*

"It's not meant to hinder your motivation. I mean to say you're a fighter. It's inherent in you so now you need to use that fight to get your body strong again. Don't give up because things seem difficult. It will get better," he assures me.

"Is that a promise?" I ask.

The doctor smiles and his eyes wrinkle in the corners. "If you put your best effort forward, I think you can do it," he says.

It isn't a straight answer, but I get it. The hospital staff have been really focused on mental health and pressing the *don't give up* theme. It's true that when the pain was bad, I just wanted to die, but now I have something to look forward to—more time with Avery. She makes me want to be a better man. It sounds like she doesn't have a whole lot of people in her life she can count on. Of course, I got my navy buds, and they are my family, but now that is going to change. Quinn is going to be a dad. Trevor is . . . I don't know, and King is dead. Sure, Liam, Jackson and Mark are good guys, but we aren't best buds.

"I'm going to give it my best." I say, finally answering the doctor.

"Good. I'm glad, Mr. Sheridan. I'll see you soon," he says. He tucks his clipboard under his arm and leaves.

That afternoon, a transporter comes for me. "I'm here to take you for PT," he says.

I can't help my smile.

CHAPTER THIRTEEN

Avery

I'm waiting in the pool area office. Halo's words ring in my mind. *It would be better to wait until Bennett is discharged from the hospital. Then we could get to know each other better.* I'm getting ahead of myself. He's only said he doesn't hit on other women. He's never mentioned dating or a future. I really need to brush up on my dating skills.

He should be here any minute. A transporter will bring him to the change room and a nurse is inside to assist him into a bathing suit. Since I was just in the water with another patient, my hair is wet and so is my bathing suit.

The pool isn't very busy today, but I do expect Kathy to stop by. She usually makes her rounds in the morning. Bennett is wheeled out to the pool area.

"Hi there. Good morning!" I smile to him like I would any patient.

"Enjoy your swim," the male nurse who brought him out says to him.

"Thanks," Bennett says with a friendly tone. He turns to look at me. "I feel like a real invalid. I can't even lean forward to get my own trunks on." He says it with a smirk, but I read between the lines. This part of the injury is always hardest on these men.

They are used to being these big, strong heroes and suddenly, they need help with mundane tasks.

"Swimming is really good for strengthening the back muscles. Let's work on getting you better," I say. My goal is to always focus on the positive so my patients can leave their negative thoughts behind.

"Okay. What should I do?" he asks.

"Let's get you standing first. You can hold on to me for support and then, when we reach the stairs to the pool, you can use the rail," I explain.

"Okay." He takes a deep breath to brace himself to stand. I help him up. "Is it okay if I help you remove your robe?"

"Yes," he answers and my mouth waters at the thought. Guilt washes over me. *Focus on your patient.*

I slip the robe off his shoulders. He looked like a big man with his clothes on—well over six feet tall for sure—but now, with his robe off and his muscles on display, I'm thrown off. I don't know why. A lot of soldiers and sailors are in peak shape. Bennett's shoulders are cut and sculpted, wide and strong.

I walk him slowly over to the rail. He doesn't say anything. When he reaches the rail, I say, "Slowly lower yourself into the water. It's a perfect temperature; I've been in today."

He does as I say and while he's entering the water, I drop my robe. I wear the most unsexy speedo bathing suit for work. It's black and plain. I get into the water after him then walk up to him.

"Geez, woman," he hisses as his eyes rake over my body. His molten eyes leave a path of heat in my own body.

I lean into him. "Please, Bennett. My supervisor could walk in any moment."

He clears his throat. "You're beautiful," he whispers. "That's it—I'll behave now."

His words wash over me like a warm salve. "Thank you. Come walk over to the wall. You should feel more stable in the water. If anything hurts, let me know," I say.

I grab a flutter board, knowing the SEALS are strong swimmers. "Hold on to this. I want you to kick your legs out. Go slow and easy."

He grabs the flutter board like I say and holds, plunging his body into the water so he can kick out his legs. It also puts his face equivalent to my chest.

"Avery, you're ruining me," he hisses. He takes me in, and I haven't felt this sexy or wanted in . . . ever.

I look down at him, proud of the progress he's made, but I also notice that my nipples have puckered involuntarily. *Oh, my.*

We move on to some more exercises. Bennett is clearly enjoying the stability the water provides and with the help of a support, he walks around the pool.

"You're doing really great," I say.

"Good morning, Avery," Kathy's voice calls to me from behind.

"Good morning, Mr. Sheridan," Kathy says. "How are you feeling today?"

"Good. The water feels nice. I can actually move," he says.

"Glad to hear," Kathy says with a small smile. "I'll catch you later, *Avery.*"

"Okay." I smile.

Kathy leaves the pool area and I breathe a sigh of relief.

"That your boss?" Bennett asks.

"Yes," I answer as he walks to me and I walk backward.

"Something is up with her. She seemed on edge," he says.

"Don't go using your SEAL skills on my boss," I say quietly, a hint of laughter in my tone.

"No, I'm telling you to raise your guard because something is up," he says.

His words jostle me. "I really hope not," I say.

"Even if it is. We're both consenting adults. Right?" he asks.

"Yes . . . but . . ."

"No buts. I won't be in here forever. I want to get to know

you better. Even outside this hospital. I know I'm injured, and I don't have much to offer," he says.

"Bennett . . ."

"Avery, please. Just hear me out fast. Give me your cell number. That way I can call you. No one would know it's me you were speaking to. I'll set my phone to unknown caller," he says.

I laugh. "Have you thought of everything?"

"Maybe." He bites his lip and a droplet of water rolls off. How I want to kiss him. Have my hands all over him. Run them over his shoulders and down to his six-pack. He has a light sprinkling of hair on his chest that runs down the center of his abs. Everything about him is sexy and masculine. My insides throb.

"Tell me your number. I'll memorize it," he says.

I shake my head. This doesn't even feel real.

I give him my number.

When I look at the clock, I see that our session is over. I help him back on the pool deck and a nurse meets us to transport him to his room.

"I want to try and walk," he says to the nurse.

The nurse turns to me for approval.

"Sure, just provide some support. He can walk to the change rooms but make sure he is in the wheelchair to transport back to his room," I say. "It's a hospital rule because they want to prevent accidents for insurance purposes, not because I don't think you can," I clarify.

"That's reassuring." He laughs with relief.

I laugh too. Bennett leaves and my stomach sinks as I consider the way Kathy said she'd catch me later emphasizing my name. I just hope I'm not in trouble.

CHAPTER FOURTEEN

Avery

I shower quickly and get my scrubs back on. I don't have a patient for another ten minutes, so I head to Kathy's office. *Deep breaths. Deep breaths.*

I reach her door and knock. She looks up from her desk. "Avery, perfect timing. Come in," she says.

I take a few steps into her office.

"Have a seat." She extends her hand for me to take one of the chairs in front of her desk.

My heart beats fast and I feel warm. *Deep, slow breaths.*

I take a seat. "Is everything okay?" I swallow hard, rubbing my sweaty palms on my thighs.

Kathy is a middle-aged woman with lots of experience here in the hospital. She's been my supervisor from day one but right now, she looks worried, or is that confused? Divided? I wish I had Bennett's skill at reading people.

"Something has been brought to my attention." She frowns. "You know I think you're a wonderful therapist and great person overall, but I wouldn't be doing my job right if I didn't take seriously what I've been told."

"And that is?" I ask, sitting on the edge of my seat.

"One of the night nurses mentioned that you have been

spending a lot of time with Mr. Sheridan and that there might be an inappropriate relationship between you," she says.

I blink. Swallow. Blink. *Fucking Monica.* "I can't imagine why someone would think that. You know I visit with most of my patients at night. You said it yourself—it helps them with recovery and makes their time spent in here more meaningful," I say. I argue but a part of me feels like a fraud. Do I come clean to Kathy? I should. I know I should. I take a deep breath. "Kathy . . . I . . ."

She puts her hand up to stop me. "Avery Malone, you're one of the nicest people I know. You're kind and sweet, and I think it's great that you're so dedicated to our patients. Now, don't say another word," she says, shutting me up. I pin my mouth shut and stare, not understanding. "This hospital has rules and I need to focus on protocol. A complaint has been brought to my attention and I have to address it. Now that being said, I will need to remove you from providing Mr. Sheridan PT. That means he is no longer your patient."

"I . . . uh . . . I don't know what to say," I murmur.

"There is a new patient that has come in today. You will meet with him at three thirty," she says.

"Okay." I nod, feeling confused. *What just happened?*

"This is a veteran's hospital, not a school playground," she says.

My eyes move from side to side as I try to decipher what she is trying to tell me in code.

No doubt seeing that I'm not getting it, she says, "Women can be catty, Avery. You need to watch your back. And if something does progress between you and the patient, please make it progress once he's left the hospital."

"Oooo-kay . . ." I nod with complete understanding. "Is that all?"

"He's a real looker. Don't let that one slip between your fingers," she says.

My face must flush so hard. My stomach bottoms out at her

words. I nod. "H-have a g-good af-fternoon," I mutter. Gosh, she has struck me stupid.

"You too, Avery." She laughs a hearty laugh.

I leave to go take care of my patient. Although I didn't get into trouble, Monica brought a complaint against me and I had a patient removed from my roster. Hospital staff will know. They will question me. Cindy will ask questions. This is really bad but at least I didn't lose my job.

I finish off the rest of my appointments for the day and head home. Things can't get any worse, right?

CHAPTER FIFTEEN

Avery

After a long day at work, I walk through the front door. Music is thumping and I am pretty sure it is coming from Jessy's room. She gets home two hours before me on most days.

I'm about to walk up the stairs when Aunt Bee walks out to me from the kitchen. "Hey there, Avery," she says.

"Hi Aunt Bee," I say. I'm tired and upset, and I hope she doesn't have a million requests for me tonight.

"What a handsome boy our little Jess found herself," she says, grinning like a Cheshire cat. She must register my confusion, because when was Dylan here? She hasn't met him. My gaze trails up the stairs where my daughter's room is, the first on the left. "He's in her room now. She actually does have a wild streak in her. She's just like us," she says. I don't know what she means. My parents were happy free-loving hippies. I'm not sure how she met Uncle Jim. I don't know why they don't have kids because I never felt it was my business to ask, but I get her little riddle. My daughter has this Dylan kid in her room and the music is loud.

I don't give Aunt Bee another glance as I take the stairs two at a time. When I reach Jess's door, I'm not sure what to do. I can't just barge in there. I don't think I am prepared to see anything not rated G. Maybe they're only listening to music and Aunt Bee has it all wrong.

This day has been one big debacle. I decide to knock. No one answers me. Okay, maybe the music is too loud. It's so unlike Jess to play such loud music. I knock harder and longer.

"One minute," my daughter shouts. With the music now turned off, I hear shuffling and whispering. My heart feels like it's beating a mile a minute. I wait. I don't know what to do as I feel a hammering in my chest. Then the door swings open and my daughter stands in front of me, bee-stung swollen lips, disheveled blond hair with strands sticking up. She's got her clothes on at least. I look over at Dylan. His floppy hair is a mess, and his lips look wet and thoroughly used. I look between them, and I don't know what to say. I've spoken to Jess about the birds and bees. She knows how old I was when she was conceived.

"What do you want, Mom?" she asks giving me an attitude I've never gotten from her before. I'd always considered myself lucky that she was this good, respectful and responsible kid, but I also wondered if she would rebel, or party, or eventually get a boyfriend.

"What do I want?" I repeat, taking a step back.

"Hi, Ms. Malone. It's good to see you again." Dylan waves to me.

Am I supposed to be cool about this? She's sixteen. She's my baby.

I finally rip my stare off my daughter and look at Dylan and say, "Hi." Hating on her boyfriend will make her hate me.

"Maybe you two should keep the music down. I need to go make dinner," I say, my voice shaking. "Will you be joining us, Dylan?" I ask, looking at him while trying to force a smile. My instinct is to tell him to get out of here and never look at my daughter again. I continue to work against what every fiber in my body is screaming to do.

"No thanks, Ms. Malone. I better be going," he says, and I watch how my daughter gets all goo-goo-eyed over him. Gah!

He walks over to Jess and kisses her on the lips. He whispers that he will call her later, and then he says 'bye to me.

Slow, deep breaths.

He grabs his coat and walks down the stairs. I stand with each of my fists on a hip, staring at my daughter like I don't know her.

When the front door closes, I walk into her room. Her bed isn't made, and I can't bring myself to sit there. I take a seat at her desk chair instead and pinch the bridge of my nose. I close my eyes for a moment, because this day is giving me whiplash.

"Please tell me you did not have sex with that boy," I say.

"Mom," she chides me.

"Jess, you've known him all of a few weeks," I say.

My daughter looks down at her feet. "I really like him. I'm going to be seventeen in a few months. It's not a big deal."

I feel steam pressing through my ears. My body is vibrating with anger but more so, fear.

I inhale and exhale, fighting to keep my tone even. I don't want to yell at my daughter. "It is a big deal. We've discussed this. Sex should be with someone you love."

"Well, I love him," she says.

"Oh, dear child. You've known him a few weeks. Your virginity isn't something you can just take back. That boy is going to be a memory to you forever," I say.

"I'm not you," she shouts at me. "You live your life alone, and that's your choice. I don't even understand why you live the way you do; it's pathetic. This whole situation. Living here with them is pathetic," she screams in my face, and I feel her words like a slap across the face.

I don't realize I'm crying until I have tears streaming down my face. "I live here because I wanted you to have an easy life. For you to have enough money to pay for college and buy yourself a small place. Do you know how much easier that makes life? I didn't bring a man into our life because I worried that no one was good enough to be your father. We were a team and we were good together. I didn't want to start another family because I feared you would feel left out. I . . . did everything I could to keep you happy," I say, as all my energy deflates. By the time I'm finished my rant, tears continue to pour down my face and snot runs from my nose. I don't think I've ever really cried in front of Jess. Well, maybe when Liam died, but she was small back then.

Jess is crying too. "I'm sorry, Mom," she says, and she rushes into my arms.

I hug my daughter tight. I thought staying here provided us with stability but now I see that living here has been more of a safeguard for me. I didn't have bills to stress about and Jess wasn't alone when she came home from school, but I also have been living half a life, which is a bad example for my daughter.

"It's okay." I hug her close and kiss the top of her head. "We are going to be okay. You're right. I've made some mistakes along the way. I'm not perfect, but I do love you dearly."

"I know. I love you too," she says through her tears. I pull back and look into her red eyes and blotchy face, knowing I must look the same way. We both burst out laughing.

"I've just been feeling overwhelmed, and I like Dylan. He makes me feel good," she says.

"I understand. I just want you to have respect for yourself. To know that sex should be about love," I say.

"It really isn't everything it's cracked up to be," she says.

"D-does that mean you had sex with Dylan?" I ask, holding my breath so hard that pressure builds in my chest.

"Almost . . . but no." She shakes her head.

I let out a long, harsh breath. I kiss her forehead.

"Your timing was close though. I got caught up in him," she says.

"Yes, but you want to be able to respect yourself after that feeling is gone," I say.

"I know. You're right. I'm not completely sure I would have gone through with it," she admits. She looks so young and vulnerable, yet I am also proud that she has a good head on her shoulders. That she was thinking and not only acting.

"Oh, baby. Life is so complicated, I get that, but sex should really be about love," I say.

"Thanks for being so understanding," she says, giving me an impish smile.

"Always." I kiss her again. My baby is growing up. It hasn't really sunk in until now.

"Dylan's really sweet. Maybe he can stay for dinner some other time and you can get to know him or something," she says.

"Sure, I'd like that," I say. "I'll go get dinner ready."

"Okay. You looked really scary, Mom," she says.

Oh, if she only knew how I felt inside.

"You're okay, right?" I confirm, just to make sure.

"I'm good. Thanks for being so understanding," she says.

"Of course, baby."

My daughter is growing up and everyone reminding of that fact is right. I need to get a life.

CHAPTER SIXTEEN

Bennett

I've been waiting all day to call her. Wondering if she is okay. If I somehow got her into trouble because I can't control what I feel around her.

I dial her number. A text message won't do it for me. I need to hear her voice.

"Hello?" she says.

"It's Bennett," I say.

"How are you?" she asks. Her voice sounds low and dreary.

"Getting there," I say. "What's going on? Did something happen?" I don't know if she will like me being this direct, but I can't help it. She sounds sad as hell.

She laughs but it's a melancholy laugh. "I got a slap on the wrist at work today. My supervisor said you can no longer be my patient."

"Damn, I'm sorry. What happened though? I never said anything, and we were discreet."

"Honestly, she said one of the night nurses had suspicions and brought her concern to Kathy. I know who it is. At least, I'm pretty sure I do," she says.

"Nurse Monica," I answer. "She was behaving weird after you

were in my room. I don't mean to sound like a prick, but I think she was hoping to win over my affections."

"I have a feeling it was Monica, too. It makes me so angry that she did that. I wish she would have come and spoke to me, even though I know that isn't how a woman like her would do things. Now my co-workers will know I had a patient taken off my roster. It just makes me look bad. I mean, thankfully, I'm not getting fired, I just . . ."

"Look, I want to say that I'm sorry for causing you trouble but I'm not sorry for meeting you, for being attracted to you. I've never met anyone like you, and I want to get to know you better," I say, laying my heart on the line. "Tell me you're feeling something too."

"I feel it," she says so softly. I imagine my fingers outlining her soft lips as she speaks.

"I almost died." My voice cracks. "I've lost friends and . . . I've been given another chance at life. When I first woke up after all my surgeries, I wanted to die. I had no reason to live, and then this sweet therapist with a heart of gold helped me with the pain. Got me to see how special she was . . ." *What am I doing?*

What feels right.

"Bennett . . . I'm feeling this too, but my life is complicated. You know I have a teenage daughter and—"

"And I love that you're such a good mom. That you care so much about your daughter. In the little time we've known each other, I know that about you for sure. That makes me want you more. I don't know if I sound like a crazy person. Gosh, Avery, I never thought about kids or a serious relationship until you," I say. She's quiet. "I've hijacked this conversation and I need you to say something." I laugh, but it's insecure because I'm completely out of my element.

"I feel something too. I've been alone since my husband died, and I was okay with that. Then you became my patient and I was just so drawn to you too. I want to get to know you better, but I can't visit you in the hospital anymore. Our conversations need to be kept to the phone. I can't risk my job."

"I know. I'm good with that. I'm going to work hard on my therapy, even though I loved working with you. I loved the way you got close to me and I could smell your hair, look into your eyes," I say, picturing her tiny button nose, rosy lips and soft, blond hair.

"I think you'll be working with Rob now," she says. "You'll be in good hands with him."

"I don't like the sound of that, but I'll take it. I need to get better and figure out what I'm supposed to do with the rest of my life."

"You'll figure it out. I haven't known you long, but I can see you're a fighter and you go after what you want. You'll be just fine, Bennett Sheridan," she says.

"Thanks. That means a lot," I say with a smile even though she can't see me. Talking to her makes me feel at peace. "Avery? I don't mean to pry, but is something else going on? I mean, is something else bothering you?"

She giggles. "Do you have a sixth sense or something?"

"Maybe," I say, my voice flirtatious.

"Just had an overwhelming night with my daughter too but we've figured things out," she says.

"I'm glad. I can imagine being a single mom isn't easy," I say.

"No, definitely not, and tonight was one of those trying nights. I need to make some changes in my life," she says, and I hear her yawn.

"You're tired. I don't want to keep you," I say.

"Have a good night. I'm glad we had a chance to talk," she says.

"I think you should take my cell number. If you need anything, I want you to call me. You can input me on your phone using a pseudonym," I say, and give her my number. "So what are you going to call me?"

She laughs. "I don't know. I haven't come up with anything yet."

"Let me help you then. What do you think of Rambo or Superman?" I ask.

She laughs; it's such a sweet sound. "What was your call sign in the navy?"

"I don't think we are at the point of our relationship where I should share that," I answer, knowing I pretty much set myself up for that one. Did I really just tell her we are in a relationship?

"Aw! Now you've got me curious. Tell me now," she says, her tone demanding and playful.

"Fine, but don't judge," I warn.

"You have my word," she says.

"When we were in boot camp, we were bored one night just lying around our sleeping quarters when this one guy pulled out a pellet gun. We made a game where we tried to shoot a bull's-eye we set up on the wall. I had gone to the washroom in the middle of the game. As I was walking out, the asshole shot me in the butt. It was an accident, but the name stuck. It's . . ." *Don't tell her. You want to win this woman over, not scare her off.*

"You can't just stop there. I'm guessing it has something to do with your butt." She laughs.

"Fine. Here goes . . . it's Asshat," I say, pinching my eyes shut. "I'd really like to see the look on your face now that I've made a fool of myself."

"You're adorable, Asshat."

"Hell, no. You aren't calling me that," I say.

"Fine. Fine." She laughs even harder.

"I love that sound," I say into the phone. She stops laughing. "I said that because I didn't want you to stop," I chide.

"You're so sweet. What should I call you?" she asks.

"How about The Mechanic?" I ask.

She giggles. "Are you a mechanic?"

"No, but I can fix whatever you have broken," I say.

"That was seriously cheesy," she says.

"Agreed. I'm still trying to recover from the fact you know my name is Asshat. Other than the guys, no one knows."

"Your secret is safe with me," she says. "I'll put you in my phone as Patricia."

"That's a woman's name," I say.

"I know but the point of putting a different name is to throw people off. That way, if my phone lights up with the name Patricia, no one will think it could be you," she says.

"Brilliant," I say.

"Bennett?" She says my name like a question.

"Yes, Avery?"

"Thank you," she says.

"For what?"

"For making me feel better," she says and yawns again.

"Anytime, day or night. Call me," I say.

"You too," she says.

"Have sweet dreams, princess," I say.

"You too," she sighs, and we end the call.

That went so much better than I could have ever imagined.

CHAPTER SEVENTEEN

Avery

Two weeks have flown by in a blur. I still go into the hospital to visit with patients in the evenings. I've managed to stay cordial with Monica. I also manage to have a phone call with Bennett every night before I go to sleep.

I wish I could see him more. At least we sneak peeks at each other when he's at the gym working with Rob on his therapy. I've learned so much about him at night when we talk in the dark. He has a bachelor pad in Virginia Beach that he stays at when he's off-duty. He loves to eat steak and mashed potatoes. He doesn't care for a tossed salad but doesn't mind to eat steamed vegetables. He doesn't know what he's going to do with his life now, and he feels like he doesn't have much to offer me.

I've never had such intense phone conversations with anyone before. He's gotten under my skin in the best way, and I don't want whatever is happening between us to end. When I hear him breathe into the phone and say how he wants to kiss me, it makes me so hot and bothered. Then I get to the hospital in the morning and I just want to go to him and jump his bones. He's awakened something inside me that has been dormant a long time. He's also up and walking with a cane now, and he's doing much better mentally too.

I head over to the rehabilitation office to check in with Kathy.

"Hey there." She smiles. "You're looking flushed this morning."

"Just came from the gym. Did a spin class. I swear it takes a couple hours for my cheeks to be less rosy when I do those classes," I say.

"We've got a big day ahead of us. Full roster of patients, then the whole department is pitching in to help set up the dinner tomorrow," she says. It's Thanksgiving tomorrow, and a lot of staff are off for the holiday.

"I'm glad to help out," I say.

"Thanks. Will you be coming into the hospital for the dinner?" she asks.

"Yeah, Jess and I will be eating here, and I have some friends coming from out of town that will join us too. My friend's husband was a SEAL; he was on the same team as Liam," I say.

"That sounds lovely, Avery," Kathy says.

"How about you?" I ask.

"Got my in-laws coming in from Philly tonight. And Arnie's brother, wife and kids are joining us, too. We're going to have a houseful."

"Do you have all the cooking done?" I ask.

"No. I'm heading out of here early today. Probably going to end up spending half the night cooking," she says.

I look at my watch. "I better head to the gym. I have a patient in a few."

I head to the gym. Sutton is already waiting for me. "How's it going?" I ask him.

"All good," he says. He wheels himself and I walk over to a set of bars. I help him get a grasp on one and he begins his reps. When he's done and out of breath, he looks at me and says, "Patricia is doing just fine. She can't wait to see you at the dinner tomorrow night."

My eyes feel like they will bug out of my head.

"Don't worry. I would never tell a soul," he says. "I knew it from that night you wanted to watch a rom-com. There was something different about you," he says.

"Sutton, we need to keep it down," I say.

"You got it. By the way, it was Nurse Monica, you know. She has the hots for your man. I heard her talking to one of the other nurses, saying what a hottie he is and how it's too bad he's so injured because he must have been an animal in bed and that he will probably get back to it with a little help." Sutton frowns.

I do too.

"I told him what I overheard. Just not the animal in bed part. I know what it feels like to be after an injury. He really likes you and he's become a good friend. I'm allowed to be happy for my friends, right?" He smiles sadly.

"Absolutely. I want to hug you right now, but I also don't want to lose my job. I'm going to miss your face around here," I say.

"I'm going to miss you too," Sutton says. "A large part of my recovery and my mental state is thanks to you."

"You're going to do great out there; I just know it," I say.

"It's going to be challenging. In here, I have my routine down pat. I just need to figure out how to navigate around people in the real world. They will treat me as incompetent," he says, and my heart breaks.

"People don't understand injuries. When they see people in a wheelchair, they will think certain things, but I do believe that there are people that will see past it. That will get to know you and see how capable you are, and what a nice guy you are," I say.

"You're like that, and I know that there will be others who see me that way too," he says.

"I'm glad you decided to stay for Thanksgiving. It wouldn't have been the same without you there." I say.

I turn around to see who's around everyone is busy and not paying us any attention. "What the heck?" I give Sutton a hug. "I'm really going to miss you, friend. You will have to stay in touch."

"Seriously Avery, I want to be invited to the wedding, and I want the first child named after me," he scoffs.

I whack him lightly in the shoulder. "You're nuts. We're nowhere near anything like that."

"Maybe not but you'll get there," he says.

We definitely aren't there yet, but for the first time in my life I'm open to the possibility.

The next morning, I sleep in. It's Thanksgiving, and I don't have work. I peek into Jess's room and she's fast asleep. Aunt Bee and Uncle Jim are talking loudly in their room.

I tiptoe downstairs and head to the kitchen. I get a text message from Bennett.

Bennett: *Are you awake?*

Me: *Yes.*

My cell rings and I pick it up right away.

"Good morning, beautiful," he says.

"Good morning to you," I answer.

"I can't wait to see you later on," he says.

"Me too, but you know we have to be careful. I heard Monica is going to be at the dinner tonight," I say.

"Don't worry so much," he says easily.

"You told Sutton about us," I say.

"Come on. You know he would never tell anyone. I'm feeling good about us and I wanted to share it with someone. I don't know what's going on, but my friend Quinn is MIA," he says.

"What does that mean? Is he still active?" I ask.

"No, he got a full discharge. He's working for a security company in Virginia Beach," he says. "It doesn't make sense. I just can't get a hold of him and he hasn't been around to see me either. I asked my friend Trev, but he doesn't know anything."

"That's strange. Is there anyone else you can call?" I ask.

"Yeah, I'll do that soon. I just wanted to hear your voice," he says, and he does that constantly—he says sweet things that make me fall for him even more.

"That's sweet," I say.

Jess walks into the kitchen.

"I got to go," I say quickly.

"Okay, see you later," he says.

"Bye."

I place the phone down on the counter and turn to my daughter. "Hey sweetie. I was just about to make some eggs would you like some?" My cheeks feel like they are burning.

"Sure," she says, rubbing sleep from her eyes. "Who were you just talking to?" she asks. She knows me well enough to know I was just behaving super weird.

"I met a man," I say, trying to contain my smile.

"Seriously, Mom? That's awesome. Where did you meet him?" she asks.

My lips twist and I mumble, "The hospital."

Her eyes widen. "Um, like he's your patient?"

"He *was* my patient," I say, bracing my palm against my forehead. "I know it was wrong of me to fall for my patient, but he's really a great guy. We've just been talking on the phone—at least until he gets out of the hospital."

"Yay." She jumps up and down, and then walks over to me and gives me a hug.

"When your dad passed away, he left me a letter. In it, he asked me to remarry and find you a good daddy. Now you're all grown up and I feel like I failed you," I admit. "Just, life was busy, and my focus was you and then work. There was no time, and no one really caught my eye."

"But this guy did? Wow! He must be something." She grins.

"He's great. Nice and handsome. Honestly, though, I don't

know where we are headed but he will be at the dinner tonight and you may get to meet him. We've been acting like strangers because of the hospital fraternization policies," I explain.

"Ohhh, Mom, you're a rebel," Jess jokes.

"Well, I try not to be," I say, because, well, since I've had her, I've become a responsible person.

"I know. I'm just joking. I'm seriously happy for you. I hope it works out," she says.

"Thanks, sweetie. How are things going with Dylan?" I ask.

"Good. I told him I think we should wait a little before we, you know . . ." She moves her eyes back and forth.

"Got it. That's probably a good idea," I say.

"Yeah, he was cool with it," she says. *Good.* I exhale.

I scramble up some eggs and warm some bagels and Jess and I sit to eat. I think how Jess and I have our own special routine, our life together. It's what we know. How will me being with Bennett change our dynamic? Will he want to live in Jersey when he's out of the hospital? We haven't discussed anything yet. I just hope that we will both be on the same page.

CHAPTER EIGHTEEN

Bennett

"Good morning, Mr. Sheridan," Nurse Peterson says.

"Good morning." I smile.

"How was your night?" she asks.

"Not bad. I'll be happy when I don't have to sleep in a hospital bed anymore," I say.

"I'm sure." She comes around my bed and conducts a neurological test. She does this every morning because of the initial concussion I had from the blast.

"Can I ask you for a favor?" I ask her.

"Sure. What can I help you with?" she asks.

"I need a pair of scissors and a razor," I say.

She frowns. They limit which personal belongings we are allowed in here. Given the suicide rates among veterans, certain items are not permitted.

"I want to shave my beard, possibly give myself a haircut. I want to look human," I explain, since my hair has started to grow wild.

"I see. That is no problem. We have a barber available who can take care of you. Only he isn't working today," she says.

"This is really important to me. I'd like it done today," I say.

"I really don't think . . .wait a sec. My nephew Michael is in hairdressing school. If you don't mind an amateur, I could call him and see if he'll do us a favor. I'd need to stay here to supervise," she explains.

"I'll take what I can get. I'm not picky."

"Okay. Let me go make the call and I'll let you know," she says.

"Thanks so much, Nurse Peterson," I say. I want to look good for my woman tonight.

I try calling Quinn again for the umpteenth time.

He finally answers, "Hello."

"Quinn, is everything okay?" I ask, sitting upright in my hospital bed.

"Bennett?" he asks, sounding confused.

"Yeah, it's me."

"Things have been messed up. Sorry I haven't been by," he says, his voice sounding hoarse.

"What's going on?"

"A lot," he answers curtly.

"Care to elaborate?"

"Not on the phone. Look, I know it's Thanksgiving. I'm in Jersey. I'll come by and visit you later," he says.

"Okay," I say, not wanting to push.

We end the call. I get out of bed and begin to look through the box of clothes I ordered online. Thankfully, they got here on time. Now I just need to decide what to wear. I've never cared how I looked but Avery has only seen me in hospital gowns and shitty joggers. I want to show that I can clean up well. Just hope she'll like what she sees.

"You . . . look real nice, Mr. Sheridan," Nurse Peterson says as she helps me up out of bed and passes me my cane.

"Thank you for all your help. Your nephew is a great kid," I say. He came in gave me a haircut and shaved my face. I wanted to transfer him payment to his bank account, but he refused to take my money.

"Thank you. He's going to graduate beauty school soon. He does my hair and my daughter's, and he's really great," she says.

"I appreciate everything you've done. All your help. I know I was a pest when I first got here. I'm sorry," I say as I stand and take hold of my cane.

"Pain can be really stressful," she says, giving me an out. "I'm not holding you responsible for anything you said or did during that time."

"I do appreciate that but I still feel the need to apologize. I'm usually not so nasty," I say.

The door swings open and Quinn stands there, tall and brooding. "No, he isn't nasty; he's just a jerk." He chuckles, walking in with a few plastic bags, like he's been grocery shopping.

Nurse Peterson smiles.

"Quinn, play nice," I say.

"Sorry, my apologies. I appreciate everything you've done for him. He isn't a jerk. He's an honorable man. I'm alive and in one piece because of him," he says to Nurse Peterson.

"I could tell. He has kind eyes." She smiles, pressing her lips together.

"Thank you, ma'am," I say.

"If you don't need anything else for now. I'll go on the rest of my rounds," she says.

"I'm good and thanks again," I say.

"Of course, Mr. Sheridan. You have yourself an enjoyable Thanksgiving," she leaves the room.

"Wow. You look like yourself again and not like some psych hermit," Quinn scoffs playfully.

"Good to know that's what you thought of me." I laugh.

"Here. I brought you some food," Quinn says, holding up a bag. "Didn't think you would want hospital food on Thanksgiving."

"Thanks, man, but the hospital is hosting a big dinner. Apparently, we're getting real food. They're bringing all the patients to the main lunchroom. You're more than welcome to join," I say.

I peek into the paper bag he brought.

"Okay, but we're still eating those subs. They're meatball. Ashton introduced me to this place. These sandwiches are like crack," Quinn says, licking his bottom lip.

"Hey, I think I lost a ton of weight being in here so I'm not opposed to eating two meals." I reach into the bag, take a sandwich and pass it to Quinn, then I grab one for myself and limp my way back to my bed since Quinn is sitting in the only chair in the room.

Getting back on the bed is a tough process. I finally get myself upright and bite into the sandwich. My eyes roll to the back of my head and I groan. "Oh, this is good."

"I told you," Quinn says, opening his mouth wide for a large bite.

We eat in silence and I savor every bite.

When I'm done, I tell him I need to get dressed for the dinner tonight.

"Oh yeah? Why?" he asks looking down at me. I'm wearing a t-shirt and jogging pants.

"Because it's Thanksgiving," I say.

"It's a hospital," he retorts, and then his gaze narrows on me. "Is this about that leggy blonde?"

"Don't call her that," I snap.

"Seems like I hit a nerve." He grins mischievously.

"Don't be a jerk. I'd never refer to Ashton that way," I tell him.

His face turns somber. "We lost the baby."

"Sorry, man. Shit. I didn't know," I say, sitting up straighter.

"It was messed up. Some stuff happened with work. She couldn't get a hold of me and now we're on rocky ground," he explains.

"So you aren't going back to Virginia Beach?" I ask.

"I'm here for now. Ashton and I have been through a lot. She's trying to push me away, but I won't let her," he says. He looks completely torn.

"Is there anything I can do?" I ask.

"No, man. I'll just hang out here a bit," he says.

"'Kay. I'm just going to change," I say. I grab some clothes I prepared and head into the bathroom, wishing I could do something to cheer Quinn up.

I pull on the grey sweater, followed by changing my boxers which is a little more challenging because I have to reach forward. I am definitely in much better shape than I was but recovery is going to be a long process. I manage to get the jeans on my bad leg first and then slide them over my behind. I grab my cane and stand, feeling winded from the simple act of getting dressed. How is this my life now?

Stop it. You need to be grateful for what you have.

I step out of the washroom.

"All good, man?" he asks.

"Yeah, thanks for dropping by. I do appreciate it. I know I've been an asshole," I say, rubbing the back of my neck. "Everything, including the pain, was very overwhelming."

He claps me softly on the back and doesn't say a word, but his eyes speak volumes. They tell me he will always have my back.

"So what's going on with you?" he asks as I walk with my cane toward the bed.

"I'm falling hard. It's crazy. I don't even know how it happened." I snicker.

"Tell me about it," he says knowingly.

"She's . . . just perfect," I say of Avery.

"Good for you," he says.

"She's coming for the Thanksgiving meal with her daughter. Thing is, we aren't allowed to be together because of hospital fraternization policies and all," I explain.

"That's tough. Wait a minute. Did you just say she has a daughter?" he asks with surprise.

"Yeah. She's sixteen. What of it?" I ask defensively.

"Easy there, slugger. I don't see a problem. I'm just surprised that you, of all people, would date a single mom," he says. He isn't off-base either. The old me probably would have been too scared to get involved with a woman who had a daughter because of the extra responsibility.

"That was the old me. The new me wants to see where this goes," I say.

"Then I'm happy for you, bro," he says.

"Thanks, man. I want to meet her daughter and get a few minutes alone with her but it's like all eyes are on us. She already had a slap on the wrist because someone reported to her superior that there may be something going on between us," I explain.

"A fucking rat. Hate those," he scoffs. "Man, you were a fucking SEAL. You're suave and stealth. You want to see your woman alone? Make it happen," he says.

"This isn't a mission," I scold him.

"Make it one," he says. "Come on, man. When you want something, you go after it; you don't cower."

"That's some pep talk." I roll my eyes.

"I'm being serious. You're both adults." He nods assuredly. He's right; us staying apart is crazy. She isn't my therapist anymore. We are two consenting adults.

"You're right. I'm going to need your help," I say.

He stands and moves to clap me on the back again but then withdraws his hand, and I know it's because he doesn't want to hurt me.

"I'm not fucking made of porcelain, asshole."

He laughs. "Sorry, man." He has the decency to wince.

I can't get on his case because I know my body is still weak. I've been working hard in therapy, building my upper-body strength and strengthening my leg muscles, but I know recovery isn't a race but a marathon.

Quinn and I come up with a plan. Nurse Peterson stops by my room to get me. Sutton and some other patients are with her, along with some transporters. We head down to the cafeteria with Quinn but when I get there, the air is sucked from my lungs.

CHAPTER NINETEEN

Avery

"Halo! Over here," I call out, waving while standing beside a long table. She sees me and waves back. Jessy went to the washroom for a minute and I don't want someone to snatch up this table. It can fit all of us.

"Avery, it's so good to see you," she says. She looks beautiful, her auburn hair longer than it was the last time I saw her on a visit to Chicago. "It was a long, crazy drive, but we made it."

I hug her, and then hug her kids.

"Hey there, Avery," Thomas says. "It's good to see you." He gives me a hug. "There she is. Look at you, all grown up," he says to Jessy as she strides back to the table.

"Hi Uncle Thomas," she says, giving him a hug.

"You're taller than your mom," he says, and I see the way he looks at her with sadness in his eyes. She's a clear mix of me and Liam.

Jessy smiles. "I'm so happy you guys came to visit."

"I'm glad we made it, but a thirteen-hour drive turned into a sixteen-hour drive," Halo says. "Macy needed pee breaks every two hours. It's like her bladder has an alarm attached to it."

"Mom," Macy whines, and gives her mom the stink eye.

"I love you and your bladder." Halo smiles.

"I don't," Brandon groans.

"The same thing happened to Jessy and me when we came to visit a few years back. It was a long drive. Not one I was excited to take again soon after, even though we loved spending time with you guys," I say.

"I drove the whole way. I don't know why she's complaining. She had Netflix on the entire time," Thomas says of his wife.

Halo rolls her eyes and swats him on the chest. "Whatever."

He laughs and kisses her cheek. They are this awesome inspirational couple. I used to watch the way they looked at each other and think *wow*.

"Dave and Jenny were driving just behind us. We got in this morning and had some time to rest, which is definitely a good thing," she explains.

"Cool. I think that's Jenny there," I say, tilting my chin to the entryway of the cafeteria. Her husband and kids are following behind. We met on mine and Jess's last trip to Chicago.

Jenny comes up and we say our hellos and hug. "I'm really so glad you all could make it," I say. I've spent a few Thanksgivings with Cindy and her sister at her apartment, but it didn't feel warm and welcoming like this.

"This is really great," Thomas says, looking around. There are long tables lined up with food in the middle. We didn't want to have a cafeteria vibe to the meal, so we set up all the dishes in the middle of the table to give the place a homey feel.

"Yeah, it's the first year we're doing it," I say. "Seems to be a hit so far."

Thomas leads our table in saying grace, then we all dig in. Of course, my eyes roam the room for Bennett. I don't see him.

A tall, big guy walks up to our table. "I'm looking for an Avery Malone," he says.

"Who's asking?" Thomas asks with an authoritative tone.

"Is she here?" the man asks, ignoring Thomas.

"I'm Avery. Can I help you?" I ask.

"I need you to come with me. My name is Quinn," he says.

"She isn't going anywhere with you." Thomas stands from the table, no doubt sensing something is off.

The men look at each other like they are in the middle of a pissing contest. "Do I know you?" Thomas suddenly asks, furrowing his brows.

Halo looks at me and shrugs, like she has no clue what is going on with her husband.

"No," Quinn snaps but then it's like he gives Thomas another look and his gaze softens. "Wells? Is that you?" he asks.

"Holy shit. It's been years," Thomas says, and shakes the man's hand.

"How have you been?" Quinn asks. I suddenly realize why he looks so familiar. I remember seeing him in Bennett's room. They're friends.

"Good, man, raising a family. Working as an EMT," Thomas says. He was put on a medical discharge years ago.

"That's great," Quinn says, but then his gaze drops to me.

I stand and turn to my guests. "I'll be back in a moment."

"Sorry about my . . ." Thomas begins to apologize.

"That's okay. I'm just going to check on someone," I say. "Continue to eat. I'll be back soon," I say as I walk away from the table.

"Sorry about that, Avery," Quinn says, as we head toward the cafeteria exit. "I'm Bennett's friend. He, uh, wanted to see you," he says. "I'm supposed to bring you to him."

I follow Quinn to the elevator and up to the second floor, past a corridor and into a sheet closet. I cock a brow and say, "Seriously?"

"He's waiting for you inside. It was the best location I could scout. Least amount of foot traffic this way. Lesser chance of getting caught." He winks and opens the door. "See ya," he says and walks away. SEALs—they really are a breed of their own.

My breath catches like it's been sucked from my lungs. Bennett stands there dressed in a sweater that hugs his wide shoulders and shows off his strong arms. His jeans aren't loose, but they aren't fitted either. They showcase strong thighs and long legs. It's a body I came to know well through therapy, but it's different when a patient is in a hospital gown. Now . . . this . . . he . . . .his face is shaved; his hair is cut.

"Say something," he says, his shoulders rising and falling rapidly.

I take a step into the very large closet that has shelves on each of the walls with folded sheets. Bennett steps around me to close the door then turns back to me. "I always wondered what you looked like under that wild beard and hair," I say pensively.

He laughs. "Do you like what you see?" he asks, his throat bobbing.

I take a few steps to close the space between us. My palm reaches out to touch his face. "You're so handsome," I say. His cheekbones are more visible and pronounced. I touch his smooth skin. He has a cleft on his chin that adds to his ruggedly handsome look. His brown eyes look more of light chocolate mocha as he takes me in. My other palm touches his cheek and my heart picks up pace, beating at a prestissimo pace.

"You look so beautiful," he says. I tuck a piece of my long blonde brushed out hair behind my ear and twirl. My printed chiffon dress sways above my knees while my cheeks flush with warmth. I knew I'd be seeing him tonight and I wanted to look good for him.

"I thought I would be seeing you from across the room," I say, swallowing the excess of saliva building up in my mouth.

"I needed to see you closer. To touch you," he says, rubbing my cheek with the back of his hand. His skin feels rough, like he's worked with his hands. My body feels alert and alive. My gaze falls to his lips. Without the beard, I see how perfect and full they are. I've had such naughty thoughts in bed at night, wondering what those full lips could do. What his mouth could do to me.

He places his palm on my chest and looks into my eyes. "Breathe, Avery."

"My heart is beating so fast," I admit with a nervous laugh.

He places my palm on his chest, and I feel the strength of his heart as it beats ferociously against my hand. We look into each other's eyes and Bennett dips his head slowly, moving closer to me. My lips ache for his touch and when he presses his warm lips against mine it feels so right. Electricity courses throughout my body, waking up every sense inside me that has lain dormant for more than a decade, or maybe even a lifetime, because nothing has ever felt like this.

My hands come up and my fingers move through his short hair. He deepens the kiss, our tongues moving in sync as wanton heat travels to my core. I moan into his mouth, feeling like my skin is burning, like an inferno is about to explode inside me and I have no control.

"Bennett," I mutter his name as if it's a question, a prayer, and my breathe all at once.

"I know," he groans as he moves his body flush with mine. "I feel your hardened nipples against me. You are making me crazy. I want you so bad," he says.

I slow the kiss, my entire body throbbing with need. "I haven't . . . I mean . . . I . . . there's been no one since my husband."

His molten eyes round. "That's fourteen years," he says, sounding shocked.

"I know," I say, feeling self-conscious. "There hasn't been anyone I was interested in. I had been a stupid teenager and I was bent on not repeating my bad choices." I pull my gaze away from him and look at the floor.

He takes my chin with his pointer and thumb and tilts my head back to him. "I'm not judging you. I'm crazy about you. I don't want to be a bad choice," he says, his cheeks flushing. Without the beard, I read the emotions on his face so easily.

"You could never be a bad choice," I assure him. He's been sweet, supportive and understanding. I bite my lip.

He exhales and it looks like he is deep in thought. "Thank you," he presses a soft quick kiss on my lips.

I smile bashfully.

"I don't want to get you fired," he says, brushing his thumb against my cheek. "I just wanted to touch you and be close to you."

"This was nice. Thank you," I say.

We kiss briefly again, and sparks between us erupt consuming me.

"I better get you back downstairs," he says breaking the kiss. "I could kiss you all night but. . ."

"You're right. I don't want trouble," I say. "Shoot." I touch my lips and I know they are swollen. I can only imagine how my face looks. "I'll stop by the ladies' room before heading back to the lunchroom."

"I'll head up to my room. I'll pick up my phone, then I'll head into the lunchroom. Quinn is having dinner probably all on his lonesome," he says.

"He actually knows my friend Thomas somehow," I say.

"Really? I guess that makes sense. You mentioned he was a SEAL, and we're close in age," he says.

"Yeah," I say.

We kiss again, stand, and face each other. "I better get back. I've been an awful host. Thanks for doing this Bennett," I say, running my hands over my dress to smooth it out.

"Yes." He smiles. "Talk soon, sweetheart," he says, winks and slips out the door.

My heart flutters but I wait a couple moments to give him a head start. I head to the ladies' room down the hall to freshen up, and then I head back down to the lunchroom.

"Um . . . hey there," Halo says.

"Where have you been?" Jessy asks with an accusatory motherly tone.

"Is everything okay, Avery?" Jenny asks.

Oh, dear. This is embarrassing.

"Everything is fine," I say, taking my seat next to Jessy. I load up my plate with turkey and begin to stuff my face, figuring if I'm eating, no one can ask me any further questions.

Halo raises and lowers her brows as she gives Thomas a look. He stares back at her with a deer-in-the-headlights, frantic expression, like he doesn't want to know.

As I'm stuffing my face, I look up and Jenny winks. I look off to the entrance of the lunchroom to see Bennett walking in, perfectly handsome and stealth. My heart skips a beat.

"Is that him, Mom?" Jessy asks.

I nod. Halo and Jenny catch on.

"Nice," Jenny says.

"Guys, please. I'm at work," I whisper.

Halo bursts into laughter.

"Looks like that secret is out," I say jokingly but, I feel the burn in my cheeks.

Bennett takes a seat by his friend and his friend claps him on the back. It seems like all our close friends know what we were up to. I hope that no hospital employees have taken notice.

"Why don't you and Jessy come back to Jenny's aunt's house for dessert?" Halo suggests.

"Yes, come. We can hang and talk," Jenny insists.

I look at Jess, and she shrugs. "Sure. I'm good with that."

"Okay, yeah, sure. I just need to see if the volunteers need any help before we take off," I say.

I stand and walk over to the kitchen. The volunteers say they have everything under control. When I leave the kitchen, I see Thomas over at Bennett's table, speaking with Quinn and Sutton. I don't walk over even though I really want to. Thomas is smiling wide and nodding his head. Bennett is smiling too. Then Thomas shakes Sutton's hand.

When Thomas walks back to the table, he just winks at me. I blush. What on earth did Bennett say about me? Or about us?

CHAPTER TWENTY

Bennett

"How did it go?" Quinn asks. Sutton is sitting across from me, and I know he heard too.

"Perfectly," I say.

"Glad to see things working out. She's such a good person and hard worker; she deserves more than the life she has," he says.

"I know. I want to give her that," I say quietly. "I want to give her everything, but we can't talk here."

"I know." Sutton nods and takes a mouthful of stuffing.

"When are you out of here?" Quinn asks.

"Probably by next week," I say.

"That's awesome," Quinn says.

"I'm out of here tomorrow. It's scary—not going to lie. I'm heading into a life I'm not used to, having to navigate a territory I don't know," Sutton says.

"It's tough," Quinn says. "Look, I know I wasn't injured, but I did leave the navy. I've been working for Cole Security. It's all ex-SEALs so it still feels like the navy. We take a lot of contracts the navy can't dip their hands in. I thought it would suck but I love it."

"It's in Virginia Beach," I remind him.

"Headquarters are in Virginia Beach, but I just had a contract here in Jersey. But yeah, I hear what you're saying. If things work out between Ashton and I, I'm hoping she may be up for a move," he says.

"I need to stay in Jersey. And let me remind you that I'm injured. I walk with a freaking cane. What would they want with me?" I ask, and then I feel like an insensitive prick. "Sorry, I wasn't thinking," I say to Sutton, feeling like hitting myself in the head.

"It's fine. I'm going to have to get used to it . . . I was thinking about going back to school and getting a degree, but your job with Cole sounds badass," Sutton says.

"We need a lot of work done behind the scenes. We're connected to satellites. We need to gather intelligence—the list goes on," Quinn says.

"That's what I was training for—before my accident," Sutton says glancing at his inert legs. "Do you think they may want a guy in a wheelchair?" I can't believe he's considering this. He's told me all about his plans for when he leaves.

"Seriously?" I ask him, cocking a brow.

"Yeah, I mean, it would be cool. I would do badass things . . . I'm kind of starting to freak out about leaving. It was easy to make all kinds of plans in this place. We're separated from the rest of society here. We're all veterans suffering from one thing or another. Heading out there is scary," he says.

"Yeah, I mean I have some money saved up, but I don't have a plan. How am I supposed to make a woman fall in love with me when I have nothing to offer?" I ask my two friends.

"She isn't like that," Sutton says quietly.

"I know that, but I need to know I can support a wife, a family. No way will I depend on anyone," I say.

"To answer your question, yes, we would hire a guy in a wheelchair," Quinn says pointedly, looking at Sutton. He turns his attention on me. "You know Cole is the right place for you too."

"Maybe." I shrug. It would be nice to do something important and get paid well.

"You could fly back here to visit or make arrangements," Quinn adds. But the thought of leaving Avery sickens me. "Look, Jackson is out in California. His main office is in Virginia Beach. Where there's a will, there's a way. He's busy with his family now because of the holiday, but I want to ask him to come out here and interview you. Talk to him; he's a pretty fucking cool guy. You too, Sutton. Maybe you can come back in and meet with him. See what he can offer you."

"That would be great," Sutton says.

His anxiety about leaving rubs off on me. "Jackson isn't going to come here to interview a bunch of wounded vets."

"He scheduled to come out here early tomorrow morning. There's a situation that has to be taken care of," Quinn says.

"I was an asshole to him last time he was in town," I remind him.

"You were a mess after getting hurt in an IED. You know he isn't going to hold it against you," he says. He's right. From what I know about Jackson and the times we've met, he's been a stand-up guy.

"Okay. Let's do this," I say to Quinn.

Sutton chimes in with a, "Yeah, let's do this."

"Good. I'll set things up and let you know." Quinn nods, taking a mouth full of turkey. "This stuff isn't half bad," he says. "That meatball sandwich was killer though, right?" he asks, looking to me and speaking with his mouthful.

"Yeah, man, that sandwich was the bomb," I say, polishing off my own plate. My life might be in limbo but today I am grateful for what I have—a special woman and good friends who have my back. Hopefully, I don't do anything to mess it up.

CHAPTER TWENTY-ONE

Avery

The next day I come into work even though I'm not on the schedule because of the holiday weekend. Sutton is leaving and I have to say goodbye.

His sister is out in the hall, waiting while we talk. "I'm going to miss you," I tell him.

"Me too. I was a mess when I first got here, and you showed me how to take care of myself. How to have a life while being in this chair," he says and his lip quivers.

"Oh, Sutton," I say.

"It's going to be hard out there," he says, taking a long breath.

"Yeah, it's going to be hard, but you're so strong and so exceptional. I don't think there's anything you can't do," I tell him.

"Thanks. I'm going to need all the confidence I can muster," he says on a shaky breath.

"Don't pay attention to the jerks. Just be you," I say.

He laughs. "I had everything planned out when I was in here but now all my plans seem jumbled up in my mind."

"It's scary. There's no point sugarcoating it. You're also one of the strongest men I know. You've accomplished so much in so little time. Just take things one day at a time. It's the best you can do," I say.

"Thanks, Avery. For everything. I'm also really glad that you and the SEAL seem to be getting along well," he says.

"We shouldn't talk about that here," I whisper even though my heart kicks up a beat at the mention of Bennett.

"Relax there are no cameras in these rooms," he says. "I'm happy for the two of you. It's nice that you can lean on each other."

"Things are still so undefined between us."

"Yeah, but he'll be out of here next week," he reminds me.

"And he doesn't have a plan. I know how scary it can be. Don't forget, I've been working here for seven years. I've seen my share of wounded vets."

"It's really hard to get back out there. I mean, it's hard when your body is in one piece but with an injury it's even harder," he says. "I don't need to tell you that your patience will be required because you get this life."

"I do but I've never really dealt with a wounded soldier on a personal level. My husband had been deployed once before his second deployment and he came back to us in a pretty good headspace. Well, actually, no, that's not true. Liam was always in a kind of a bad headspace because of the way he grew up. He was closed up and didn't show much affection. Then he died," I say, a familiar numbness overtaking my body and soul. "I haven't dealt with a wounded soldier. My good friend went through a very rough time with her husband and his PTSD."

"I hear that. I mean, the good part about being in here is that we've had time with therapists and stuff. We've been able to talk and figure out the stuff in our head. Problem is, some stuff you can't unsee or undo," he says.

"I know, and that makes me so nervous. Everything has been relatively easy with Bennett I don't know what road we face ahead," I say.

"Whatever it is, I think you two have something worth fighting for," Sutton says, and his words speak to my heart.

"We do," I say. I give his hand a squeeze. "I'm going to miss you, my friend."

"Me too, Avery. We'll be in touch. I don't want to leave my sister waiting too long," he says.

"You take care and good luck." I stand as he wheels himself out of the room and just like that, 4C is empty.

I head home. First, I stop in Jess's room. "Hey, sweet pea." I kiss the top of her head.

"Got a functions test on Monday," she explains.

"I won't keep you," I say.

"That's okay. I kind of wanted to take a break anyway," she says. She presses her lips together. "So what's going on with you and the guy?"

I was grilled by Jenny and Halo when we got back to Jenny's aunt's house. Jess went with Brandon, Macy and Jenny's kids to watch a *Star Wars* movie. Thomas and Dave joined them, thankfully, because I still feel kind of awkward speaking of another man around Thomas because he does things to honor Liam's memory which is amazing and awkward for me all at once.

"He's great and I really like him, but he's got a lot on his plate. He was injured and he's been through a lot emotionally. I don't want to set myself up to get hurt," I admit.

"You need to take a chance, Mom. Otherwise you'll never know," Jess says.

"When did you become so smart about relationships?" I ask.

"I'm not. I'm just telling you what I think you would say to me." She grins.

"Thanks." I take a seat on her bed and fall back. "Things are just so complicated."

"But you really like him," Jess says.

I sit back up. "How do you feel about that? I know you haven't met him, but he's getting out of the hospital this week. I was thinking we could have dinner in a restaurant together," I say.

"That sounds great." She smiles. "I've always worried about you being alone when I left for college," she admits.

"Aw, sweetie. You don't have to worry about me."

"But I do," she says.

I take a breath. "You know the letter your dad left me?"

"I know all about the letter," she says blandly. The guilt of not finding her a daddy always ate away at me.

"I just feel like I've let both of you down and now that you're leaving in a year and a half, I've gone and fallen hard for a man." I frown.

"You can't control when feelings happen. I think I'm the only girl in my school that waited until junior year to kiss a boy," she says.

"Yeah, I guess you're right. It just feels like everything is up in the air. I also want to go looking for an apartment. I always wanted to buy a house around here, but I don't think I want to make a permanent decision now even though I want us to have our own place."

Jessy stands from her desk and walks over to me. "Having our own place would be completely awesome." She wraps her arms around me, and I cherish these moments with my daughter.

I hug her back and when she pulls away, I stand. "I'm going to go get ready for bed."

"You're going to go talk to your boyfriend," she says, waggling her brows.

"Yeah, I am," I say. I don't know if Bennett is even my boyfriend, but he is very special to me. "Study away."

"On it." She winks. I kiss the top of her head. "Love you."

"Love you too," she says, and she picks up her pencil and starts an equation.

Back in my room I fall back on my bed. I think of my conversation with Halo and Jenny yesterday. I had told Jenny and Halo about the amazing kiss I shared with Bennett in the sheet closet while I was over for dessert at Jenny's aunt's mansion. I also told them how we haven't discussed a future together, despite the fact that we both have strong feelings for each other. Halo said to give him time to adjust to the outside. I sure don't want to pressure him either—I just wonder where his head is at. I definitely know what my heart's been feeling. I just wish things weren't so up in the air. If there was one thing I liked about my life it's that it was predictable and stable. Now, it feels like anything but.

CHAPTER TWENTY-TWO

Bennett

I dial *my girl*. Thinking those words have me feeling heady. I was never this guy. I didn't make promises I couldn't keep. I told women upfront that my job came first. Until her and now.

I don't know what to do. She doesn't pressure me or ask me what my plans are.

The phone rings three times. "Hello," she says out of breath.

"Where did I catch you, baby?" I ask. Looking at my watch, I see it's half past nine.

"I made Aunt Bee and Uncle Jim a late-night snack. Just brought it to their bedroom and I left my phone in the kitchen, so I ran back down here," she says.

"Can't they make their own damn snack?" I ask, unable to hide my irritation. From our nightly calls I'm getting the feeling these people are real users.

"It's no big deal," she says.

"Fine, but when I'm out of here I want to come over there and meet them. I want to see how you're living. Why you've chosen to come into this hospital nights your daughter isn't home," I say.

"Bennett, honey," she says, and the way she sing-songs my name and calls me 'honey' gets me all riled up. It makes me feel like I've found my home. "They aren't the friendliest people. I usually don't bring guests around. It's more like a place that Jessy and I crash."

"That's how you've been living for the past twelve years? Baby, I told you how shitty my time in foster care was. You need a home. A place you're comfortable, for you and your daughter," I say.

"I know, it's just that I've been saving money and Jessy leaves for college after next year. I always figured I'd make the move at some point. Now, I've realized that living here has become stressful for my daughter so I'll be moving out soon," I say.

"Why do I get the feeling you've been planning a move for years?" I ask. "I don't want to step on your toes. I just want you to be happy."

She doesn't answer.

"I'm right. Aren't I?" I ask.

"Maybe," she mutters quietly.

I don't like that she feels stuck in her situation. I know all about being in a place you don't like and not having a way out. Avery is a grown woman, but given her childhood, I am not surprised she is scared to take a risk and be on her own.

I don't want to push the matter further and make her feel bad so I drive the conversation toward the one thing I know puts a smile on her face. "I can't wait to meet Jessy."

"I can't wait for you to meet her either," she says, her tone perks up. If there's one thing I know, it's that you don't meet a single mother's kid unless you're an important part of her life.

"Maybe we can do dinner when you get out," she says.

I laugh. "You make it sound like I'm doing time in prison."

"Not what I meant," she says in a chiding tone.

"I know," I say. "So, what are you wearing?" I ask, my voice turning gruff at the thought of her luscious lips.

"Honestly?" she asks, sounding hesitant.

"Yeah, honestly. Whatever you're wearing, I'll find sexy. Hell,

I saw you in your scrubs the first time and felt breathless, and those things do nothing to show off your curves."

"Bennett," she sing-songs my name.

"It's true. Now tell me," I insist.

"A Snoopy pajama shirt," she says, sounding embarrassed.

"Hmm, I bet you look so hot. I can't wait to get my hands on you . . ."

"Bennett, stop . . . I . . ."

"Let yourself get turned on," I say.

"It's been so long. I'm . . ."

"What are you going to say?" My voice dips deep as heat swirls into my stomach and down to my cock. I'm rock hard.

"I want you so bad," she says.

"Are you wet?" I ask.

"Bennett," she chides. "I can't answer that."

There is something so pure and unadulterated about Avery that makes me crazy hot. Knowing she hasn't had sex in eons just makes me want to take her more.

"If I wasn't scared of someone walking in here, I'd tell you to touch yourself while I rub myself. I'm rock hard for you, baby," I say.

She breathes fast into the phone. "I never touch myself," she admits, shocking me. "I've just shut that part of myself off," she says, and my heart hurts for her. What has she been through that she's stopped herself from satisfying her needs?

"It means a lot to me that you're sharing that with me. I want to take care of you like you deserve to be taken care of. I just need to get the hell out of here," I say. I'll probably need to rub one out in the washroom after this call.

"I can't wait for you to get out of there," she says. "And Bennett, I am wet. So wet at the thought of you having your hands on me," she says, and I know it wasn't easy for her to say that out loud. I heard the hesitation in her voice.

I hiss. "Avery, touch yourself. Now. Put your fingers between your thighs and rub," I order.

"Bennett, Monica could walk into your room. You need to be careful. Stop saying my name," she chides me.

"She's already been here. She was curious as to when I was leaving. Suggested that me and her grab a cup of coffee together after I'm released," I say.

"What?" Avery snaps. "You're kidding me. She hit on you?"

"Yeah, baby, she did," I say.

"And what did you do?" She asks.

"I told her I didn't think that was a good idea. She walked over to my bed and placed her hand on my arm," I say.

"She what?" Avery practically shrieks. "That woman got me in trouble at work. She almost cost me my job and then she has the nerve to hit on you?"

"Relax. I told her to take her hand off me. That I wasn't interested. I would have told her I was taken but I didn't want to set off any warning signals in her mind," I say.

I hear her blow out a breath. I love how jealous and possessive she just became.

"Now take a deep breath and close your eyes. Where were we? Oh, yes. You are dipping your fingers into your warmth," I say.

The phone is quiet and then I hear Avery breathing hard. I begin to rub my cock a little then slip my hand under the sheet, squeezing my girth and pumping.

"Bennett," she moans.

"I'm so hard for you. I'm getting myself off Avery. I'm thinking that it's my fingers touching you between your thighs. I'm dreaming about how wet you are. How bad I want my mouth between your thighs, my tongue licking your sweet pussy."

She moans louder. "I can't do this," she pants.

"Let go, baby. Fall with me," I say, and she does. She falls into orgasm and I blow my load in my hands like a fucking teenage boy.

After we've had some time to recover, we stay on the phone chatting some more. Avery's voice has grown low and tired. She sounds sexy as hell and I wonder what it would feel like to have her in my bed all night. Every night.

"I can't wait to get out of this place so I can spend more time with you," I say. I don't know how and what that will look like, but I want it like my next breath.

"I want that too," she says.

"Do you know where you'll stay?" she asks.

"No, not yet. I wanted something close by to you, but I don't know how to make that work. My place is in Virginia Beach. I have some money, but I don't want to waste it on a rental if I don't have to. I don't have any job prospects lined up. I need to come up with a plan and fast; it's just not so easy," I explain.

"I understand," she says, and I appreciate her understanding.

"Thank you. I want you in my life, Avery. I just don't know what my life out there is going to look like."

"We'll figure something out," she says.

"Yeah, okay." I rake the fingers on my free hand through my hair, wishing we had a better plan than this.

"Have a good night," she says.

"You too, baby," I say. "I wish you were in my arms so that I could kiss you goodnight."

"I'm here waiting," she says, sounding so pliant and relaxed.

It doesn't seem fair to talk to her this way when I don't have a plan of how to keep her in my life. Yet I'm determined to make sure that Avery Malone stays in my life.

CHAPTER TWENTY-THREE

Bennett

I hop out of the shower after my physical therapy appointment. I dry my body and turn my head so I can see the scars down my back. There's one that is more pronounced, long and jagged. Memories from the IED explosion threaten to surface making my body feel too hot and palpitations make me feel woozy. No, I won't think about it. I'm lucky things didn't end up worse for me.

After drying my body, I slip on a pair of boxers and lounge pants followed by a T-shirt. My anxiety is high this morning. Sutton should be here any minute, and Quinn and Jackson are due to arrive within the hour. Quinn seems to think that Cole Security is the right place for me and maybe it is, but how do I include Avery and her daughter in my life from freaking Virginia Beach? We haven't known each other long, and yet we're very much a couple with strong feelings for each other. Still, if I don't have a job or a way to support myself and a family then what kind of man would I be?

I never knew who my father was—I only knew he didn't give a shit about sticking around. He must have been a loser with no job and no sense of responsibility. I can't be that man.

"Hello," Sutton's voice calls me from inside my room.

I inhale and exhale, and open the bathroom door. "Hey, man," I say. I limp toward my bed since I don't use the cane for short distances; it makes me feel like an old guy.

"What's wrong with you?" he asks. His sister came to take him back to Alabama a couple days ago and he sent her home on her own. He's been staying in a hotel while waiting for this meeting.

"Nothing." I walk over to the only chair in the room and take a seat.

"It doesn't look like you have nothing on your mind," he says, crossing his arms in front of his chest.

"How are you? How's the hotel?" I ask.

"It's good. Easy, with an elevator, but pricey as hell. I hope this Jackson can offer me a good job," he says.

I laugh sardonically. "What is it about us guys that we need these complicated jobs? We need to save the world."

"I don't know about you, but I was always proud to serve my country and it was a way for me to get away from farm life," he says.

"For me, it was a place to go after foster care ended. Then I saw I could be someone people respected. Do things to keep people safe, and it fed something inside me that I always needed," I admit.

"And you want that feeling to continue." He has me pegged.

"Yeah, man." I blow out a breath. "Problem is . . ."

"A particular blonde with a heart of gold," he says.

"I don't know what to do. There's no way I can lose her," I say, my chest growing tight at the thought.

"You two have something special. You'll figure it out," he says.

"I sure hope so." I know it's messed up, but I need more time with her. When I get out of here, we can really be together, and I can show her that we are meant to be. I just hope that she will be up to moving to Virginia Beach with me because if Jackson makes me the right offer, I don't think I'll be able to reject it.

CHAPTER TWENTY-FOUR

Avery

I've just finished with a patient in the gym area and I'm heading to the cafeteria for a coffee and snack when I pass the front entrance to the hospital and see Sutton speaking with one of the nurses. I do a double take. I thought he left town. I saw his sister pick him up.

I wait off to the side until he's done.

"Hey, you." I lean over and give him a hug.

"Hi, Avery. Good to see you again," he says warily.

"What brings you in? I thought you were all clear." I grin.

"I am. Just met up with a friend. Your old patient Mr. Sheridan. We had a job interview," Sutton says.

"Really?" I spoke to Bennett last night. He didn't mention anything at all. "What kind of a job?"

"For me it would be strictly office work for Cole Security. The owner is a friend of Quinn. You know, the guy who came for Thanksgiving dinner," Sutton says.

My stomach sinks. "I remember Quinn." Thomas said he was an ex-SEAL.

"So his friend has this huge security company. They have government contracts and it sounds really cool. I told him I'm in," Sutton says.

Sutton always spoke about becoming a therapist. He was so good with so many of the patients but maybe he wasn't really into it. Maybe, like everyone else around here, he was searching for a place to fit in in his new life.

"I'm happy for you," I tell him.

"Me too. I won't feel like a broken soldier there. I'll be doing work that matters and getting paid well," he says, his excitement transparent. I want to ask him about Bennett, but it seems inappropriate.

Why didn't he mention any of this to me?

"So, you'll be staying in Jersey then. That's great news," I say.

Sutton's face falls. "The job is in Virginia Beach," he says sympathetically.

It feels like a knife has been put through my chest. Bennett lives in Virginia Beach. It would make sense that he would want to work there.

I want to ask Sutton if Bennett was offered a job there too, but I should give the man I'm in a relationship with the chance to breaks the news to me. I bid my friend goodbye and wish him luck. I continue on with my day but the sinking feeling in my stomach doesn't cease.

CHAPTER TWENTY-FIVE

Bennett

"You'll need to have semi-annual check-ups with an orthopedic specialist and find yourself a physical therapist to continue working on your knee and back," Dr. Simmons says.

"Got it," I say. I'm hoping to have one particular physical therapist around a lot.

"Well, if that will be all, I wish you the best of luck," the doctor says.

I shake his hand. "Thank you for everything."

"My pleasure, Mr. Sheridan," Dr. Simmons says and leaves the room.

I pick up a small gym bag that has pretty much everything I own and prop it on my shoulder. With my cane in hand, I head out of the room. Leaving this place feels good.

Quinn had wanted to pick me up, but he had something work-related to take care of and anyway, I need to get by on my own. I head down the elevator, saying goodbye to the hospital staff I've befriended during my stay.

Avery stands just inside the hospital doors, speaking with a patient. Our eyes meet and my heart melts. *Soon.* Soon we won't have to hide.

We hold each other's gaze. Her eyes say more than words

ever could. They tell me I'm going to be okay. They tell me she'll be by my side.

I turn away, not wanting to draw attention to us. I leave through the hospital doors and fresh, cool air hits my face. It's daunting and exhilarating, scary and euphoric. It reminds me of all the times I left a foster parent and was transferred to another home. The unknown had been scary as a child. It's scary now.

An Uber is waiting for me. He already has the address for the Airbnb I've rented for the next few weeks. It isn't far from Avery's aunt and uncle's house, where I've been invited for dinner tonight.

My cell rings and Quinn's name is on the screen.

"Hello."

"Hey, man," he says. "You out of the hospital?"

"Yeah, it feels good," I admit as I unpack my clothes and familiarize myself with my new basement apartment.

"So, what's the plan?" he asks.

"I'm seeing Avery for dinner at her house tonight. Going to meet her daughter," I say heading into the small kitchen area which is modern and clean.

He snickers. "You sound nervous."

"That's 'cause I am," I say. "I don't know anything about kids."

"You said she was a teenager. Just talk to her about regular stuff," he says.

"And that would be . . ."

"School . . . sports. I don't know. Just regular conversation," he says.

"Yeah, yeah."

"Jackson told me you're coming aboard," he says.

"Told him I'll be out there in one month," I say.

"So you spoke to Avery and she's cool with you leaving," he says, but it sounds like a question.

"Not exactly. That's why I need a month," I say hesitantly.

"Dude, you're asking for trouble. She has a kid she's responsible for. She can't just pick up and leave," Quinn says.

"I haven't thought it all through, but her daughter is going off to college," I remind him.

"You said she's a junior. That's a year and a half away. A long fucking time," he scoffs.

"I'll figure it out, okay?"

"The job with Jackson is serious. You have to get security clearance and . . . let's just say if you aren't committed, you should tell him," he says.

"I'm serious," I assure him.

"Okay. I have a call coming in that I have to take. Laters," he says.

"Later." We end the call. And I head to the bedroom and lie back on the bed.

I'm driving in a Jeep. Sand dunes surround us. The wheels fight through the sand leaving behind a cloud of dust. We're headed on a mission. Everyone is on high alert. I'm sitting by the window, Quinn beside me and Trevor beside him. A chinook sounds overhead and King gives me a nod. We are close to our location. The old run down two story buildings come into view.

"Something is wrong," I say, the Chinook has changed direction.

"What?" King shouts, slowing down.

"Something . . ." A kid wearing shorts and a t-shirt with no shoes begins to wave at us. What the fuck? Something is going to happen. I shove Quinn out of the moving vehicle. "King, stop!"

I think I push Trevor and then there's a blast and I'm catapulted out of the vehicle. My body smashes to the ground—crack, bang, boom. Fire erupts around me and smoke fills my lungs. I'm in the dirt and lift my head to see. My eyes feel gritty and it takes me time to focus.

When I do, I see King hunched over the wheel . . . flames lick along his spine. No. No. I need to get to him. He can't die.

I cough. I try to stand up. Trevor, Quinn where are you? Sand fills my mouth. I don't know if I've screamed their names. I squeeze my eyes shut 'cause they sting so bad. Turning on my stomach is nearly impossible. Pain cuts like a knife across my back and I can barely use my legs. Fuuuuck, it hurts so much. AHHHHHHHHH!

My eyes fly open. I'm breathing hard and drenched in sweat. My heart races at dangerous speeds. I had a couple dreams in the hospital, but none were as vivid as this one.

My therapist told me the dreams may come or I may be one of the lucky ones who don't relive a nightmare.

It takes me time to get my bearings. When I do, I head to the washroom and shower. Then I put on a load of laundry. The image of King lying there helpless fills my mind. It's like I can smell the smoke, feel the gritty sand between my teeth. *Why is this happening now?*

I take a few deep breaths. I want a drink to ease the anxiety I'm feeling, but I won't go there. I won't allow myself to turn into my mother. Instead, I head out into the freezing cold day. Walking to the corner store with a cane and a bad knee feels like a daunting task. I order an Uber. I'm a fucking mess. I try talking myself out of this anxiety, reminding myself I'm lucky to be alive. I'm lucky to have found Avery but why would she want to settle down with a broken man?

The Uber arrives and takes me to the larger supermarket. I buy some groceries for my place and two bouquets of flowers for Avery and her daughter. My head still feels cloudy with the remnants of my dream, and I try to clear it away unsuccessfully. Suddenly, dinner with strangers doesn't sound like such a good idea. I'm a fucking mess.

CHAPTER TWENTY-SIX

Bennett

A teenage girl opens the door with a smile so similar to her mom's.

"Hi, you must be Bennett," she says.

"Yes. Nice to meet you," I say, passing her the flowers. *Keep your shit together.* The way I feel about Avery scares me. I've never felt this way before and because of that I need to be here. I want to meet her daughter and get to know her life even if mine is a mess.

"Thanks. That's nice of you," she says and takes a sniff. "Mom loves roses."

She seems to be happy to meet me, which I'm taking as a good sign. "Come on in." She waves me in. I take off my runners and follow her inside. "Mom just ran up to take a shower. Can I offer you a drink?"

"Do you have Coke?" I ask, feeling like I need a pick-me-up.

"No Coke in this house. Mom is a health freak. Is water okay?" she asks. I follow her into the kitchen area.

"That will do," I say.

Jessy sets the flowers in a vase.

"So, how's school?" I ask awkwardly.

She gives me a weird look, which only enhances how I'm feeling. "School is good. How does it feel to be out of the hospital? Mom said you were released today."

"It feels weird. I don't know. I guess it feels good," I say.

"That's nice," she replies. I don't think this is going well and I want to make a good impression on the kid.

She walks over to a kitchen cabinet and takes out plates. She sets five plates down.

"Can I help you with the cutlery?" I ask.

"It's okay. I got it." She smiles.

I hear the front door open. Jessy's eyes turn wide. "Must be Tom and Bee," she says quietly.

"It's okay. Your mom has told me a little about them," I say.

"And you still wanted to meet them?" she asks, looking at me, perplexed.

"Yes," I say. I want to understand the dynamic of Avery's life. She and Jessy are a team. I don't want to come between them but I sure as hell want to be a part of their little family. The thought is sobering. My dream from earlier feels less significant as my focus switches to Avery and her daughter's wellbeing.

A tall man with dark hair lined with grey strands walks into the kitchen. He looks at me, nods, and extends his hand. "Tom."

I reach out to shake his hand. "Bennett."

"Oh, you must be Avery's friend." A middle-aged woman with long grey hair and a smile reaches out to shake my hand. "Nice to meet ya. I'm Bee."

I shake her hand. "Bennett. It's a pleasure to meet you, ma'am."

We stare at each other awkwardly for a few beats when Avery walks into the kitchen. Her wet hair hangs over her shoulders. In a simple pink long-sleeve T-shirt and a pair of washed out jeans she takes my breath away.

"Hey Bennett. Sorry. I left work a little late. I'm running behind," she says, leaning up and giving me a kiss on the cheek.

"No worries. I'm actually a little early," I say taking in her scent. The tension I was feeling earlier leaves my body.

"Mom, Bennett brought us both flowers," Jessy says, pointing to where the two vases sit on the kitchen table.

"They're beautiful. How sweet of you," Avery says, smiling to me. Her smile is warm and personal. It reminds me why I've fallen so hard, so fast for her.

"You're welcome," I say.

We stare at each other. A long beat passes and then Avery turns and begins to take some dishes out of the oven.

"Can I help with anything?" I offer.

"We got it covered," Avery says and winks to Jessy.

Jessy stands by the counter, chopping a salad, while Avery puts some dishes on the table.

"Let's sit down," her aunt says, and I follow Avery to the table and wait for her to take a seat. She pats the chair beside her, so she is situated between me and Jessy. Her aunt and uncle sit across from us.

We begin to eat. Avery has made some tofu and chicken, Chinese style, along with a shrimp dish and a beef dish that has green peas.

"I don't remember the last time I had a home-cooked meal. Thanks so much for having me," I say to Avery and her aunt and uncle. There's a quiet tension around the table, an unease that feels all too familiar to me and reminds me of times when I arrived at a new foster home and ate the first meal. It was always so awkward. In most cases, that feeling stayed because the foster parents were in it for the money and didn't care about parenting.

"My pleasure," Avery says.

"Mom is a really good cook," Jessy says.

"My nephew was a SEAL. Died way too young," Tom says.

I don't know why, but when Avery said she was living with family I'd thought it was hers, and not her deceased husband's.

"I'm sorry. That's tough," I say.

"The boy never had a father. My sister raised him. Did the best she could," Aunt Bee says.

"Aunt Bee, I don't think this is the best time to speak of Liam," Avery says politely.

She and Jessy give each other a WTF look.

I stay quiet.

"My sister had a hard time. Couldn't take care of the boy herself," Aunt Bee goes on.

Jessy and Avery stop eating their food.

"Avery, dear, would you mind bringing the soy sauce to the table. You know how I like to dip my food," her aunt says.

Avery leaves the table for soy sauce. She returns a few moments later and places the bottle in front of her aunt. Her aunt doesn't say thank you.

"What happened to you?" Tom asks me straight out.

I take a sip of water. "I was involved in an IED explosion."

Avery places her hand on my forearm. "You don't need to talk about that now."

"It's okay," I say, smiling to her reassuringly. I don't know what's up with her aunt and uncle, but they aren't fazing me.

We begin to eat quietly.

"Avery, would you mind bringing me the club soda? This food is going to give me heartburn," her uncle says.

Jessy stands. "It's okay, Mom. I'll get it," she says. Something about the way she responds tells me this kind of thing happens often, and that's why Avery doesn't like to be home.

Jessy leaves the table and the grip on my fork tightens. She returns with a can of club soda.

"Me too, dear, if you don't mind," Bee says to Jessy.

Are these people for real?

"What is it that you do, Jim?" I ask.

"Me?" he asks, like I have some nerve asking him a direct question.

"Yeah." I nod.

"I dabble in this and that," he says.

"And you, Bee? Are you working?" I ask, wondering how they

keep up this home. I know Avery pays their food expenses, but it costs much more to hold a place like this.

"I work at the Walgreens," she says.

I nod. "Nice."

"You going to be walking with that cane forever?" Aunt Bee asks me in return. I know I just got personal with asking about jobs, so she clearly feels like she has a right, too.

"Hopefully not." I nod.

Avery's knee knocks into mine under the table. I look at her and she whispers, "Sorry."

The rest of the meal is uneventful. When it's time to clear, her aunt and uncle sit and don't offer to help.

"You relax. I'll clear the table," I say to Avery. She must be exhausted after a long day at work and cooking such a fine meal.

"It's okay." She begins to stand.

I place my hand on hers. "Sit," I tell her with a smile.

She stands and so does Jessy.

"Let us just help you," Jessy says. They both stand and begin to clear the table. I help too and follow them to the sink area. Next to the sink, Jessy whispers, "Leaving Mom at the table with them is worse torture than cleaning off the table."

"Uh, got it," I nod.

"What's for dessert?" Uncle Jim asks, rubbing his rounded belly.

"I didn't get dessert. I didn't have time," Avery explains.

"You know that we're supposed to get full meals Avery," he says in such a demeaning way.

"Buddy, if you want dessert, take your car around the corner. Pretty sure I saw a Dairy Queen close by," I snap.

Avery looks at me like I just told her that her puppy is dying. Jessy mutters something I don't understand but she has a full-blown smile on her face.

Shit! What have I done?

"Are you going to allow your guest to speak to us this way?" Aunt Bee asks Avery, her chin tilted to the ceiling.

Avery's mouth draws open and shut. Open and shut.

"It should've happened a long time ago," Jessy says. "You and Uncle Jim think my mom is your slave and she isn't. So what if you're my dad's aunt? It doesn't give you a right to behave shitty," Jessy finishes, her cheeks red, her chest heaving.

"Jessy," Avery chides, placing her hands on her hips.

"Not this time, Mom," Jessy says. "Let's leave now. Let's just go. Let them clean their own dinner and get their own stupid dessert and make their own stupid evening tea."

Avery looks frozen.

"Babe. Talk to me," I whisper against her ear.

Avery is at a loss of words.

"Come. Let's go. Both of you," I say feeling the need to take charge. I take Avery by her hand and Jess follows us. We grab jackets by the door and Jessy takes the car keys.

"I can drive," she says.

Avery looks shell-shocked, but she nods.

We head outside.

"I'm sorry, but they're thoughtless pricks," I say. Then I look at Jessy. "Shoot, I'm sorry. I need to learn to use better language."

Jessy laughs. "I'm not five. I hear much worse at school." She presses her lips together and looks to her mom. "Mom, it's fine. Stop freaking out. If it were up to me, I would've told them off a long time ago. Bennett was right to do what he did. Thank you, Bennett," she says, giving me an assured nod.

"Avery, I'm sorry. I overstepped. It's hard to watch how they treat you. Their lack of respect for you and your daughter is completely appalling. They're shitty people, I couldn't stand by and do nothing," I say, knowing I'm being a little harsh, but honesty does always work best.

"They are," Jessy agrees.

"I know that. Don't you think I know that?" Avery snaps. "They're the only family we have," Avery says to Jessy.

"Mom, they were Dad's family, and he really hasn't been a part of our lives in forever," Jessy says.

"I know that, but now we don't have a place to stay. How can we go back in there? It would've made more sense to find our own place. I told you I was working on it," Avery says to Jessy. "And you . . ." She turns to me, her eyes darkening with wrath. I cower in front of this woman who holds my heart in her hands. "You can't just bulldoze my life."

"You're right and I'm sorry. But I'm also not sorry for standing up for you. I always want to stand up for you. I finally understood why you spent most nights out of the house, and it got to me. I know I need to control my temper and not act on impulse. I'm truly sorry for that," I say.

Avery's tight brows and narrowed eyes relax into a soft smile and warm gaze.

"I'm sorry. I messed up. You and Jessy can stay at my place. You can both have the bedroom and I'll take the couch. You will find a place soon, I'm sure, and we can send for your things. Is it so bad that I want better for you?" I ask.

"Bennett, you're all right in my book," Jessy says.

Avery laughs.

I laugh.

Jessy laughs.

Everything feels a little lighter.

I head back inside with Jessy and Avery so they can pack a bag. I may look injured, but I'm still a big, strong guy. The aunt and uncle aren't anywhere to be seen. Avery and her daughter return downstairs each with a large duffle on their back. Something about it reminds me of my deployments.

The three of us get into Avery's car, and we head back to my place. I've rocked Avery's entire world. There is no way I can leave now.

CHAPTER TWENTY-SEVEN
Avery

"I really like him, Mom. Now I understand why you've been so smitten," Jess says, lying in the dark beside me in Bennett's room.

"Jess, we don't have a place to live right now," I remind her. "What he did was irresponsible."

"The way he stood up for you is something I should've done ions ago," she says, and her words hit me hard. I've always tried to do right by my daughter.

"I've failed you. I just had this vision in my head that you could do great things with all the money that was left behind from Daddy's death. I pictured these great scenarios in my head about giving you an easy life. I've had to work so hard and I guess, for some reason, staying with Uncle Jim and Aunt Bee gave me a false sense of support and comfort." I sigh.

"You haven't failed me. I'm just fine. *We're* fine. It's just been time to move on for a while now. We've been stuck. I have to thank Bennett for unsticking us." She laughs and yawns at the same time.

"I'll take the day off tomorrow and go house-hunting," I say, looking at her with such pride. "By the way, when did you grow up?"

"Funny."

"Get some rest. I don't want you to be tired," I say, giving her forehead a kiss.

"I love you, Mom," she says with her eyes closed.

"Love you too."

Jessy falls asleep and I stare at the ceiling replaying the conversation I had with Sutton about him taking a job out of state. Bennett hasn't mentioned anything to me. He's only told me how he wants us to be together, how his feelings for me grow every day. I figure it means that he didn't take the job and doesn't want me to worry.

A long drawn out groan that sounds agonizing pierces the quiet of the room and startles me. Bennett shouts, "No."

I worry that he's having a night tremor. My stomach sinks and I slip out of bed and tiptoe over to him in the family room. His head jerks from left to right quickly and he's screaming, "No, no, please don't take me."

I walk over to him and touch his shoulder.

"Bennett. It's Avery. Everything is okay," I say. His dream has a strong grip on him, and he doesn't snap out of it. He starts to cry and my heart breaks. "Bennett, please open your eyes." I shake his shoulder harder. "Bennett, it's a bad dream. It's Avery. I'm here." My palm comes up and brushes his forehead. His eyes open but he looks at me like he can see right through me. "You were having a bad dream," I say.

He nods, but he still looks spacy. I caress his forehead. "Do you want to talk about it?"

He shakes his head.

He lifts his blanket. "Come in here. I want to hold you," he says.

I climb in beside him on the couch and he covers the two of us. I wrap my arms around him tight and he wraps his arms around me, and we hold each other in the silence of night, not a word spoken between us. With his arms holding me tight and his lips breathing against my forehead I feel safe, wanted. When have I ever felt this way? I meant to come in here and soothe him and yet he is soothing me.

"I remember when social services came and took me away from my mother," he suddenly says. "I don't know where that dream came from, but it was so real and vivid. I've never dreamt that before. It was something about tonight. Being in that home with your aunt and uncle, watching how they treat you and your daughter . . . I couldn't stomach it."

I tilt my head up a little so I can look into his eyes. "I don't know how I expected dinner to go. I knew you wanted to see where I lived and how I lived. I knew you wouldn't like it. Maybe there was some small part of me that hoped it would end this way. I wasn't brave enough to do it myself. I let my daughter down by living in such an uncomfortable and passive-aggressive atmosphere. I just didn't know how to take that step. How to make that change," I admit.

Our bodies are already flush together but somehow Bennett pulls me even closer and kisses my forehead. "You're so brave. You got pregnant at sixteen and had a kid basically on your own," he says, because he knows that Liam was rarely around. "You had no one to rely on and you did such an amazing job with Jessy. You put yourself through school and you have a great job. I think you're being too hard on yourself. We all want to feel safe and a part of something. For me, I found that with the navy. It scares the hell out of me that I don't have that anymore, so I know what it's like to have comfort ripped out from under you. What happened tonight isn't the same thing but in a way, it is. Like I said, I'm sorry, but I'm not really sorry." His voice is gruff. The timbre low and smooth. He smells of fresh shower gel and something distinctly him. I want us to get lost together but not with Jess in the next room.

"Thanks, Bennett. I really needed to hear that." I press a kiss to his lips. He's slowly stealing my heart. I want to ask him what the future holds, what his plans are, but he just left the hospital. It's a big step in a new life. I don't want to pressure him.

"I want to always be around to reassure you," he says. *Can he sense my anxieties over us?* Over the job that Sutton mentioned. There's no way he took a job. He just assured me that he wants to always be around.

"I hope you will be," I say, wanting him to stick around so badly. "I should get back into bed with Jess." I slide off the couch and out of his warmth.

"I hope so, Avery," he answers into the darkness. I tiptoe back into bed with Jess and I fall asleep easily this time.

CHAPTER TWENTY-EIGHT
Bennett

It's been two weeks since Avery and Jess moved out of her aunt and uncle's house. They stayed with me a few nights and then found their own cute little two-bedroom apartment close to Jess's school.

I lean back in my chair and stare at the woman who owns every piece of my heart. "Do you like the linguine?" I ask.

Avery takes a sip of her wine and swallows a bite. "It's delicious. Thanks so much for doing this. It was a long day at work. I spent half the time in the pool, which always makes me more tired."

"I hope you aren't too tired. I've been waiting for tonight for a while." I smile. Jess is staying at friend's place tonight which means Avery and I have her place to ourselves.

"Me too. It'll be nice to have alone time. Don't worry—the pasta is giving me just the right amount of carbs to restore my energy," she says and takes another sip of wine. "This is really delicious," she says, and forks another mouthful.

"Thanks. I'm glad I went for the roasted vegetables and linguine and not the pork in a gravy sauce like I planned," I say, knowing Avery likes to eat healthily.

"Definitely the better choice in my book," Avery says.

We finish eating and we both just sit back in our chairs, drink wine and laugh.

I take her hand and caress it in mine. "I've still got dessert," I say.

"Hmm, dessert sounds good, but I may have other things on my mind," she says with her cheeks flushed.

"Oh yeah. What did you have in mind?" I ask, taking a sip of my wine. It's fun to flirt with her. To watch her chest rise and fall faster as my words excite her.

"I was hoping you could offer some suggestions," she says.

"Well," I say, standing from my chair. I walk around the table. "I was thinking that there was something I wanted to taste . . .or I do have a chocolate lava cake in the fridge. I can warm it up and we can share." I stand in front of her. I would like to kneel in front of her and bury my head between her thighs, but I can't kneel yet.

"I think I may be more interested in hearing what it was you wanted to taste?" She smiles devilishly. I love that there are no boundaries between us. Her shyness is fading away. The fact that she feels safe with me does something to my insides. Everything about her calls me to on a deep level.

"Sure. I can tell you a little about what I was thinking," I say.

She takes a sip of wine. "I'm all ears."

I take the wine from her hand and drink from her glass. Wanting the taste of her on my lips, I lick my lips slowly and watch as her pupils dilate. Then I give her both of my hands. "I'm going to need you to come with me."

She places each of her hands in each of my palms, and I pull her gently to a standing position. She tilts her head up to me and our lips almost connect.

"How I would love to take you here on the kitchen table," I say.

"Soon. We'll get there."

"Yes, we will. I want to kiss you so bad, but I know if we kiss here both of us will lose control, and there is so much I want to do to you that I need you on the bed for," I say.

"Lead the way, sailor." She smirks.

"Did I mention how beautiful you look tonight?" I ask as I lead her to the bedroom. She's wearing a tight black shirt that dips in the front. Her tits look full and her skin is milky white. She doesn't normally dress in such a revealing manner, which tells me she's dressed like this for me.

"About three times." She laughs.

We reach the bedroom where I set up some candles. "Give me a sec," I say as I make my way around the room, lighting them.

"This is so perfect," Avery says.

"I want our first time to be memorable," I explain.

"It will be." She smiles.

"I want you so bad," I admit.

After I light the last candle, I walk over to her and take her in. Avery is beautiful on the inside and outside but tonight, her hair catches the glow of the flames and her eyes glimmer like cognac and I find myself swimming inside them. She looks at me too and I lift my hand and touch her breast over her shirt. Her breaths quicken and we hold eye contact.

"Just touching you like this makes me crazy," I say.

She doesn't respond but her gaze tells me more than words ever could. My hand moves from her breast and I lay it flat where her heart is. It's beating fast and hard. I take her palm and lay it against my chest so she can feel what she does to me. Her eyes hold mine. Both of us are breathing erratically and my restraint snaps. My lips connect with hers and her hands come up and hold the back of my neck. Our lips move in sync, like we were always meant to be like this. She tastes of wine and sweetness. My tongue comes up to tangle with hers. My hands land on her shoulders and move down her arms across her stomach. I look for a way to lift this shirt off of her but there isn't an edge to pull over her head.

She senses my confusion. "It's a bodysuit. I have to remove my jeans to take it off."

"Is this supposed to be like a chastity belt or something?" I snicker.

She doesn't answer as she pops the button on her jeans and begins to lower them over her behind.

I mutter expletives under my breath, thanking the powers that be for putting this woman in my life. With her jeans removed, she stands in front of me in this little body-suit number. It's high cut on her legs, showing off her long legs and slim waist.

"You're stunning," I say.

"I stopped after work to pick it up. I wanted to get something sexy. I don't own anything sexy," she says softly, like she's apologizing.

"Babe, you hit jackpot," I say. "Lie back on the bed."

She does as I say. "There are clips between my legs to open it. The lady in the store said these were a big seller."

"That lady was right." I lie beside her and my hand dips between her thighs. I begin to rub her over the fabric.

"Bennett," she pants. I love how responsive she is. Thinking how long she went without sex almost causes me to blow my load.

"I got you," I say as I slip my finger inside the body suit and dip a finger inside her. A soft moan leaves her lips and her eyes fall closed. She breathes heavily and moans as I work her over. I can't let her come before I get my mouth on her though.

I unbutton the snaps between her legs. She isn't wearing panties, or maybe this thing is panties—I don't know. She's mostly bare except for a small strip of hair. Her pussy is wet and pulsing. Just watching her causes my cock to throb against my jeans. I ask her to shift up the bed and then I situate myself between her legs on my stomach. I want to drink her in, taste her juices.

My tongue connects with her clit as I lick down her opening, and her body jerks beneath me. I work my tongue up and down. "I've been dreaming about this," I say as I put a finger inside her. "You taste like heaven."

"Bennett," she moans my name.

"Say it again," I urge her as I work my tongue faster. She is swollen and so close to coming.

"Bennett," she says, and inhale and exhale to slow myself down because the breathless way she says my name makes me lose my mind.

I pick up speed and she begins to come. "Holy smokes, this is so much better than I thought it would be," she says. I continue to lick her as her hips move with my tongue, her whole body jerking. I don't relent as I suck every last bit of her juices. When she comes down from her high, I use my arms to shift my body up next to hers. I put my arm around her and she curls into me, fitting perfectly.

I kiss her forehead. "When you said it was so much better than you thought it would be, what did you mean?" I ask lazily, dragging my finger up her arm.

"Did I say that?" She laughs, giving me a feigned innocence look.

"Yes." I raise my brows, waiting expectantly for her to explain.

"Okay, well let's just say that high school boys don't know what they are doing so none of them . . ." She tilts her chin and nods.

"You mean no one ever went down on you before?" I ask, perplexed.

Her cheeks turn ashen. "Bennett, don't look at me like that." She lifts the blanket to cover her face.

"Don't hide from me," I say.

She peeks out from under the blanket, only showing me her eyes.

"I'm sorry. I didn't mean to sound shocked. I actually kind of like the idea of me being your first," I say and feel my chest puff out a little larger.

She laughs and moves the blankets to under her arms, "I'm glad you're proud of yourself. That was . . ."

"That was what?" I ask, waiting for an answer.

Her eyes glow with mischief and she doesn't give me an answer. Damn, woman.

CHAPTER TWENTY-NINE

Avery

"You lie back and let me take care of you," I say, pressing on his chest as I crawl out from the covers and straddle him.

"Take off your top," he says.

I lift the body suit over my head. I got a new lacy bra too. After never treating myself, it was time.

His dark eyes turn to molten pools of lava.

"Like what you see?"

"You know I do," he says on a groan as the palms of his hands knead each of my breasts. I press my breasts against him.

"You're going to make me come in my pants," he says.

"Well, we better take care of that," I say, shifting to the side so I can remove his jeans. I pop the button and lower them along with his boxers. His cock is large and thick. I was expecting him to be big, given his size, but this is . . . My insides clench.

I lean down and take him in my mouth. He's too big for me to take him all in so the part that doesn't fit my mouth, I fist with my hand. His fingers work into my hair and he groans. "So good. Yeah, baby, like that," he says as my tongue swirls around him. He lengthens and stiffens in my mouth.

I bob my head up and down sucking him off. With my other hand I cup his balls. "Fuck this feels good."

His words spur me on and I move faster. Watching the affect I have on him turns me on more and the ache between my thighs grows stronger.

"I want to come inside you. I need to feel you around me," he says. He pulls his cock out of my mouth and I move up his body to straddle him.

"I'm on the pill. Are you clean?" I ask.

"I'm clean. I've had every blood test known to man in the last couple months," he scoffs.

"We can still use a condom. I just figured . . . you should . . . ah . . . know."

"Avery." His hand comes up and he cups my chin. "The thought of going bareback with you is making me crazy. Don't make me wait another second," he says.

I guide his cock inside me and we moan together. I begin to move, and his palms come up and work my breasts. He lowers the bra so that my tits sit above it in the air. "Come here." He guides me forward and he takes one of my nipples in his mouth.

I moan, feeling wetness pooling between my thighs. His tongue does a circle, licking around one nipple, and then he moves to the other one. I watch him, in a daze. Something about his thick lips, high cheekbones and big, manly hands has me under a spell.

We move faster. He thrusts up inside me and I move myself faster and faster against him.

"You feel so good. Being inside you like this . . ." he pants. "I've never done this with anyone. Ever," he says, and his words hit me in the middle of my chest and warm my heart. His head falls back on the pillow and I move on top of him, and we get lost in the lust, in the fire that burns between us. I begin to come first, and Bennett follows soon after. As his come shoots inside me, my body combusts, and I can't take it. Everything feels like too much, too real, too everything... We both fall into ecstasy. And it's absolutely perfect.

I fall beside him, and we catch our breath together. It almost feels like our hearts are beating to the same rhythm.

We fall asleep at one point and when my phone beeps after one a.m., I check it. Jessy writes that she is at her friend's house and going to sleep. I'm glad she didn't forget to text me.

As I put my phone down, Bennett wraps his arm around my waist, his erection pressing on my back, and we make love again. This time he rolls on top of me, using his arms to brace himself. He enters me slowly, moving his hips in a slow roll. His torturous rhythm rubs my clit in all the right places. We come again together, falling into this beautiful ecstasy, this place where I feel safe beneath him. To this place where we feel like one.

CHAPTER THIRTY

Avery

My phone alarm goes off. I had to set an alarm so Bennett and I wouldn't be in bed together if Jessy decided to come home early. I turn to see that Bennett isn't in bed. He's awake which means I can steal a few extra minutes of sleep.

I press the snooze button. Another five minutes won't hurt. My body feels tired and well used. My eyes close and I fall into a blissful sleep.

The alarm goes off, scaring the crap out of me.

I sit and rub my eyes, then I run my fingers through my hair to tame it. I walk over to my dresser and take out a large football jersey I have from college. It hits my knees. Then I trudge over to the kitchen. My muscles ache. I can feel Bennett everywhere. It's a heady feeling. I've never had such a strong connection with a man before. It's like Bennett and I get each other. It helps that our chemistry is certifiably explosive, and he and Jessy get along so well.

I'm falling for him and that terrifies me, yet I don't want to stop myself from falling. I hit the kettle and look in the fridge to see what our breakfast options are. A phone beeps and I automatically turn to its sound. It's Bennett's phone. Sutton's name lights up the screen, along with a message. *Can't wait to see you in two weeks. This place is freaking awesome.*

See him in two weeks? What the . . .?

My heart beats faster. Sutton said he took the job, but Bennett never mentioned it. I assumed he declined. *Is he leaving me in two weeks?*

I reread the message, thinking that maybe I read it wrong, but no—the words are there in fine print. With all the drama with my aunt and uncle, and finding a new place to live, I forgot about the whole job thing. Bennett would have said something if there were, in fact, something to say. I feel like such a fool, allowing myself to live in this perfect bubble where I believed I'd met a great man who liked me a lot and got along with my daughter. I've gone and fallen in love with him, for crying out loud. *You stupid fool,* I shout in my head, and my palms begin to sweat. The thought of losing Bennett guts me. Did he even plan on saying goodbye? I think back to all the messed-up situations I had with Liam. How he shut down before leaving on a deployment. He never gave me the love and attention I needed, and I somehow convinced myself that Bennet was the real deal. That he'd be different. How could he be so cruel?

He isn't, Avery.

The voice in my mind is unconvincing. That text message speaks volumes. Sutton and Bennett bonded, and they are meeting up in Virginia fucking Beach.

"Avery?" Bennett's voice breaks into the internal meltdown I'm having. I am holding his phone and staring at it, probably like it's a lethal weapon hellbent on destruction. He's freshly showered, wearing one of those sweaters that hugs his thick arms. His jeans hang on him just right—narrow on the waist, not too tight in the thighs.

My head snaps up to his eyes and I remember how they first made me fall for him. His molten eyes carried so much emotion, but it was all a lie.

"When were you going to tell me you were leaving?" I snap,

passing him the phone. I watch as his eyes widen and he takes a deep breath. He takes the phone, and I walk out of the kitchen.

"Avery, it's not what you think," he says.

"Oh, really? You didn't take a job at the other end of the country. And you won't be starting in two weeks. And, let me guess—you've known for a while and didn't want to enlighten me. Hmm, what could that mean?" I tap my fingers against my chin. "What was I—just some piece of ass to you? I know how SEALs can be. I've heard stories around the hospital. I've seen my friends' marriages fall apart. You guys go overseas, and you think you can do whatever the hell you like. Doesn't matter who's home waiting for you."

"That isn't fair." Bennett takes a step back like I've wounded him.

"Ha! That's funny. You've been telling me how much you care about me. I let you meet my daughter, for fuck's sake," I say, waving my hands in the air like a crazed person. "There was a reason I didn't date. There was a reason I didn't let anyone into our lives."

"Would you please let me explain?" he pleads, his mocha eyes holding a torrent of emotion.

"What is there to explain? Did you take a job in Virginia Beach?" I ask, crossing my arms over my chest. Anger pulses through me. I don't know who I am madder at—him or me.

"Yes, but—"

"Are you leaving in two weeks?" I ask.

"Yes, but let me explain," he says, his voice low and broken.

"Just leave. Get out. I don't ever want to see you again," I say.

"Avery, please," he says.

Tears run down my cheeks and blur my vision. This is too painful. I'm a mess and Jess may be home soon.

"Leave." I point to the door.

Bennett walks over to the door. He opens the closet and takes his jacket and cane, and he walks out.

I fall to the couch and bawl my eyes out. What was I thinking, falling for a man like him? What a colossal mistake.

CHAPTER THIRTY-ONE

Avery

After spending all day Sunday watching movies in bed, I head back to work on Monday determined to get my life back on track. I get through my morning appointments.

I'm leaving the gym area on my way to the lockers to eat my lunch in solitude when Cindy stops me.

"Hey, you. Mind telling me why you were MIA all weekend?" She waggles her brows like I would have some juicy details. I never told her about Bennett, and for that, I feel like an awful friend. My eyes begin to water. Her face falls. "I'm sorry. What's going on? Did something happen?" she asks.

"A lot." I nod.

"Do you want to get out of here?" she asks, clearly reading my distress.

"Yes," I sigh.

"I'll drive. Let me just go up and grab my purse. I'll meet you out front?"

"Okay." I head to the locker-room, grab my purse and meet her outside.

We walk over to her car in silence then get in. She starts the engine but before she puts the car in drive, she looks at me thoughtfully. "Is this about him?"

"Him?" I ask, feigning confusion.

"Aw, come on. Give me a little more credit than that," she says.

I remain quiet.

"Avery, we've been good friends a while. I know what your life has been like. I've seen you trudge through your time at work, passing another day and another day. Then suddenly there was a pep in your step," she says.

"I'm always smiling at work. I'm happy to be helping my patients," I say.

"I never said that you weren't good at what you do or weren't committed. Everyone knows how committed you are, but you suddenly had something more," she says.

My stomach sinks. She knows about Bennett. "Does the whole hospital know?"

Her right eye pinches slightly shut, and she tilts her head from side to side. "I wouldn't say everyone, but some people are talking. It's only hearsay though. No one has proof."

I blow out a breath.

"Avery, you could've trusted me. I would've never told your secret. I thought we were good friends," she says.

"I'm sorry. I feel terrible."

"I can see, and I don't intend to guilt you now. All I'm saying is I'm here for you if you need me. You can talk to me. I would never do anything to jeopardize your livelihood. I know I say stupid shit sometimes and get caught up in the gossip mill at work, but I do have boundaries." She laughs sadly.

"I'm sorry. I didn't mean to hurt your feelings by not sharing. I was just terrified of what was happening between Bennett and me. I've never felt this way before and . . ." I search for the right words.

"You fell in love with him," she says.

The tears I was holding back begin to fall. I hate to admit it, but I did exactly that. I nod because words are just too hard.

"Oh, honey." She leans over to hug me.

"He's leaving," I say. Sure, he's been calling my phone non-stop and sending messages, but nothing he can say will fix the broken inside me.

"You mean he isn't planning on staying in Jersey?" she asks.

"No," I say. "He didn't even tell me he was planning to leave." Sutton had let the job interview slip. I should've confronted Bennett though. I should've called him on it. "I feel stupid and weak."

"Hon, you are anything but that. You're kind and smart. You're a kickass PT and an amazing mom," she says.

"I let my daughter down too. I stayed with Aunt Bee and Uncle Jim too long. I knew they were toxic . . ."

"They provided you a safety net. You got to save your money, and I've met Jessy how many times? Right, like a million. That girl is smart and stable. That's all on you. Don't you forget that. I know it's shitty to have your heart broken. How many times have you given me pep talks over the years?" She looks to me with her lips tilted down, her eyes creasing in the corners.

"Enough times," I answer knowingly.

"'Cause I put myself out there. I allow myself to feel, and yeah, it's scary, and I do get hurt, but I can tell you what I don't want in a man. I can also tell you what I do want. I just haven't found it yet," she says.

"I know what I don't want either. Life with Liam was mediocre, but I had Jess to think of and I wanted her to have her daddy around," I say.

"From the stories you told me, you put up with too much," Cindy says. "No disrespect to the dead, but it's true, Avery."

"I know. You're right. I was young and alone with a baby. I put up with too much crap. I'm not that woman anymore though. I won't be left behind or manipulated. I just won't have it," I say.

"Hear, hear," Cindy says.

I look at her and burst out laughing. I feel manic, but with the overload of emotions inside me, I need a release. She laughs too and things just feel lighter.

"We got half an hour. How about we go indulge in some cheeseburgers, fries, and maybe some gravy?" she says, and she licks her lips.

"That sounds perfect, minus the gravy for me." I smile.

She drives off, and even though I'm still feeling glum she's reminded me that I am not the woman I once was. I won't put up with the things I used to put up with.

My phone beeps in my hand and I see another text message from Bennett. I've been ignoring them. I told myself that if I read them, I will lower my defenses and I don't want that.

My phone beeps again.

Bennett: Please meet with me. I need you, Avery. Please.

His simple words break my heart in two. I put the phone away and have lunch with my friend. I won't let another SEAL turn me into a fool.

CHAPTER THIRTY-TWO

Bennett

"I've tried texting and calling. She won't even answer my calls," I say, pacing back and forth in my apartment.

"Man, I told you to be up front with her. Trust me, after everything Ashton and I have been through, I can finally say I know how to stay out of the doghouse," Quinn says.

I scoff. "Why do I find that unlikely."

"Hey, don't start. Ashton and I have been through a lot, but the main thing is that I am trying to show her I'm here for the long run. I'm not cutting out," he says, sounding like a man I don't even know. I would make fun of him and tell him he's lost his nuts only I totally get how he feels. I'd say and do anything to win back Avery's trust right now.

"How can I show her when she won't answer my calls?" I ask.

"Go to her work, find her at home. Do whatever you need to do," he says.

"Work is out of the question. I don't want her getting fired. She was already warned about me," I mumble, mostly to myself.

"I've got to go. Keep me posted."

"Talk to you later."

"Bye." He ends the call.

I think of how my life could have taken a very different route had my angel not walked into my hospital room when she did. The pain was unbearable and all I saw was black. Then Avery came into my life like a ray of sunshine. She saved me that day. I can't lose her.

I call Sutton because I still haven't returned his text message.

"Hello," he answers, sounding cheerful. I'm happy for him.

"Hey, man," I say.

"Is everything okay?" he asks. I haven't known him very long and he's much younger, but this kid feels like he could've been my brother. Maybe it's the military connection.

"Well, I kind of messed up with Avery," I say.

"Shoot. I hope I didn't have anything to do with it," he says.

None of this is his fault. I take the blame for holding back. "Why would you say that?" I ask, because it is an odd thing for him to say.

"The day Jackson and Quinn came into the hospital to interview us, I bumped into Avery on my way out. I assumed you told her about the interview, so I mentioned it," he says.

Fuck me. She knew and didn't say anything. She must have thought I was keeping it from her all this time.

"It's no worries. I didn't tell her about it because I wanted more time with her. I handled things badly, but I plan on fixing it," I say.

"You know, that night she invited you along for the movie night she thought I'd be a good influence on you. At least, that's why I think she introduced us. Reality is meeting you was the best thing that could've happened to me. I'm really happy here at Cole," he says.

"I'm happy for you, brother," I say, and I truly mean it.

"Thanks, man. Will I still be seeing you soon?" he asks.

"I hope so, but I'm honestly not sure," I say.

I don't want to screw Jackson over because he's amazing and I'm so grateful, but I can't walk away from what I have with Avery. We just mesh together. Nothing like this has happened to me before.

"Don't say anything to anyone, okay? I'm working on getting there," I add.

"Mum's the word. Avery is special. Hope it all works out," he says.

"Thanks, Sutton. Take care and kick ass out there," I say.

"Right back at you."

We end the call and I look at the clock on my phone. She usually gets home after six. I take a seat on the couch and wait. With all this time on my hands, I try to find a way to win her back. I only hope that I can.

CHAPTER THIRTY-THREE

Avery

I leave the gym and head home. I was hoping a spin class would increase my endorphins and make me happy, but it didn't work.

I pull into the parking lot of my new building. Jess is standing next to Dylan's car. They're kissing, mouths meshed together. *Young love.* I try to push my own anxieties aside so I can be happy for my daughter. Just because I haven't had luck in love doesn't mean Jess will have the same fate.

I leave the car and carry my gym bag on my shoulder. Snow sprinkles down, the air is fresh and crisp, and everything looks so pretty and serene. Too bad my mood doesn't match.

I clear my throat. "Hey, Jess."

She jerks back at the sound of my voice. She was clearly too busy to notice me. "Mom," she says, in a very high-pitched voice. "Hi."

"Hi Dylan." I wave.

"Good to see you again, Ms. Malone," he says with his accent.

"I best be going," he says to Jess, eyeing me out of the corner of his eye.

"If you like you can stay for dinner. I'm making turkey chili," I offer.

Dylan looks to Jess, and she shrugs and nods.

"Sure, I'd love to," he says.

"I'll see you upstairs then," I say.

I leave the lovebirds on their own. It's freezing outside, and I need a cup of tea to warm up. I'm glad that Jess has been bringing friends over. She never had the option to do that while growing up, and I still feel guilty about it.

I hang my jacket and leave my gym bag on the floor. I'm a sweaty mess but I figure I'll start on dinner and then go shower. I hit the kettle and take out a large pot and pan, since I like to cook the turkey thoroughly.

I check my phone. There hasn't been a single message from Bennett all afternoon. Not since he sent me that desperate message when I was out with Cindy. A part of me is sad that he's stopped trying even though we would have never worked out in the long run anyway. I see that now. He was recently injured and happy to be alive. He wasn't planning on settling down. Not with a single mother, and maybe not ever.

With the pot simmering on the stove I head to the shower. As I pass the closed door to Jess's room, I hear laughter through the door. I smile as I head to the washroom to take a shower. With time on my hands I wash my hair and massage a treatment through my ends. My stomach feels hollow and I wish it would go away.

I throw on an oversized hoodie and a pair of jogging pants, and tie my hair up in a loose bun. When I leave the bathroom, the door to Jess's room is still closed. Hopefully, my daughter heeded my advice about being careful or practicing abstinence, which is the best way to go. I would know, since I perfected it with more than a decade of no sex.

I walk through the family room toward the kitchen and—

What the heck?

Someone is sitting on the couch.

My heart jumps and I am about to yelp when I turn around and realize it's Bennett.

"What are you doing here?" I ask, looking around. "How did you get in?"

He winces. "I knocked. No one answered. I tried the door and it was open. You really should lock your door at all times," he says like he cares.

"You shouldn't be here," I answer. I'll need to remember to tell Jess to be more careful with locking the door.

"We need to talk. I need to explain. You won't answer my calls," he says, using his cane to get up.

"There's a reason for that," I remind him.

"Look, you have every right to be upset but would you at least . . ."

Jess walks into the hall. "Oh, hi Bennett. Are you joining us for dinner?" she asks him.

My daughter full-out knows we broke up. She saw me pouting all weekend. What on earth is she doing? I eye her, giving her a *what the hell* look.

She raises her brows at me then looks back to Bennett. "This is Dylan, my boyfriend," she says to him as Dylan walks up behind her. *Traitor.*

"Nice to meet you, Dylan," Bennett says, shaking his hand. "I'm Bennett."

Dylan shakes his hand, and I drink Bennett in. He's wearing one of his sweaters that fits snugly to his frame. Maybe he's so built that they don't make them that large and that's why it's snug. Either way, it shows off his broad shoulders, muscular arms and a narrow waist. I realize he must have been sitting here for a while because his jacket is resting on the side of the couch.

Bennett looks to me. "I'll leave," he says.

"You should stay," Jess says.

My daughter and I will be having some choice words later.

Bennett smirks and Jess smirks. I don't even know what is going on.

"Fine, I'll stay," he says. "How can I help?" He looks to me.

Wonderful, sweet Bennett, always wanting to help. I can't tell him to leave because I don't want to make a scene in front of Dylan or my traitorous daughter, for that matter.

"We can set the table," Jess says to him.

"Okay, sure," he says. He follows her to the kitchen.

"I'll check on the chili. It should be about ready," I say, turning away from Dylan.

I follow my daughter and Bennett to the kitchen. This is one of the times where the age difference between Jess and I seems minimal. I was basically a child raising one.

Bennett asks Jess how school is going. He remembers which subjects she's taking which surprises me. He asks her how her driving is coming along, and then she asks him if he can take her driving again. It's like they've developed a whole relationship apart from me. I stir the chili in the pot and then I slice up the baguette I bought to eat with the meal.

I pass Jess the plate with the sliced bread and then I pour the chili into a bowl. We all sit at the table and I don't make eye contact with Bennett. Dylan and Bennett begin to talk, which I guess eases some of the tension in the room.

Bennett asks Dylan where in Australia he's from. Dylan tells him he heard he was in the navy. My daughter has clearly spoken to her boyfriend about Bennett. He somehow managed to penetrate my life. Why did I have to fall for another man who was going to leave me?

I fork the food on my plate. Bennett's presence has made me lose my appetite. What could he possibly say to fix all that's broken between us? Nothing. There is no way he could. He kept me in the dark and strung me along.

"The meal was delicious. Thanks, Ms. Malone," Dylan says, standing with his plate. Jess takes hers then asks Bennett if he's done.

"It's fine. I can take my own plate." He smiles at her. They have this friendly comradery happening.

"I'll take it," Jess insists. She walks over to me and asks me if I'm done and I nod.

It leaves me sitting side by side with Bennett, alone at the table. I can't look at him. I keep my hands in my lap and twiddle my thumbs. A few seconds later, Jess walks back to the table.

"Dishwasher is loaded. Is it okay if I go back to Dylan's house to study?" she asks.

Gah! I hope that isn't code for something else. I hate that he seems like a nice kid.

"Okay." I nod. She wants me to talk to Bennett. She clearly thinks there is something to talk about. She doesn't realize that we are totally over.

Jess leaves and I pick up my head. Our gazes lock and my heart sinks. Looks like I just signed myself up for a whole evening of trouble.

CHAPTER THIRTY-FOUR

Bennett

"Look at me, please," I beg.

She shakes her head. "I don't know what you want. We had a good run and it's over," she says.

I hate that she can't look me in the eyes. "We are far from over."

She looks at me like she doesn't understand me. "What is it you want from me?"

I want to tell her everything. I want a life with her and her daughter. I want to wake up every morning beside her.

"I made a mistake. I should've told you about the job interview. I was in the hospital and I was feeling low on myself. Here I had this beautiful smart woman who was interested in me and I was a cripple without a job. Without options," I say.

"That's never what I saw," she says, and I hate how sad she looks. I hate myself for making her feel this way.

"My whole life got sideswiped in the blink of an eye. I saw myself staying in the military, maybe forever. It was everything to me. Then I felt alone and broken, and I met you. I don't know what would've come of me if I didn't have you to look forward to. You were the highlight of my day. You made me want to get better. I wanted to become a better man for you but how could I do that without a respectable job?" I say.

"You could've told me how you were feeling. You shared so much of your past with me. *We* shared so much and you kind of left out a super-important detail," she says.

"I know." I rub my temple. "I messed up. I was scared of losing you. I thought if we had more time together out of the hospital that . . ."

She snaps to a standing position. "What, Bennett? What did you think? That a little more time and I would fall in love with you only to have you leave me? I've been on that roller coaster before. I'm not interested in getting back on."

I realize that there are things about her deceased husband she hasn't told me, because the woman standing in front of me looks terrified and broken. "I'm not him. I don't know exactly what happened with him, but don't compare us," I say. "I want you, Avery Malone. I'm falling in love with you."

She burst into laughter as tears stream down her cheeks. "Are you even listening to yourself? You can't say those things. You penetrated my life, my bed and my heart, and you were planning on leaving in two weeks. When exactly did you plan on telling me? Or didn't you? Was I going to get a letter? Or maybe a text message?" she asks, pacing back and forth. Her hurt and anger towards me breaks my heart.

"I was planning on telling you soon. I never planned on leaving you without notice. Jesus, woman." I shake my head. "I want us to stay together. I knew it would be hard, but I told myself we could have a long-distance relationship—well, at least until Jessy left for college, or I figured maybe you could just move to Virginia Beach with me. It's great out there, and family-friendly, and you could find a job out there too," I say, getting carried away with myself. Her jaw is dropped, and she looks at me incredulously.

"Are you listening to yourself?" she huffs and throws her hands up in the air. "You can't just go and plan my life. I don't know where my daughter will apply for college or where she'll get in. You know I need to put Jess first. I . . . I . . ." words seem lost on her tongue. She stalks off to the family room and falls back on the couch.

I'm a fucking idiot.

I use my cane to stand and follow her. "I messed up. I see that now. I've never been in a serious relationship. I've never had to care for anyone outside of myself. And, of course, my team on deployments, but that's different. I never meant to overstep or decide for you. I just can't see my life without you in it. And that job was a solid offer. I'd do something I'd feel good about and get paid well. There aren't many options out there for an injured SEAL who still needs a shit-ton of therapy," I say.

She exhales and it seems like some of her anger deflates too. "If I was so important to you then why didn't you just share this with me?"

"Because at that point we were hiding our relationship. We only had stolen moments together. I didn't feel secure that it was enough. That you would choose me," I admit.

Her brows draw together. Her brown eyes are red from crying and she looks at me with I don't know what in her expression. Pity? Remorse? I don't like it.

"Our time together in the hospital was special," she says.

"And our time together out of the hospital has brought us so much closer. We have shared and been through so much in such a short time. You can't deny it. We've had a chance to see how much we mesh. That we're really good together," I say.

She swipes at some fallen tears on her cheek. "But how could I ever trust you? You hid so much from me."

"I'm sorry. I messed up. I won't deny it. You can trust me. Give me a chance to prove it to you. If I need to, I'll tell Jackson and Quinn I won't take the job. I'll stay here in Jersey and find what I can," I say.

She shakes her head. "I don't want you to take some half-ass job. I want you to feel good about what you're doing," she says, and of course my angel is thinking of everyone but herself.

"I don't want to leave you. I want you in my life. You're more important to me than some job. If it means I risk losing you then it isn't worth it," I say.

"That's sweet, but I can't leave. Jess has to finish school here. Our life is here, and her friends are here," she says. "It seems like we're at an impasse."

"With you by my side, nothing is impossible." I reach for her hand and look into her eyes.

"Bennett, I..."

"Kiss me, Avery," I say breathlessly. My gaze drops to her plump lips.

She moves slowly toward me and my body buzzes with anticipation. I read fear in her eyes and yet she still moves closer to me. Her mouth touches mine, warm and welcoming, and peace washes over me. My hand comes up to touch her cheek as I deepen the kiss. My tongue dives into her mouth like I am claiming what's mine, and she lets me, taking what I have to give. I drop my cane and it hits the floor, and I use my other arm to wrap around her waist and pull her flush with me. We are both breathing hard. My heartbeat is erratic and all I want to do is take off all her clothes and sink inside her, remind her how it feels when we are connected.

My lips move to her neck as I nip and suck at her delicate skin.

"What are we doing?" she asks.

"Let me show you how I feel about you. You drive me crazy with need. Everything about you draws me in. Your perfect breasts," I say, grabbing a handful of her breast and kneading it in my hands. "Your soft skin," I say as I slowly run my fingers down the milky skin of her neck. "Open your eyes. Look at me, Avery. Look me in the eyes and see how broken I've been these last few days without you," I rasp. I drop my hand into the waistband of her sweatpants and rub my finger on her panties between her thighs. Her eyes are open. They look like warm milk chocolate as she stares at me. Her breaths are shallow. I push her panties aside and dip a finger inside her.

Her hands grasp my shoulders and her chest rises and falls. I give her clit a pinch and her eyes fall closed. Her head tilts back and she moans. "I can't stand. My legs will give out on me."

"I've got you, babe," I say, taking a few steps forward. I walk her back until her back hits the wall. Then I lift one of her legs and wrap it around my waist. If I wasn't injured, I would hoist her up so she could wrap her legs around me easily, but I don't want to aggravate my back injury. Instead, I press myself against her center. I'm so painfully hard right now, but nothing matters to me except her pleasure. I trace her underwear with my fingers and feel her dampness.

"You are so wet for me. I love it," I hiss against her ear. My finger dips inside her. I pull it out and rub her wetness over her clit. She's soaked for me.

Avery moans. I can feel her swelling beneath my touch. "I can't do it. I can't come like this. It's too much."

"Trust me, Avery," I say, and I dip my finger in and out of her faster. I slip my other hand into her pants and rub her clit with my thumb, and then I give her a soft pinch and she cries out, falling into bliss as I pump my finger into her. Her cries of passion are so freaking sexy that my cock bobs against my jeans, threatening to rip the fabric.

"That's it, baby. Take it," I tell her, rubbing her clit in circles. Her whole body is shaking. Her breaths are frantic. Her mouth is open in an *O* as the sweetest sounds escape her. I pull one hand out of her pants and hold her up as her legs give out. When she comes down from her high, she melts into me, her head resting against my chest.

"That was . . ." She's speechless. Good.

I want to lift her in my arms and carry her to bed but that still isn't possible because of my back. I wait for her breathing to even out. The fact that she is trusting me to hold her, to give this to her, means everything. "Let's go to bed, babe. I need to have more of you," I say.

She shakes her head.

"No?" I ask, feeling confused.

"I want to stay right here," she says, and then she drops to her knees. She unbuttons my belt and unzips my zipper. My cock must look like a ferocious beast right now because I am hard as fuck.

"You don't have to do that," I say.

She licks some pre-cum off my tip and moans. I hiss. Fuck, that was hot.

"You really don't though," I say.

"I want to," she says, sounding very much like a seductress. She moves me so that my back is to the wall, and then she guides me to her mouth. It feels like my eyes will roll back into my head, but I keep them open and run my hands into her hair, watching how her plump lips wrap around my girth. She takes me in and I feel myself hit the back of her throat, her mouth hollowing. She lifts a hand and grips me, giving a squeeze as she pumps me inside her mouth and with her hand. The simultaneous motion is dizzying.

"I won't last long," I grit out.

She pulls back and her tongue licks my crown.

"You'll be the end of me," I say, leaning back against the wall. My balls turn heavy as she creates a rhythm of licking my girth and taking me back. I groan and my hips begin to rock in and out of her mouth. She got control of her gag reflex, that's for darn sure.

"If you don't want me coming in your mouth, you'll need to stop now," I warn her. Fuck, this is the best blow job of my life. Watching her on her knees, knowing this is Avery giving me her trust, has me completely undone.

"Come in my mouth," she says as she licks a bead of come off my crown. "I need to taste you."

She picks up pace and my head hits the wall as my eyes shut, and I let her take over. Electricity shoots down my spine as the liquid heat of her warm, wet mouth engulfs me. I shoot into her mouth as my heart hammers and ecstasy overtakes me. I grunt and groan, and she milks my every last drop. I'm fucking ruined. This woman has me wrapped around her finger.

When I come to, she stands and watches me with wide eyes and a big smile.

"Your wish is my command, princess," I say.

"Very funny." She laughs.

I wrap my arm around her and pull her to my chest, and we stand like that, hugging. A part of me just wants to keep her wrapped up in my arms forever.

I tilt my chin to look at her. "You okay, babe?"

"I don't know," she answers, looking a little solemn.

"Avery, as long as I have you in my life, we will figure it out. I made a mistake by not sharing with you. And I get that now. I know I can't expect you to move. I just want to be with you," I say.

She gives me one of her warm signature smiles. I kiss the top of her head and then I take her hand and guide her to her room.

"Bennett, Jess's curfew is in an hour. We should just get cleaned up," she says.

"An hour is all I need. Trust me."

CHAPTER THIRTY-FIVE

Avery

"You look . . . relaxed," Cindy says, waggling her brows.

I roll my eyes, staring at the chart in my hands. "Buzz off," I say, looking at the chart one more time before I go to meet a new patient.

"No way. You aren't getting off the hook so easy," she says. "Now spill. How sorry was he? Is he still planning on leaving?"

My lips turn down. "I honestly don't know. We don't have a plan. All I know is that we want to be together. He apologized and he's aware he overstepped and screwed up by not telling me about the job, and he is sorry, and he admitted he was wrong. He was open with me, Cindy, and it felt so good," I say. Liam had been closed down all the time. He'd screw up one way or another and say *sorry, I messed up,* and then he would just go and make the same mistake all over. He sure as hell didn't care to make it up to me in the bedroom or any other way.

"I'm sure it was, girlfriend." She smirks, giving me a knowing grin.

"Not like that." I wave my hand at her. It was exactly like that but I'm not up for sharing details.

"Yeah, right, okay," she concedes. "I'm glad he's turning out to be a nice guy."

"Me too. I just hope that we will find a way to make us both happy," I say. Bennett and I are stuck between a rock and a hard place. There doesn't seem to be a good answer for us.

"Me too, sweets." She smiles.

"How is your sister doing? I'm sorry I didn't ask before. I feel like an awful friend, making everything about me," I say. Last I remember, Cindy was helping her with a resume.

"Well, she left the last job because her and her boss were hooking up, and then it ended. Now she's working in a new place. You should check it out," she says.

"I'm sure it's a cool place, but you know I'm not getting a tattoo," I tell her.

"You never know. Maybe the sexy SEAL will have you engrave his name or call sign on your behind," she says, and then she laughs.

"Yeah, not happening," I say. Bennett's call sign is Asshat. "I better get going. I hope everything works out for Ella."

"Me too, but who knows? The girl falls in and out of love so easily. It's hard not to get whiplash," she says.

"Ah! So it runs in the family," I say, and give her a playful wink.

"Unfortunately, there are just so many handsome men out there. Problem is, most of them are frogs," she says.

"Hear, hear to that," I say.

"Aw! Come on. You found yourself a good one," she says.

"I did," I say. I really want to believe Bennett and I can make this work because I've never had this type of connection with someone before.

"Oh, Avery. You're just the person I need to see." Dr. Rudgers stops in front of Cindy and me.

"Hello, Dr. Rudgers. How can I help you?" I ask, using my professional tone.

He frowns.

I look to Cindy. She raises her eyebrows. "Gotta go." She turns on her heel.

"There's a new patient in 4E; he's still in recovery, but I want to set him up with PT in a couple weeks. Problem is he's rejecting therapy right now," he says.

It's my turn for my lips to turn down. It's sad when a patient feels like they have nothing to work towards. "I can look over the file and see what I can do," I offer. There have been times when I can get through to a patient.

"Thanks. I've had Vivian speak with him a few times. It wasn't helping and I don't want to push too hard," he says. Vivian is one of the psychologists we have on-site. She's wonderful but I get that some personalities just respond differently to different people.

"I understand," I say. "So I'll keep a look out for the file then," I say, turning to leave.

"Ah! Avery, I . . . uh, was thinking we never did get a chance to go out for our dinner," he says.

Right. The dinner I had agreed to as friends. Dr. Rudgers is clearly not interested in me as a friend.

Monica walks by and smiles to me. Great timing, she has.

"I'm. . . kind of seeing someone," I say. Geez! That sounds bad.

"Oh, I see. It isn't Mr. Sheridan, is it? Because that would be against hospital rules," he says, surprising the bejesus out of me.

"Um . . .well. It is Mr. Sheridan. He is no longer a patient at this hospital. We didn't connect until after he was discharged," I say. It isn't completely true, but . . .

"Well, that isn't my business, I guess. I just thought I should tell you that HR frowns upon such things, and I've heard employees can lose their job," he says.

I'm not sure if he's threatening me or giving me a friendly warning. "I appreciate your concern, but Mr. Sheridan is an adult. We are both consenting adults and I don't see that it is anyone's business," I say. My cheeks are burning hot and my heart is racing a mile a minute. "If you'll excuse me, I'm late for my next patient." I take a deep breath and walk a few steps away.

"Avery?" His voice stops me in my tracks. Why doesn't he call me Ms. Malone? I preferred it when he did. It meant there was a professional boundary between us.

I stop and turn around, "Yes?"

"I meant no offense. I honestly wish you the best of luck." He grins, flashing his perfectly white smile.

"Thank you." I smile back. "You have yourself a good day."

I turn to head to my next patient. My head is swimming. Should I have lied about Bennett? How would I have gotten out of the date? He didn't need to know who I was seeing. It's none of his business.

I take a deep breath and knock on the door of my new patient's room. I clear my mind to focus on my patient. I just hope I didn't get myself into a whole lot of trouble.

CHAPTER THIRTY-SIX

Bennett

"Bennett, I can appreciate where you're coming from," Jackson says after I give him a speech about why I have to back out of the job.

"You do?" I ask, surprised. I'd heard he was super understanding and nice, but this is above and beyond. I committed to the job. I gave my word, and now I'm backing out. This is something I would never do.

"Yeah." He laughs. "Dude, I relocated to California for my wife while the main headquarters of my business was in Virginia. After what guys like us have been through, I'm all for finding a woman you love and starting a life."

"Fuck." I breathe out a sigh of relief. "You don't know how much your understanding means to me. I'm not a man who goes back on his word. I want you to know that."

"Quinn told me you're a good guy. Look, I'm going to be frank with you. I know what it feels like to lose people, to leave the navy. I wasn't injured, but I have the stain of blood on my hands. I know what's it's like to suddenly find yourself in a life you know nothing about," he says.

"It's like you can read my mind. I'm falling in love with Avery, and I don't want to lose her, but I also feel like I'm losing myself," I admit. So many SEALs leave the navy and get fucked up in the head. There are too many stories of alcoholism, drug addiction and suicide. Jackson has given people purpose. That's why I feel comfortable opening up to him.

"It's good that you can admit that out loud. Does your woman know how you feel?" he asks.

"In a way. I messed up with her, and I'm treading on shaky ground. She knows I'm at a loss about what to do. We need to talk some more and figure things out," I say.

"Okay, here's what we're going to do," he says, sounding very much in control. "Quinn said you've got a lot of experience with cybersecurity. How about I send a member of my team to set you up remotely? You can work from out there for now. Let's see how it goes. You'll still need to sign off on all the legal paperwork, NDAs and such, but I want you on my team. What do you think?"

"I think you're a saint," I say.

He laughs. "Far from it. Talk to your woman and get back to me."

"Thanks, man. You have no idea how much I appreciate this," I say.

"I think I do," he says. "Be in touch. I've got another call coming in."

He ends the call and I blow out a breath. I always felt like my life was one long stretch of bad luck. It seems like that streak has ended. First Avery came into my life, and now I've been given a second chance. I just hope this streak continues.

CHAPTER THIRTY-SEVEN

Avery

For the next two weeks, I feel like I am walking on eggshells at work. Something is up, and I just don't know what. Kathy hasn't been her regular cheerful self. I wonder if she is mad at me. I don't know if it's something personal that I've done or if she is having personal issues and it really has nothing to do with me at all. It feels like nothing in my life can be smooth sailing at the same time.

Bennett and I are stronger than we've ever been. He's happy to be working for Cole. He goes for physical therapy three times a week, he's rented himself a studio apartment, and he's over every night for dinner at my place. He and Jessy are getting along great too, and it's a relief that he's teaching her how to drive because teaching her was making me want to take Valium. Everything feels right except for this uneasy feeling I get when I come into work.

After dropping off my personal belongings in the locker room, I head to the rehabilitation services office to check in with Kathy.

"Hi. Good morning," I say cheerfully.

"Morning." She lifts her gaze briefly from her spot behind her desk while she types away on her computer.

I can't take the tension between us any longer. "Kathy, is there something wrong? I . . . I mean, did I do something to offend you?"

Her lips press together, and she looks pensive. Her gaze goes from me to her desk. "I received this envelope here. I'm supposed to pass it on to you," she says hesitantly. We've always had a really good working relationship so her cool demeanor throws me off.

I stare at the manila envelope and take it from her. It's from HR. My stomach sinks. "What's this about?"

Her cool demeanor morphs into a look of remorse. "I like you Avery. You are one of my best physical therapists. I even consider you a friend. That's why I tried to warn you in a nice way about staying away from Mr. Sheridan. You, more than anyone I know, deserves happiness, but the hospital has rules and it was brought to someone's attention that you broke them. Your case is being investigated by the hospital."

Blood drains from my face and a cool sweat pops on my forehead. "Seriously?" I open the envelope and read its contents. It's a letter basically stating what Kathy just said. I am under investigation for breaking the employee-patient fraternization policy, and if I was found guilty, the result would be termination.

I fall into the chair in front of Kathy's desk.

"I'm sorry, Avery. I did warn you. I didn't want to come down hard on you but maybe I should've. HR takes these things seriously and apparently, there's a witness."

A witness? Damn. Who could it be? Dr. Rudgers? Why would he do this? I think back to the day I told him Bennett and I were together. What a colossal mistake. Or maybe it was Monica. She couldn't get her claws into Bennett so she doesn't want anyone to have him.

"I'm sorry Kathy," I say, looking up. Tears flood my eyes. "I really didn't mean to cause any trouble."

"Honestly, I was a little angry these last couple weeks that you didn't take my warning seriously. I really had your best intentions at heart," she says.

"I did take them seriously. I stayed away from Mr. Sheridan. We only reconnected after he left the hospital," I say. Gah! I've become a big fat liar too. There was Thanksgiving. That passionate kiss. The way he kissed me that day branded me. But, I would never want to take it back. Bennett has brought so much good into my life and Jessy's. I think of the way he helped her with science homework after dinner last night. How my heart fluttered at the sight.

I can't be a liar. I won't.

"You know what . . . it's not entirely true. I kissed him days before he was released. I'm sorry, Kathy. I never meant to cause any trouble. I will head over to HR and resign," I say.

"I'm sorry, Avery. I can't say that I completely understand the policy. You're both adults but the rules are the rules and they are meant to be followed," she says.

"I understand. I want to thank you for being an amazing boss," I say.

"Aw, sweetheart." She stands from behind her desk and walks around to me. She opens her arms wide and gives me a big hug. The tears I was holding back break free and slide down my cheeks.

"I'll be fine," I say, unsure if I'm reassuring her or myself.

After leaving Kathy's office, I head back to the locker room to wash my face in the bathroom. Mascara runs down my cheeks, making me look like a crazy clown. I reach for some paper towel when Monica leaves a bathroom stall.

"Avery." She smiles. She sees I'm clearly upset, and she smiles.

"Monica." I nod.

That's when it hits me. The day I told Dr. Rudgers that Bennett and I were together, Monica walked by. She must have overheard.

"Everything okay, doll?" she asks while soaping up her hands.

"You know there isn't anything I hate more than a fake

person," I say, and her jaw drops as she rinses her hands. "Wait, actually, there is. A jealous person."

"I have no idea what you're talking about," she huffs as she takes paper towels to dry her hands.

"Sure you don't. It was you, wasn't it? You're the one who went to HR and said I was having an inappropriate relationship," I say.

"You're crazy," she says, shaking her head at me.

"I don't think so. Bennett told me that you inquired about us. He would never go for a woman like you," I say. I know it's cold, but this bitch has gone too far.

"Oh, and you think he's going to stick with a Goody Two-shoes like you?" she huffs. "Men like him get bored easy. He needs someone experienced," she says, showing her true colors.

"Oh, and I suppose you're that kind of woman?" I ask.

She looks at her red fake nails and an evil smile spreads her lips. "Dr. Rudgers sure thinks so."

That's when it hits me. She's sleeping with the good doctor. "Did you hear him ask me out? Is that what this is about? Because he was interested in me while sleeping with you?"

Her brows draw together and her smile falters. No, that wasn't it. She didn't know he asked me out. She just overheard the part about me and Bennett being together.

"What's your problem, Monica? Why do you have to cause shit for other people?" I ask.

She laughs, throwing her head back. "That's funny. You, Little Miss Prissy, have everyone after you. I saw Mr. Sheridan first. He should've been mine," she says, and I feel my eyes bulging from their sockets. I want to counter her stupid argument but she continues. "Clearly Mr. Sheridan isn't enough for you because you had to go grabbing Dr. Rudgers' attention. I didn't know he asked you out. Although I was a little confused as to why you had to tell him you were in a relationship with someone. It's like you were trying to make him jealous or something."

"Oh, so you're certifiably insane. Just because you notice

someone first doesn't mean you can claim them, and not that you deserve this explanation, but I told Dr. Rudgers I was in a relationship because he asked me out and I wanted to make it clear I wasn't available," I say.

"You're a bitch," she snaps. "I hate girls like you. Getting everything they want on a silver platter. You seriously think I believe that you would go for a broken SEAL and give up on an opportunity to be with a doctor?"

Okay, so she is nuts. "I have no interest in Dr. Rudgers. I have not pursued him at all. How can I spell this out for you?" I counter.

She rolls her eyes. "Whatever, bitch. I'm not blind. I watched the way Dr. Rudgers looked at you. With you gone, it will be out of sight, out of mind." She gives me a smirk and walks out of the bathroom.

I look in the mirror. I can't even blame her for what happened. It was all on me. I broke the rules. I gave a crazy woman like her ammunition.

I've always tried to be the best I could be at work and at home to Jessy as a mom. When Bennett came along, I suddenly wanted more. I knew the risks and I took them anyway. These last few weeks, Bennett's been so loving and dedicated. So caring, thoughtful and loving. My list could go on but what stands out the most is that I don't feel alone. I don't feel like it's me against the world, doing my best to raise a daughter well. With Bennett by my side, I have this renewed sense of self. Like he was the other half of me that's been missing.

I fix my mascara, take a few deep breaths, hold my chin up high and pull my shoulders back. Then I take the envelope and walk over to HR.

CHAPTER THIRTY-EIGHT

Avery

"What are you going to do?" Jess asks me after I finish telling her that I resigned. I lie back on our living room couch, staring at the ceiling. I must be in shock.

"I don't know." I shrug. "I have money saved up, so we aren't in any trouble."

"There's also the trust account you set up for me," she says.

"You know that money is for you." I pull my gaze from the ceiling and stare at my daughter who is sitting at the end of the couch cross-legged.

She rolls her eyes at me playfully.

"I'm going to start job-hunting soon. I know of a few private clinics—maybe I can swing by and see if they're looking for a therapist," I say. I wonder if Kathy would be willing to give me a reference since I resigned.

"Are you sure you should've resigned? I mean you said they wanted to investigate you, but it doesn't mean you would've lost your job," she says.

"I know that, but there was a part of me that felt like I was on this running belt. I've been doing the same thing the last seven years, and yeah, I liked working there, but I also had this weird attachment to wanting to help all the veterans," I say.

"Because of Daddy," she says, pressing her lips together in a soft frown.

"I think so. He gave his life for our country. It was my way of giving back but in doing the best I can for the veterans I also wasn't moving forward with my own life," I say.

"And you're finally moving forward." She gasps cheerfully.

"I am, and it feels good," I say. "How about we get out of here for Christmas?" I ask, my daughter. I need a break from life.

"What did you have in mind?" she asks.

"I was thinking of Chicago to stay with Halo and Thomas, but then Bennett mentioned Virginia Beach and it also sounded interesting. His place is being rented out right now but he has a lot of friends with families out there. It could be nice," I say. A part of me wants to leave Jersey all together, but I don't want to uproot my daughter's life.

"Virginia Beach, huh? Is that the place where Cole Security is located?" she asks. Clearly, her and Bennett have been talking.

"Yes." I'm not sure where she's going with this.

"Bennett was telling me about it. He kind of told me what he could about his job. It's cool that he deals with all this top-secret stuff," she says.

I laugh. "Yeah, he's got a pretty cool job."

"Do you think you would want to move there after I graduate?" she asks.

I sit up straight. "Where is this coming from?" I ask, feeling guilty.

"It wasn't Bennett. Don't worry. I just feel like you are sick of Jersey, and with me leaving in like a year and a half, it may not be a bad idea."

"Great, so now we're back to you doing a countdown until you leave," I huff, and push out my lower lip and laugh.

"Mom, you know it's my dream to go to Yale," she says.

"And Connecticut is so much closer to Jersey than it is to Virginia Beach," I say.

"That's why there are airplanes. You know there's enough money in my trust to take a plane to visit you often. Thanks to your stubbornness in not spending the money, I'll be able to see you often," she says.

"Well, then, I did good by not spending it," I say. I watch my daughter pensively. "Sweetie, I know you worry about me. I worry about you too, but I'm good."

"I know you are," she counters quickly. "I'm happy you found Bennett."

"I'm happy too," I agree.

"So let's go see Virginia Beach. I heard it's pretty out there, and they have better weather," she says.

"They still get snow. It isn't Florida," I say. And that's when it hits me. We need to go to Disney World during Christmas break.

"Mom," Jess says, staring at me like I've grown two heads. In her defense, I am sure my eyes are bugging out of my head.

"I have the best idea." I clap my hands together.

"What?" she asks excitedly, no doubt anticipating what I'll say.

"Let's spend Christmas in Virginia Beach and then let's head to Disney World," I say, my voice high-pitched and filled with so much enthusiasm it feels like I'm bursting at the seams.

"Mom, you don't vacation, like, at all. You've had a rough day—I get it. Let's just chill and not make any plans. Let what happened today sink in and then we can decide where to go," she says.

"When did you become the adult?" I ask.

"Do I need to remind you that I'm all grown up? You've clearly done a good job raising me," she says.

"Thanks, sweets." I lean up on my knees to kiss her forehead. My heart bursts with joy. When I sit back down, I stare at my daughter. "I loved raising you here. I love being your mom, but I was always worried about what was going to happen next. I always wanted to play things safe, so we didn't vacation and I worked overtime, and life was good, but now you're growing up and, like you say, you'll be leaving me soon. I really want to do this. Let's go to Virginia Beach and spend Christmas with Bennett and his friends, and then you and I will head to Florida together. Just me and you. It'll be perfect. I always wanted to see Disney World, and when you were little and going through your princess phase, I wanted to take you there so bad, but I was in school at that point. Let's do it now," I say, hoping I've convinced her.

"Okay, yeah. I'm in," she says, and we hold hands and bounce together.

"It means we need to get on a plane," I say as butterflies swim in my stomach.

"You'll be fine," Jess says. She's never been on a plane either but she doesn't seem nervous at all.

"I'm not so excited about the flying part, but this is going to be really great," I say. I'm finally stepping out of my safety zone and taking hold of my life. Resigning from my job is a good thing. It's the first step to the new life I want. A life that's in arm's reach.

CHAPTER THIRTY-NINE

Avery

"Hon, it's going to be fine," Bennett says, looking at me with concern. We are sitting on a plane headed to Virginia Beach. I have Bennett on one side of me and Jess on the other. I am freaking the heck out. Bennett takes my hand in his and gives it a squeeze.

"Mom, it's going to be fine. Flying is safer than driving." Jess's words don't calm me either, although I am proud about all the facts my girl knows.

My heart beats fast and I'm trembling.

Bennett leans over. "You're safe. We're going to have a great time together. Deep, slow breaths," he says, watching me. He takes a slow breath in and I follow, staring into his eyes. This man. He grounds me and makes me feel like everything's going to be okay. I follow his slow breaths in and out, and tension slowly leaves my body.

"Are you sure it was a good idea to leave the cane behind?" I ask.

"Yes, I'm fine without it. You see how good I'm doing. I may always have a slight limp to my gait, but I don't need a cane to support me anymore," he says. I know the cane is a sore spot for him, so I don't push. I just hope his knee is strong enough to carry his weight.

The pilot comes on the intercom and speaks. The plane begins to move.

"Is that normal?" I ask.

Bennett laughs. "We're reversing. If we actually want to leave this place, it's very normal."

The plane heads toward the runway and in minutes we are speeding up, up, up, into the air like birds.

"This is so much fun," my daughter says. "What a rush."

Bennett leans into my ear. "If we were alone, I'd want to make you a member of the mile-high club."

Heat gushes between my thighs from the promise of pleasure his words bring. The tilt of the plane causes any feeling of arousal to dim.

Bennett brings my hand to his mouth and places a soft kiss to the back of it.

The plane levels.

"Should we watch a movie or something?" Jess asks, pulling out her laptop.

"Sure. What do you have in mind?" I ask. Now that we are up in the air, I let out a heavy breath and feel the tightness in my chest easing up.

"I don't know. How about *After*?" she asks. It's a romance movie with two people in college. Jess has been telling me she's wanted to see it.

"Okay," I answer.

"Is this a chick flick?" Bennett asks. "Because if it is, I have some work to do. I'll let you ladies get to it."

I love how he gives Jess and I our space to just be mom and daughter. He gets how close we are, and he doesn't come between us. In the past, I'd worried about bringing a man into our lives in case he was needy and tried to take me away from my daughter. Bennett isn't like that all. When I am free or when Jess is out, he has me, but when Jess is there, he makes things all about her. I'd like to believe her dad would have been that way, too.

I sit back and share headphones with Jess. Our heads are tilted together so that we can hear and watch the movie together. A few minutes into the movie and I start to sweat. What if my daughter leaves for college and finds a bad boy with tattoos and piercings? I look over to Bennett briefly. I bet he was the stereotypical bad boy when he was younger, and he has tattoos. He's also a great man.

"Mom, don't look so worried," Jess says, looking over to me like she can read my mind.

"Me?" I feign innocence. "I'm not worried."

"Ha, funny. I would say the male lead isn't my type but look how cute he is," she says.

"Dylan doesn't look like him," I say. Dylan looks like a quintessential surfer. Longish floppy brown hair, tall and muscular.

"I don't plan on marrying Dylan. We're just dating. He wants to go to college on the West Coast so he can spend his time surfing. Don't get me wrong, I like him a lot, but I don't know what I want," she says, sounding very much like a teenager.

"You have all the time in the world to figure it out," I say.

We get back to watching the movie and before I know it, we are landing in Virginia Beach. Nerves bubble inside me. This is Bennett's hometown. His friends are here and technically, his job is here. How will I fit in with his friends wives? What is Bennett like around his people?

I take a deep breath. Showtime.

CHAPTER FORTY

Bennett

I head into the kitchen at Liam and Nat Dempseys' house, and grab a beer from the fridge for Liam and me. The ladies are situated at the kitchen table, and when I walk over, everyone hushes.

"Don't keep quiet on my account," I say, looking at Avery. Her cheeks flame red.

"Stop thinking that everything is about you," Avery says, smiling wide while shaking her head.

"Isn't it, though?" I smile.

"Get out of here." She waves me off.

I'm glad to see Jess and Avery getting along so well with everyone. We just enjoyed a nice Christmas dinner at the Dempseys', and now the men are in the family room, chatting, while the women are at the kitchen table having a gossip session, which I seriously think is about me.

I walk back into the family room and pass Liam his beer.

"Thanks, man."

I twist my bottle cap open and take a seat on the couch before sipping my own. The guys have been left in charge of watching the kids, which means that we have to keep our talk clean.

"Avery and Jess are really cool," Liam says.

"Yeah," Mark nods as he chases his daughter and son around the couch.

"Thanks. I'm just really glad she agreed to come out here for the holidays," I say.

"She seems to be fitting in," Mark says, and I know what he is insinuating, what all the guys seem to be hoping for.

"I can't pressure her now. She's been through a lot. She's lost her job, and she has Jess to worry about. I can't go bulldozing her life." *Again.*

"I totally get that," Jackson says. Since I've been working at Cole, we've gotten a lot closer. Of course, I am his employee, but Jackson has also become a good friend.

"Thanks," I say, then pause. I swipe a hand over my mouth. I do have something on my mind, and I could use some relationship advice.

"What is it?" Quinn asks, staring right at me. Of course, he'd be the one to notice my discomfort. We were on the same team for years.

"It's fine," I say, looking around at all these men with their children. I was never surrounded by families before. Most of the guys had been single, and then Quinn went and fell hard for Ashton. Trevor was the only married guy on our team, and his wife left him more than a year ago.

"Spit it out, Asshat." Liam smirks.

"Don't go calling me that here," I say. Avery knows why it's my call sign but I don't need the kids hearing it too. "I think we should change it to Studmuffin or something, so my woman thinks I'm all that."

They all burst out laughing.

"Thanks . . ." I'm about to say assholes but then think better of it with all these kids running around us.

"You've clearly got something on your mind, so just spit it out," Quinn says. I know he's not going to leave well enough alone.

"Fine. I haven't told her I love her yet. I'm not sure how to do it," I say.

Jackson raises one eyebrow and takes a deep breath. Liam sighs beside me. Quinn gives me a wide-eyed look, and Mark just laughs at everyone.

"What the hell, guys? Was it that bad?" I ask.

"Not per se," Mark begins.

"Can someone say something helpful?" I ask, looking at these grinning idiots.

"Fine. Look, there never is a good time," Liam says, looking pensive.

"Shit, you guys are making it sound like I just asked you how I should tell her about a critical illness. All I want to do is tell Avery that I'm completely in love with her," I say, my volume a little louder than I intend. The guys suddenly look a little wide-eyed.

"What?" I snap. They are clearly fucking with me.

Liam tilts his chin to something behind me. I turn around slowly because I am sensing that I'm being watched. When I turn, I see all the ladies have walked into the room. Natalie has a dreamy look on her face. Catherine is smiling from cheek to cheek. Ashton has a hand clapped over her mouth. Jess is smiling from ear to ear, and my woman has the brightest smile and her eyes are filled with tears.

I just told her I loved her in front of all of my friends.

My jaw goes slack. It wasn't what I intended, but it's done, I better own up and make it right. I stand from the couch and slowly walk over to her. "I love you, Avery Malone."

"I love you too." She beams, and I give her a quick peck on the lips.

Everyone cheers and I take her by the hand and lead her over to the couch. My idiot friends continue to whistle and holler, and Avery blushes, but she takes it well. She laughs as I pull her down to sit beside me. "Sorry. I'll try to make it up to you," I whisper against her ear.

"No, this was perfect," she says.

Jess takes a seat on the couch on the other side of us. "I'm really happy for you guys."

"Thanks, Jess. That means a lot." I smile.

"Aw! You guys are completely adorable," Nat says.

Avery leans into my chest, and I lay my arm around her shoulder. We all start playing charades with the kids. Everyone is laughing and having a good time. Sitting here in Liam's family room with my arm around Avery, I finally feel at home. I kiss her forehead, and she gets up when it's her turn to act something out. I can't believe that this beautiful, good-hearted woman is mine.

CHAPTER FORTY-ONE

Avery

Since Jess and I leave for Disney World tomorrow, Bennett asked if we could have one night alone. Jess agreed to stay with the Dempsey's, since Arabelle took a liking to her and says my daughter reminds her of Princess Elsa because of her long, blond hair.

"Where are we going?" I ask Bennett.

"You'll see when we get there," he says. Nat lent us her car for the drive, since Liam has some kind of obsession with his car that is apparently named Robin.

"Okay." I lean back in my chair. Bennett takes my hand and brings it to his lips. I can't believe he told me he loved me in front of a group of people I just met. I mean, his friends are amazing, but it was awkward and perfect at the same time. Nothing has gone simply for Bennett and me, but we seem to work regardless.

The sun is setting, creating beautiful hues of pink and peach sorbet across the sky. The weather in Virginia is definitely warmer than Jersey but it's still cold.

"How much longer?" I ask. He looks at his GPS, which has been deliberately angled away from me.

"Almost there." He grins. We drive through a range of mountains, winding up and up then when we crest, the turquoise ocean stretches out from the cliffs before us.

"You know it's too cold to go to the beach," I joke.

"I don't plan on leaving the bed for the next twenty-four hours," he says.

I squirm in my seat. The promise in his words sends a jolt of liquid heat between my thighs and up into my stomach.

His hand drops between my legs, and he rubs me there. Breath flees my lungs. "Bennett," I warn.

"I want to get you off," he says. "I want to see you really squirming."

"Bennett," I say, losing my train of thought.

"I wanted to have you naked under me the first time I told you I loved you," he says, rubbing faster. My hips gyrate against him. He flattens his palm against me and rubs faster.

"I'm going to . . . you need to drive . . . bad idea . . ." He's made me forget how to speak.

He smiles. "My focus is on the road and I can drive with one hand."

I grab the handle above my head as sweat breaks out over my body. Suddenly, he slips his hand into my leggings and beneath my panties.

"Fuck, you're soaked," he hisses.

I moan. He rubs me with his finger, moving my wetness around. "I want to get inside you so bad."

My head falls back against the headrest and my eyes shut as he rubs me relentlessly. I come hard and fast, pressing against him with wanton abandon. My heart beats rapidly and my insides contract, making me feel like it's too much and too good all at once.

When I come down off my high, he pulls his hand out of my panties, sucks his finger into his mouth, and says, "Yummy."

This man. He's amazing. He's everything.

We turn right, drive along a road, and then pull up to a beach house. "What is this place?" I ask, my voice raspy from my recent orgasm.

"The town is called Corolla. This place belongs to Quinn's grandmother. He gave me the key for us to stay here tonight." A blue two-story house on stilts with plantation shutters and a wrap-around porch sits on a large piece of land far off from the road. It's close to the water. The view from inside must be spectacular. "Nat and Liam got married here, and Quinn and Ashton spent time here. This place is supposed to be magical."

"Oh, yeah?" I ask intrigued.

"Well, I just had my appetizer. Let's get in there because I'm ready for the main course," he says, sliding the car into park.

I give him a stupid grin, probably because I am still high off the orgasm he just gave me.

He leans over to the back seat and grabs the overnight bag I packed us.

"Come on, baby. Let's go make our own magic." We leave the car and I follow him toward the picturesque beach house.

CHAPTER FORTY-TWO

Bennett

I turn the key and open the door.

"This place is perfect," Avery says, walking in after me.

"You're perfect, babe," I say, pulling her into me from her waist.

Her eyes soften and she gives me one of her warm smiles. "Thanks. You aren't so bad yourself," she says, and presses a kiss to my lips.

My stomach grumbles. "I better whip up something to eat," I tell her. "We both need our energy for what I have planned." I wink and head deeper into the house. While I take the grocery bags and situate them on the kitchen counter, Avery walks over to the floor-to-ceiling windows that overlook the ocean.

"What a view," she murmurs, her shoulders rising and falling.

"Tell me about it," I say, but I am looking right at her.

She tilts her head to the side. "Thank you."

"For what? You can't thank me 'cause I like looking at you," I say as I take out the potatoes we bought and situate the steaks on the counter.

"Thank you for making me feel good about myself," she says, and it makes my heart ache. I'm beginning to understand that even though she and her husband had only been together a short time, most of which he was gone on deployments, he didn't make her feel special or wanted. She was basically trudging through life as a great mother but neglected as a woman with needs.

"Sweetheart, you are so beautiful," I say, walking over to her by the window. She watches me with warmth and heat in her eyes. "Keep looking at me like that and we will never eat dinner." I take a small nip at her bottom lip.

She wraps her arms around me. "I need you well fed, that's for sure." She grins mischievously. "I better help you cook so we can get this show on the road." She unwraps her arms from around my neck and saunters over to the counter, swaying her ass.

I follow her and give her a light slap on the butt. She yelps but then she smiles. It gives me some ideas for later on.

Avery peels the potatoes while I baste the steak with a rub I got at the supermarket. This all feels very domestic. It's weird, yet perfect because everything with Avery just feels right.

I head back to the front door and take out some candles I borrowed from Liam while we were there last night. He may ride my ass about all kinds of shit, but the guy is a romantic at heart and definitely a family man.

I light candles and turn off the lights. It's dark outside, but the view of the ocean and the countless stars is incredible.

Avery and I sit to eat. Steak and mashed potatoes is my ideal meal. "Do you like it?"

"It's delicious. Everything is perfect," she says. She's been saying that a lot. It makes me nervous because nothing in my life has been smooth sailing.

"It is," I agree.

"You said Nat and Liam got married here?" She looks around at the high rafters of the house. I bet this place is even more beautiful in the daylight," she says.

"Yeah, Quinn was always talking about this place when we were deployed. He described it to all of us. He used to say it's like a little piece of heaven," I say. "When you're deployed in the middle of nowhere it's always nice to picture this peaceful place."

"I'm glad we came," she says, and takes a bite of her steak.

"Me too. I guess there was a time I didn't think I would make it, you know." I take a deep breath. "After everything I've been through, I'm just glad to be here. To have this chance with you."

Avery's eyes begin to water. "Oh, Bennett."

"Shit! I've gone and made you cry," I say, chiding myself.

"You make me happy. These are happy tears," she says, swiping at one that rolls down her cheek.

"I guess it was fate. If I hadn't been in the accident to begin with then we would never have met," I say.

"No, I guess we wouldn't have. I'm just happy you're doing so much better," she says, and the passion and love in her eyes— it makes me want her even more.

We finish our meal and Avery stands to clean up.

"Leave the dishes for tomorrow. If I don't have you now, I may explode," I say. I take her hand and pull her into my body. Heat floods her gaze as her eyes drop to my lips. I thrust my hands into her hair, cupping the back of her head and pulling her against my lips. We kiss hungrily as our lips mesh and our tongues entwine. I want to devour her. We kiss until we are both breathless and panting, and then we break apart. Our chests heave.

"Should we take this to the bedroom? Or maybe the kitchen counter is closer." Her eyes flash at option two. "Kitchen counter it is." I take her by the hand and when we reach the counter, I take her by the hips and lift her.

"Bennett, you shouldn't lift me. At least not yet," she says in her therapist tone.

"Take off your jeans and your panties," I say, taking a step back so that I can watch her undress. She squiggles out of her jeans and lowers her panties.

"The counter is cool," she says.

"Lean back and spread your legs," I tell her.

Her eyes turn round.

"Avery, we are completely alone here. No chance of anyone interrupting us. Now, do you trust me to bring you pleasure?"

She nods, and I love how much she trusts me because I know how hard it was for her to give me her trust. She places her feet on the counter so she is spread wide.

"Touch yourself," I say.

"Bennett I don't . . . I mean . . . I don't do that kind of thing in front of you," she mutters.

"Touch yourself the way you think I would touch you," I say.

She dips a finger between her thighs. Even in the candlelit kitchen I can see how wet her folds are. She rubs herself with a finger and I feel like I'm going to blow my load. "That's it, baby. Now put a finger inside," I say, low and demanding.

She does as I say and dips her finger inside herself. Her head tilts back and she moans.

"Do you want to make yourself come like this?" I ask as my dick throbs against my jeans.

She shakes her head.

I smile deviously loving how much she is changing and finding herself as a woman with needs. She went without sex or the touch of a man for so many years. It boggles my mind and warms my heart that she chose me, chose *us*.

"What do you want me to do?" I ask, taking a step toward her, my body humming with need.

"I want your mouth on me," she says.

I drop to my knees and my head is eye level with her sweet pussy. She is so wet that before I even taste her, I lick my lips at the thought of her sweetness.

My tongue runs through her folds and she quivers. I run my tongue slowly up and down, up and down, over her clit which is so engorged she is going to detonate any minute. "You want to come. Don't you?" I say, and I look up at her.

"Yes, I need to. Yes," she moans.

"I don't want you coming," I say.

I insert a finger inside her while I use my thumb to rub her clit.

"Bennett, I can't hold off," she pants, looking down at me.

"Wait," I say, withdrawing my finger. I give her my mouth again.

"Bennett," she moans. Her voice is thick as honey.

"Don't come," I demand.

I lick her up, dipping my tongue between her folds, lapping the sweet nectar that drips from her.

"I can't, Bennett," she says. I feel her insides begin to quake against my tongue.

I rear back and slap her pussy. Not hard, but not soft either. She looks at me with her eyes round.

"Did you like it?" I ask.

Her breaths are ragged as she says, "Yes, can you do that again?"

I want to laugh but I hold back, not wanting to break the moment. "Wait, sweetheart." I get to work undoing my jeans and removing my boxers. "Take off your shirt and bra," I tell her, and I remove my own shirt.

My dick stands to attention, throbbing. Avery looks at me and she sucks on her bottom lip.

"Like what you see?" I cock my right brow.

"I need you inside me," she says.

"That's what I want, too," I say, taking a step toward her.

I rub my cock against her folds, her wetness coating me.

"Bennett, please," she says, her voice filled with lust and sex.

I thrust inside her, holding her hips against me, using the friction to go deep. She cries out, "I need to come."

"I know, but hold on a little longer," I tell her.

"This is torture, you know," she says.

"It's the sweetest kind of torture. Trust me," I say as I thrust again, going deep and slow.

"Faster," she says, and I love how hungry she is for me.

I take her command and I thrust faster and harder. Avery

cries out, falling into an orgasm. It's beautiful, the way her mouth falls open. Her body quakes beneath my rhythm, my touch. My own eyes fall shut and I ride the wave, burying myself inside her deep and rough. She loves it, crying out over and over, and I fall over the edge with her.

CHAPTER FORTY-THREE

Avery

The sun peeks in through the blinds. It's so bright, you wouldn't think it was the middle of winter. I sit up because my bladder is screaming.

I rush to the bathroom my body sore in the best way possible. After Bennett and I made love on the kitchen counter, we moved to the bedroom where he showed me all kinds of new things. Who would have thought that I liked my vagina slapped? Or my butt, for that matter. Bennett taking command in the bedroom is such a turn-on, too.

After using the toilet, washing my hands and brushing my teeth, I saunter back to bed.

"Get your cute butt back in here," Bennett says with his raspy morning voice. He holds up the covers for me to slide in. I cuddle against his warm body. "I'm not going to see you for a full week. I still need my fill."

"We made love three times last night," I remind him. Even my vagina is tired, but I am not complaining.

Bennett makes love to me again. This morning, he is slow and sweet. When we are done, we shower together. He soaps up my body, and as he washes my breasts, he leans in and kisses me.

"I know I've said this a few times already, but I love you," he says.

His sincerity means so much to me. From the sounds of it, Bennett didn't have much love growing up. He has also never been in love before. Bringing out this emotion inside him makes me feel special and wanted in a way I've never felt before either.

"I love you, too." I kiss him back. "And there is no rule for the amount of times we can say it either," I say.

After the shower, we get dressed and have breakfast. As we are loading up the car, Bennett says, "We definitely have to come back here. I'm having fantasies about us making love on that beach in the summer."

His heated words get me all hot and bothered. "I'd like that very much."

We get into Nat's car and drive back to Virginia Beach. Bennett plays some music and we take in the picturesque scenery along the coast. I even like the quiet moments with Bennett—the moments where he allows me to be inside my head and just think. His friends seem wonderful. What would it be like to move out here?

Bennett turns down the music and gives me a quick glance. "What are you thinking?"

I grin. "I was just thinking that I like Virginia Beach. I like all your friends too," I say.

"Thank you," he says carefully. Ever since he withheld the truth from me about taking a job in Virginia Beach, he hasn't brought it up again, even though I think he would like too.

"I don't want to make any promises but maybe I could see myself moving out here after Jess leaves for college. I mean, it's only a plane ride away," I say, using my daughter's words.

"Seriously?" Bennett asks, sounded elated.

"Yeah." I nod.

He goes quiet and gets the pensive look he usually gets when he's thinking too hard. He bites the side of his mouth too.

"What is it?" I ask, feeling nervous.

"Don't give me that look. I haven't made any decisions without you. I promise." He laughs nervously.

"Okay."

"I was just wondering if you would want to move in together? I mean, me, you and Jess," he says. "I mean, you pay rent, and I pay rent. Maybe we can get something a little bigger and live together."

I freeze a little. Not because I don't want to be with him, but because I have to think about Jess, too.

"You know I love both you and Jess. I know she is almost grown up and doesn't need a dad, but I'd like to be there for her," he says, gripping the wheel so hard his knuckles look white.

I take my hand and place it on his thigh. "You've been really wonderful with Jess, and she really likes you. I'd love to move in with you. I just need to talk to her. Me and her have been our own little unit ever since she was basically born. I need to make sure she is okay with it. I love you, Bennett, and I want to be with you . . ."

"I understand." His tense grip on the wheel releases. He removes one hand and takes my hand, bringing it to his lips. "I know it's a big step."

"It is but it isn't. Everything with you feels right. I know that it's time for us. I just have to consider Jess's feelings, too," I say.

"I love what a good mother you are. Honestly, when we were back in the hospital and you spoke of your daughter, I thought it was pretty cool how much you cared about her. I don't even know who my dad is," he says.

"You may have grown up in foster care, but you sure turned out alright," I say.

"I have the navy to thank for that," he says.

"You have great friends who really care about you. You're a good man, Bennett Sheridan, and I'm lucky to have you in my life," I say, knowing he needs the reassurance—just like I do.

CHAPTER FORTY-FOUR

Bennett

Avery and Jess left for Florida. Christmas is over, and all the girlfriends and wives have gone Boxing Day shopping, leaving the kids with their better halves at Liam's house.

Liam put on some Disney movie, so all the kids are occupied while we sit at the kitchen table.

"You think Avery will want to move out here?" Jackson asks.

I shrug. "I don't know, man. I can't pressure her. I just asked her to move in together," I say, and take a sip of my beer.

"That's awesome." Mark fist pumps me. "We'll have to change your call sign from Asshat to Asswhipped."

"Ha ha, smartass. What should we say about you? I've heard Charlie has you wrapped around her little finger."

"So true." Jackson chimes.

"Fuck off," Mark says, then winces. We all eye each other, anxiously, but no little kids come screaming from the other room, yelling about 'rude words'.

"I'm happy for you," Liam says.

"Well, she didn't actually agree to move in with me yet," I admit. "She's planning on bringing it up with Jess in Florida," I say. "She hasn't lived with a man since her husband died, and that was like fourteen years ago."

"Right. You mentioned he was a SEAL, right?" Quinn says.

"Oh, yeah. Do we know who he was?" Jackson asks.

"His name was Liam. I'm guessing his last name was Malone," I say. "He's a couple years older than Avery, so maybe he would've been around thirty-six if he were alive today," I say.

"So he could have been in BUD/S with me," Liam says. "I don't remember a Liam Malone."

"He was on Team Six with Thomas Wells," Quinn says. "You remember Thomas. They were hit by an IED explosion in Afghanistan."

"Yeah, that's right. I remember. What a fucking tragedy," Liam says.

"Guys, let's talk about something else. This is depressing," I say. After surviving an IED explosion myself, I feel guilty for being alive. Talking about Jess's deceased father just doesn't seem right and makes me remember things I'm trying to forget.

"Daddy, I need to go to the bathroom," Mark's son Cullen calls out.

"Duty calls." Mark laughs, saluting the table before going to help his son.

"Man, when did all you assholes grow up?" I ask.

"Hey, language," Liam chides, side-eyeing the kids.

We all burst out laughing and clink our beer bottles together.

It's been five days since Avery left. Even though I have a secure laptop with me on the trip, Jackson suggested I come into headquarters and get a taste of what it's like to work here while I'm in town. Truth is, it's fucking amazing. The guys are all business at work. There are a lot of new contracts coming in, and I've been assigned to check them out from a cybersecurity perspective before we agree to take them on as clients.

I head into Mark's office to ask him a question. After I knock on his office door, he calls me in. "Hey, man," I say.

"What's up, Asswhipped?" Marks laughs, forever the joker.

"Funny . . ." I take a seat. "Look at this." I pass him a document. It's a job for a United States governor—something about a corrupt business deal overseas.

Mark looks at the document with eagle eyes. I look down at the disaster of paperwork on his desk. He can't possibly know what is what, with all this chaos.

A piece of paper with my name on it catches my eye. It looks like some sort of background check. I'm not surprised the guys checked me out, considering the type of work we do here.

While Mark is reading the document, I read over the information on myself. My birthdate, age, height, and military status are all a given. A picture of my birth certificate shows only my mother under guardian. This information isn't new to me. My gaze continues down the legal-size document. The word 'siblings' draws my attention. It says *brother deceased*. My blood turns cold. What the fuck?

Mark looks up to me and gives me a puzzled look. I'm not sure how I come across but the blood just drained from my face. "What is wrong with you?" he asks.

I realize my mouth is hanging open. "That paper over there caught my eye. It has my name on it."

"No biggie. We check everyone out. You know this," he says.

"Can I see what you found on me . . . I mean . . . I grew up in foster care. I never really tried to find out what happened to my mother," I mutter, feeling like a basket case. Brother deceased. What the actual fuck?

"Yeah, I guess," Mark says, passing me a file. I begin to read and as I do, a cold sweat breaks out over my body. I feel cold and clammy as I read that I had a three-year-old brother who was taken to his aunt and uncle's house to live. His father was a Steven Montgomery. I was placed in foster care. It's written that my father is unknown and that my mother's maiden name was Sheridan. I had a brother who died? How do I not remember this?

"Bennett, what's happening here?" Mark is standing beside me. I hadn't even realized he was there.

"I had a brother," I say.

"I know, man. I'm sorry. He died young," he says.

"Really? How young?" I ask.

Mark looks at me with a narrowed gaze. "What do you mean? Are you saying you didn't know you had a brother?"

"I was taken out of my drug addict mother's house at age four. I don't remember much," I scoff.

"Shit," Mark hisses. "I shouldn't have given you the file."

Anger rises inside me. "I've never inquired about my family, but I have a right to know. Please. I grew up on my own. If I have family out there, I want to know."

Mark takes a deep breath. He looks like he doesn't know what to do.

"Mark, please."

He walks over to his office door and closes it.

"How old was my brother when he died?" I ask. Did he have an illness? Was he well taken care of?

"He was twenty, Bennett," he says, eyeing me in this weird way.

"Twenty?" That's fucking young.

"You said he grew up with an aunt and uncle?" I ask.

"Bennett, your brother was a SEAL," he says carefully, and my stomach bottoms out, and it's hard to breathe. I shoot up to a standing position and stare at Mark.

"My brother who was a year younger than me became a SEAL?" My heart pounds in my chest and rings in my ears. I had a brother. Why didn't they keep us together when I got put in the system?

"Yes, he was raised in Jersey. His father was a junky, but his father's sister took him in when child services came to your mother's house. You were both very neglected and undernourished," he says.

"I feel sick," I say.

"Sit, Bennett. Fuck. I'm sorry, man. I had no clue you didn't know," Mark says, sounding sympathetic.

"Tell me what you know," I insist, biting back tears. Fuck, I don't cry. What is happening? I take a seat like he says because my head is spinning.

"Not much man. I just know that his name is Liam Montgomery. Died in Afghanistan." He pauses and swipes a hand over his mouth. I look down at the paper I'm holding; it says page one of two down at the bottom.

"Where is page two?" I ask.

Mark's eyes turn wide. "My desk is a fucking mess. I can never find anything."

"Mark, from one SEAL to another, I call bullshit." My tone is stern and my gaze on him is unforgiving.

"Fuck," he mutters under his breath, and within seconds, he pulls a piece of paper out from a pile, knowing exactly what he was looking for and where it was. Organized chaos at its best.

I grab the paper out of his hand and read.

Next of kin: Avery Montgomery and daughter, Jessy.

No, no, no. A cold shiver racks my body as I read the words over and over again. There must be some mistake.

"This can't be right," I say.

"I didn't realize you were dating his widow until we were sitting at Dreamboat's kitchen table and you and Quinn brought him up. Your brother was on Thomas Wells' team. He died in the IED. I'm really sorry for withholding the information, but you know how it is. We find stuff that no one knows, and it isn't my place to let you know. Those are the rules we live by . . ." Mark tries to explain himself, but I am not hearing any of it.

I stand from the chair, take the pages with me and stalk out of his office. I walk past all the other offices.

"Hey, man." Sutton stops me to talk.

"Not now," I splutter. I walk right out the doors of Cole

Security headquarters into the brisk winter air. The cool air does nothing to release the tightness in my chest. My brother was Jess's father.

There is no way that Avery will want to be with me once she finds out.

CHAPTER FORTY-FIVE

Bennett

I reach the end of the parking lot, and my lungs burn as I hunch forward, bracing my palms on my knees. I hold onto the papers tight as the wind blows. How can this be? I had a brother I don't remember. We were separated. He had family who wanted him. Liam Montgomery, Liam Montgomery. My brother.

What would my life have been like if we hadn't been separated? Would I have felt so alone? Would we have been there to lean on each other? I'd always wanted that sense of family, yet I was too much of a coward to go out and get it. Maybe I just hadn't met the right girl until Avery, his widow. Fuuuuck. Why me?

I straighten myself out and scream at the top of my lungs. Why did she have to be his wife? Why did Jess have to be his daughter? I can't replace him, my own brother. It's so wrong. If Avery knew, she wouldn't have given me a second glance. This whole situation sickens me.

I fold the papers and tuck them into the back pocket of my jeans, then I grip the sides of my head. I'm losing it.

"Bennett," someone says my name carefully. I whirl around to see Quinn watching me like I'm a wild stallion, unpredictable and maybe a little unhinged.

"Did you know? Tell me the truth," I say, clenching my jaw. Why does this hurt so bad?

"I didn't, but Mark just updated me. He thought you might need a friend," he says.

"This is so messed up," I say.

"I met him, Bennett. I knew your brother," he says.

"What was he like?" My voice cracks, my throat as dry as sandpaper.

"He looked nothing like you, for starters," he says. "He was tall, a bit of a smart aleck." He laughs almost to himself. He pushes his hands into the pockets of his jeans. "He was a good guy, a dependable member of his team. I remember when they died. I had no idea you two were related," he says. "I'm sorry, man."

"What do I do about Avery? She won't want me. I'll lose her." I rub my hand on the back of my neck.

"If she loves you it won't matter," he says.

"He didn't treat her right. Things were messed up between them," I say.

"You're not him," Quinn says with such confidence.

"I don't know who I am. I've spent most of my life lost, searching for a place to belong. I found the woman of my dreams . . ." I snicker. "Only to find out she's my deceased brother's wife." I sigh. "I need to do the honorable thing and walk away."

Quinn takes a step toward me. "You can't make that decision for her. If you and Avery have love, then it's worth fighting for. It's not like you knew she was your brother's wife."

"It doesn't change the facts, though."

"Well, my friend. . . there is only one way to find out," he says.

"Yeah."

He claps me on the back. "Have some faith."

I nod. *If only it were that easy.*

"You good?"

"I don't know if I'm good, but I'm okay to be out here on my own if that's what you're worried about."

"Okay." He heads back toward the building. I embrace the numbing, cold air

My cell rings. Avery's name lights up the screen. She's due back in Jersey in two days.

"Hey, babe." I fight to keep my voice even.

"Hi," she says, sounding like her cheerful self. Her sing-song voice reminds me of the first time she came into my room at the hospital. She was this angel bringing me solace through the pain.

"How's it going over there?"

"Oh, you know . . . same old," I say. *How will I break this news to you?*

"I guess that's good. Jess and I are at Magic Kingdom today. This trip has been like a dream. Everything here is magical," she says.

I want to tell her that she's my magic. She fixed me, and now I'm going to lose her. I swallow down my pain.

"You're the magic, sweetheart. I can't wait to see you guys," I say.

"I miss you," she says.

My heart cracks. Will it be goodbye when I tell her the truth? "Say hi to Jess."

I hear Jess muttering in the background.

"She says hi back," Avery says.

My throat clogs. I'm really her uncle. A blood relative.

"Is everything okay?" Avery asks.

I thought I was doing a bang-up job of hiding the anxiety from my tone but apparently not.

"You're not very talkative today," she says, and the concern in her tone is crystal clear.

"I was just busy here with something." It's not really a lie. "I love you, babe."

"I love you too, Bennett," she answers. I soak in her words

and engrain them to memory. The thought of losing her rips me up inside.

"'Kay, take care. We're scheduled to be on a ride in fifteen minutes. We have to stay on schedule," she says.

"You two take care and stay safe," I say.

"Thanks. You too." She blows me a kiss through the phone and the call ends. I squeeze my eyes shut and grip my phone. *Please don't let this be the end of us.*

CHAPTER FORTY-SIX

Avery

The phone rings twice.

"Hello?" I hear Nat's voice and I take a deep breath.

"Hi." My voice shakes.

"Yes?" Nat asks.

I take another deep breath. "Hi, Nat. It's Avery." I know I sound hesitant and distracted.

"Avery?" She repeats my name. "Is everything alright?"

I only have her number because Jess stayed with her while we were in Virginia Beach.

"Sorry to bother you. Um . . . I returned from Florida yesterday. Bennett was supposed to be here, and he isn't. I've tried calling his cell, but he isn't picking up. I've called the airlines and checked the news for plane crashes. Honestly, I'm not sure what to do," I say, my insides shake. Where could he be?

I had spoken to Jess in Florida and she liked the idea of Bennett moving in. He said he would be here waiting for us when we got home. Yesterday, we spent the day traveling and he isn't here.

"Darn. I'm not sure, Avery. I can call Liam to see if he knows anything," she offers.

"That would be great," I say. "Thank you."

"Of course. Talk soon." She ends the call.

I pace the apartment. Jess is in school. I didn't want to scare her, so I didn't tell her I was worried about Bennett's absence. She was so young when Liam died but I remember the day he was killed. We had spoken by Skype. He spoke with Jess and told her how much he loved her. He'd never had done that before. I'd always wondered if maybe he felt like something may have gone wrong that day. My morbid thoughts shift to Bennett. What if he's lying in a ditch somewhere?

I pace back and forth. My nerves are on overdrive. Hopefully Nat calls me back soon. I had planned to continue job-hunting today, but how can I when I feel like such a wreck? I fall back on the couch, staring at an empty TV screen. Where the hell are you, Bennett?

CHAPTER FORTY-SEVEN

Bennett

I stand in front of my brother's grave back here in Jersey. They buried him here close to where Aunt Bee and Uncle Jim live. The Montgomerys. Those nasty people raised my brother. I stare at his name. *Liam Montgomery*. His stone doesn't say much other than his birthdate: April 26, 1984. My emotions have been all over the fucking place.

"I don't know how I don't remember you," I say to his stone. "I don't remember much from the time I lived with our birth mother. Maybe I was too young or maybe I blocked it out. Pretty sure we went through some really rough times with her. I've had some bad dreams about being younger, but they are few and far between." I sniffle. "I really would have liked to get to know you," I say, and the tears swelling in my eyes begin to fall. "It would have been nice to have a brother. I hope those jerks Bee and Tom treated you well, but I'm guessing, after meeting them, they weren't a walk in the park." I scoff. "But they were definitely better than some of the homes I landed in, that's for damn sure." I pinch my eyes shut and hold the bridge of my nose with my pointer finger and thumb. "Fuck, how do I say this?" I'm at a loss for words.

"I was caught in an IED explosion not long ago. I don't know why I had the privilege to survive and you didn't. I hate that you aren't here and that you missed your daughter growing up. Avery did a great job. Jessy's a great kid. Well-rounded and loved. You'd be proud." A loud sob escapes me. I don't remember ever crying like this in my life. I was ripped apart when King was killed but I didn't cry. I didn't shed a fucking tear, and he was my brother, too. "So, here's the thing. It seems that fate has kind of fucked us over or played roulette or I don't even know, but after I got injured, I met a woman and fell in love. I've seriously never been in love before. I had lots of female bed partners but none that were worth keeping around. Then Avery came into my life at just the right time. She saved me; she made my heart feel things it's never felt before. Problem is I didn't know she was yours. Now, I don't know what to do. I can't walk away from her and Jess. They've become my family. I don't want to walk away, but I don't think she will want me either way when she finds out we're brothers." I grip the sides of my head. "This situation is so messed up. I wish I could've met you," I say, then I realize if he were here, I wouldn't have Avery, and she has quickly become my everything.

"Okay." I suck in a breath. "I just wanted to come here. Let you know you have a brother that's grieving your loss because I feel this huge gape in my heart even though we never met."

I swipe at my damn tears and head back to my car. I need to man up and go see Avery. She needs to hear the truth and it has to be from me.

CHAPTER FORTY-EIGHT

Avery

"Thanks for getting back to me," I say to Nat.

"I'm sorry I don't have more information," she says. As far as Liam and the guys know, Bennett got on a plane back to Jersey yesterday.

"It is what it is," I say. I was hoping she would have some news. "Maybe he left me. I hadn't considered that as an option." I hiccup, trying to keep my tears at bay.

"I saw how much he loved you. I don't know what could make him just walk away without an explanation. Liam was very vague with me when I asked about Bennett. If I didn't know my husband, I'd overlook it, but something was off. Maybe something happened over at Cole while he was here. I can't pinpoint why, but I feel like all the guys have been on edge these last few days," she says.

"I wish you knew. I'm racking my brain, trying to understand why he wouldn't call. Even if he was busy, he could just text and let us know he's okay," I repeat myself. The seconds tick by but they feel like hours.

"I'm going to grill my husband later. He's at Cole this week. He doesn't leave for deployment for a few weeks, so I'll be on his case," Nat says.

"If you find anything, please call me," I say, desperate for answers.

"Of course," she reassures me.

There's a knock on my door. "Nat. There's someone at my door. Can I call you later?"

"Go ahead. Take care. And remember to keep breathing," she says.

"Yes, thank you." I end the call.

With my cell phone still in my hand, I head to the door and check in the small peephole. Bennett stands there with his head down.

I swing the door open. "Where have you been?" I ask angrily when I see he is in one piece.

"Can I come in?" he asks.

His head hangs low and he looks tired and disheveled. "What is going on, Bennett?" I ask my heart rate spiking. He also looks defeated, the way his face falls and his shoulders slump.

"You're going to want to take a seat for this," he says, walking past me into the apartment.

My stomach somersaults. "What happened?" His face looks crestfallen. "Just spit it out. I'm too tense and worked up. I seriously thought something bad happened to you," I say, closing the door and following him toward the family room area.

"Something bad did happen but not in the way you think," he says. His eerie tone does nothing to calm my nerves.

"What's going on, Bennett?" I ask. He looks like he just found out his best friend died.

He opens his mouth to speak but seems unable to find the words, then he rubs the top of his head and takes a seat on the couch. His head hangs low between his shoulders.

I take a seat beside him. Any anger I was feeling from his lack of contact melts from my body. Instead, I am filled with this sense of dread. Like something is really wrong.

I place a gentle hand on his thigh. He looks like he's struggling with something. "You know you can tell me anything," I say, then pause, because a thought comes to mind. "If this is about us moving in together . . . if it's too fast, I'll understand."

His head snaps up and his gaze holds mine. A look of bewilderment fills his eyes. "Avery, it's not that." He inhales a deep breath and looks up to the ceiling, then back to me. "Don't you understand? From the first time I saw you, you were completely irresistible to me. You breathed life back into me. I was hollow inside. After the explosion, I felt like I had nothing to live for, and then you came crashing into my life, and my heart began beating in a way it never had before. You made me want things I never dreamed I would have. You and Jess are so important to me," he says.

My own heart melts when he mentions my daughter, too. "So what is it? What on earth is going on?" I ask, feeling so on edge.

Bennett looks right at me. "A few days ago, I was at Cole Security headquarters when I accidentally came across some information."

"Okay . . ."

He takes another deep breath while I feel like I'm not really breathing at all. "It was information about my past. I was never meant to come across it. The company does security checks on all its employees. You know I grew up in foster care. I never found a family that wanted to adopt me. I went into the system when I was four and left when I was eighteen. What I didn't know was that I had a baby brother. He was a year younger than me," he says, looking at me with such heavy eyes that his pain seeps into my heart.

"Oh, Bennett." I take his hand and hold it in mine.

"I didn't even remember I had a brother," he says, his voice shaking. "How could I not remember that?"

"I don't know, sweetheart. You were so young and probably living in poor conditions. Don't be so harsh on yourself." I press a kiss to the back of his hand. "That's good news. I mean, you have family. Where is your brother?" I ask.

Bennett's eyes fill with tears, but they don't shed. His shoulders slump. "He's dead."

I lean forward and embrace him. "I'm so sorry." My hand rubs the back of his neck.

He pulls his head back to look at me. "I love you," he says. "So damn much."

"I love you too," I answer, and he leans back, pulling out of my embrace. A chill runs over my body. Why does it feel like he's saying goodbye?

"What's going on?" My brows narrow.

"Avery I . . . there's no good way to say this," he says, standing and taking a few steps away from me, and it feels like my world tilts sideways. I'm losing him.

Tears swell in my eyes and I don't even know why. "Bennett?"

"My brother's name was Liam Montgomery. He left behind a widow, Avery Montgomery, and a two-year-old daughter, Jessy Montgomery," he says.

My hand claps over my mouth as my head begins to swim. Did I hear him right?

"Avery, breathe" he says. I feel like I may pass out. He takes a seat beside me again. "I know what you're feeling, baby. I've been a mess, a complete wreck. He was my baby brother. He died and I didn't know. Then I've gone and fallen in love with his widow. I wanted to spend my future with you. I wanted to be a role model to Jess." He swipes a hand over his mouth, but I can't focus. His words swim in my mind, but they don't mean anything. How can this be?

"You're related to Aunt Bee and Uncle Jim," I say.

He shakes his head. "We didn't share the same father. Only the same mother. I went into foster care. He went to live with them."

I shoot up to my feet. "I need you to go, Bennett," I say, my entire body shaking. I need space to think.

"Avery, please. Let me be here for you. This can't be the end of us," he says.

"Bennett, please. I'm holding on by a thread. Jess is expected home in a couple hours, and I can't . . . I just . . . need you to go."

He sighs. "I'll go but I'm coming back later. I'm not leaving you, Avery. I want to be in your life. I know this is some fucked up twist of fate, but here we are. It eats me up to know that he didn't survive but I'm here, a living and breathing man, and I'm head over heels in love with you."

"Please . . . p-please go. I need . . ." I don't know what I need. "Space."

Bennett looks like I just shattered his world. But my head is too messed up to think about us when all I can think about is Liam.

"Okay." He stands and leans over to kiss me, but I feel frozen in my place like a statue.

He walks out the door, and I fall to my knees and cry. I stay like that for a while. I don't know why, but it feels like Liam has died all over again. The loss of his death washes over me, fresh and raw.

I don't know how long I am on the floor when I get myself up and trudge to my bedroom, heading toward the one thing that always brings me solace. I reach onto my closet shelf and take out the box that holds his things and take out the letter. I read the letter over and over again. I repeat his words in my head. His voice is now a distant memory I almost don't remember, yet his words are comforting, like a warm, familiar blanket. I sink down to the floor and read.

Dearest Avery,
It's funny how life turns out, isn't it?
We didn't have some full-blown love affair. I know I didn't sweep you off your feet or make your heart skip a beat but when push came to shove, we were family. We stood by one another and that meant something to me.
I love you. I loved you, and Lord knows I know I did a bad job of showing it. For that, I'm truly sorry. Maybe it was my messed-up childhood—maybe it was how much my feelings for you scared me.

Leaving you and Jessy each deployment tore me up. I wanted to open up to you and share my feelings each time I left. I tried, believe me, I tried, but there was this concrete wall inside me, tall and strong, a fortress of sorts that prevented me from showing both of you.

I know I erected that wall to protect myself as a kid. That wall kept me from feeling, and that's what saved me from my brutal childhood. I thought it would continue to save me, but it only divided me from the only family I ever knew. The pain of feeling distant from you and Jessy was like a blade cutting me open slowly, deeply.

The sad part is that I know if you're reading this letter, I'm gone. I never had a chance to make amends. I never had a chance to show you how much you both meant to me. How much I love you. Don't ever doubt it.

I'm a selfish man, Avery. I never claimed to be anything else, but you, dear wife, hold my heart.

I have one last request. I don't want you to be scared to fall in love. To give your heart. Not every man will be like me. I didn't hold you dear and it's my biggest regret. Your heart is so full of love. And Jessy? She is the best of both of us. She deserves a father and you deserve a husband who will cherish the ground you walk on. There is a man out there—believe me. Don't be scared. If I had a second chance to be a better husband, it would have been me.

My last wish, Avery, is that you give your heart. I need to know that I didn't completely shatter your trust in men, in love. I will be smiling down on you and Jessy from heaven knowing you are well taken care of. Knowing that another man could give you what I couldn't.

Love you always and forever,
Liam

"Oh, Liam. Would you feel that way if you knew I was in love with your brother?" I say to the space in front of me. What would you have been like if you survived the explosion? You and Bennett went down the same path. You were cut from the same cloth. You both became SEALs, and you both made the navy your family.

Now, Bennett's here. He sees us, he needs us. He isn't leaving. I don't know what to do.

My eyes grow tired from the tears and all the pain that courses through me. My body feels too heavy to move. Peace washes over me and my bones relax. I'm walking in a forest. The grass is green and overgrown, and the sun strobes through the trees creating a dapple of light on the ground while providing enough warmth that my skin feels warm.

"Avery? Is that you, sweetheart?" Liam asks with his arms outstretched to me.

"Yes," I say excitedly as my heart beats fast. "It's so good to see you. It's been so long," I say, taking him in. "You look not a day over twenty. Your light eyes seem translucent and your skin glows. You were always such a handsome man."

Liam smiles bashfully. "You're so beautiful. Even now, so many years later," he says, smiling, and then it falters. "Avery, I know I didn't give you that letter when I was alive, but I feel like it's been a pact between us."

"I couldn't find her another father," I say with tears streaming down my cheeks. Why am I crying so hard?

"Shhhhhhh." He rubs at my eyes with his thumb.

"I . . . was scared."

"I know. I didn't do right by you, but he will," he says.

"He?" I ask in shock. "What do you mean? Do you mean Bennett? He's your brother, Liam. I'm so sorry. I'm so, so sorry," I sob. "I never meant to fall in love with him."

"It's okay. I told you there was a man out there who would treat you better. Go to him. Love him," he says.

"How? I . . ."

Mom. Mom. Mom.

My eyes open and I startle when I see Jess hanging over me. Her dark eyes are frantic. "Geez, you scared the living daylights out of me," she says, holding her heart.

I sit up. "What's going on?"

"You tell me. I came home from school and the front door

was open. I called out to you and you didn't answer. You were passed out on the floor," she says as a hiccup escapes her, followed by tears.

"Oh, honey. I'm sorry. I didn't mean to scare you," I say.

She throws her arms over my shoulders. "You're all I have. If something happened to you . . ." A new wave of tears escapes her.

I wrap my arms around her and hold her tight. "I'm okay, but there is something I need to tell you."

She pulls back to look at me. "What's going on?"

"Come lets go to the kitchen. I could use a hot cup of tea," I say. She extends her hand to me to lift me off the floor.

"What is that?" she asks, her gaze dropping to my hand.

I hadn't realized that I was still holding the letter. I don't want her to see it. She's always thought of her dad as a superhero and I want her memory of him to stay that way.

"It's a letter your dad left me before he died," I say, and fold it up and slip it into the envelope. She doesn't ask to read it. "I have something to tell you, sweetheart."

"Is everything okay? Are you feeling okay?" she asks nervously.

"I'm feeling okay." I rub her back and reassure her.

We walk to the kitchen together. I hit the kettle.

"Take a seat," I tell her.

"You're seriously scaring me," she says, but she goes to take a seat anyway.

"I don't want to freak you out so I'll get to the point," I say.

Jess nods and laces her fingers together, settling her hands on the table.

"While Bennett was in Virginia Beach he came across a file on his background. Because he was in foster care from a young age there were things he doesn't remember from his childhood. The file said he had a brother that passed away. His brother was your father. He was a year younger than Bennett," I say quickly, holding my breath while waiting for a reaction.

Jess sits in her chair, watching me carefully. Did she hear what I said?

"Say something. Anything," I urge.

"So they were both SEALs? Dad would have been in BUD/S a year after Bennett," she says.

"Yeah, it's crazy. Bennett didn't know he existed. I'm guessing it was the same for Liam," I say.

"Do you think Aunt Bee and Uncle Jim knew?" she asks.

"You know, I have a feeling they did but they never mentioned it. They didn't think too highly of Liam's mother," I say.

"I know. They didn't like her," she says. "It's not like my grandfather was any better. He left them. Just took off. What kind of man leaves two sons behind?" she asks.

"Bennett had a different father. He doesn't know who he was," I explain.

Jess and I go back and forth, dissecting our crazy life and guessing what Aunt Bee and Uncle Jim knew. They were never ideal people to raise a child. I'm guessing that's why Liam had such a hard time with expressing his emotions. And I was young and stupid, and left Jess in their care while I got my degree. But I know it's different because she still had me. I was her primary parent, not them. A part of me wants to know why they never mentioned Liam having a brother, but then I realize that whatever they say won't matter anyway. It won't bring Liam back.

"So what now, Mom?" Jessy asks.

I set a cup of tea in front of her and one in front of me. "I don't know. Bennett was really torn up over finding out. He didn't know he had a brother. And then he found out that he's in love with his brother's wife and wants to be a part of his niece's life."

"Holy shit. He's my uncle," Jess says, her eyes bright. She's taking this news a lot better than me. "He's my blood relative."

When she was younger, she would come home from school and ask why she didn't have a sister or brother, or why she didn't have cousins like the other kids. It was always a sore point for her. She said when she grew up, she would want to have lots of kids so that she could make herself a big family.

"He is your uncle, baby." I smile to her.

She smiles back and then it falters. "You aren't going to break up with him, are you?"

It doesn't surprise me that she can practically read my mind we have always been so in sync with each other. "How can I be with my deceased husband's brother? It would be a betrayal to your father. Ever since Bennett told me the truth this overwhelming guilt is consuming me. Liam told me to find myself a new husband but I don't think he meant his own flesh and blood," I say, worried that I've overshared. Jess is so mature for her age, but this is something personal and related to a father she barely knew.

She shrugs.

I suddenly remember the dream I just had. All these years, I've never dreamed of Liam. Not even once. Shortly after he died, I wanted to dream about him so badly, needing to see his face. I wanted to yell at him for leaving Jess and me alone, but those dreams never came. Now, the dream finally came. He told me to find a better man, a man who would love me like I needed him to. Does that mean Liam would have been okay with Bennett being my boyfriend?

The dream feels like it's fading from my mind, and I panic. I want it to stay clear in my head. I don't want to forget him. Faults and all, we created a beautiful life together. Jess is my everything. The last part of the dream flashes in my mind. *"It's okay. I told you there was a man out there who would treat you better. Go to him. Love him."*

I palm my heart.

"Mom!" Jess waves a hand in front of my face.

"Sorry I just spaced," I say. "What were we talking about?" I refocus on my daughter.

"You said you didn't know how you can be with Dad's brother," she says.

I frown. "I'm sorry, honey. I know this must be so hard for you."

"Don't be sorry. I really like Bennett, and now that I know he's my uncle I like him even more. He and Dad shared the same mom. He has my genes. My dad's genes. This is so cool. I never thought I would meet anyone I was related to. I never liked to think of Uncle Jim as a relative," she says, rolling her eyes.

I can't blame her for that one.

"Bennett's a good guy, Mom," she says.

"Are you sure you would be okay if we were together?" I ask.

"I'd be more than okay. You told me that Dad would have wanted you to move on. You felt bad about not finding me a father. Well, Bennett has been the closest thing I've had to a dad, and he was related to my dad. I wonder if they were alike. They must have been. Bennett was a SEAL too," she says.

"Oh, honey." I wrap her up in a hug. "I love you so much."

"I love you too," she answers.

We break apart. "I need to get my homework done," she says.

"Okay, but are you sure you're okay with all this?" I ask.

"What were the chances you'd meet Dad's long-lost brother in a veterans' hospital after he'd been injured?" she asks.

I shrug. "One in a million."

"Mom. He was sent here to us. Dad sent him from heaven. I just know it," she says. "He wanted his brother, his family, to take care of us. Bennett—he's good."

Tears spill down my cheeks. "Bennett is good." I feel that with every fiber of my being.

CHAPTER FORTY-NINE

Bennett

I sit back in my apartment, feeling like I am losing my mind. She kicked me out. I knew she wouldn't want to be together after she found out about Liam and me being brothers.

My cell rings and Liam Dempsey's name lights the screen. I don't want to talk to anyone. I decline the call. A second later, it starts ringing again. I press decline. I just want to be left alone. If I lose Avery, I don't know what I'll do. The damn phone rings again. Stubborn bastard. I answer.

"Hello," I bark.

"Finally," he says. "Where the fuck are you, Sheridan? Avery called Nat asking all kinds of questions. I haven't said anything to her, but she knows something is up. You need to go to Avery and talk to her. You can't just go MIA."

"I was there. I saw her. Told her the truth," I say, kicking the wall. I stub my toe and want to yelp, but I suck it back.

"And?" he asks.

"She kicked me out," I say.

"Fuck," he hisses.

"Yeah, man. I mean, I was expecting it, but it still stings. I'm not giving up though. My brother's been gone a long time, and I would never mean him any disrespect, but what are the chances that I'd fall for his widow? You know how I was with the ladies. There was no woman who could tame me," I say.

"Until you wanted to be tamed," Liam answers.

"Look, the accident changed my life. It opened my eyes. There were nurses in that hospital hitting on me and I didn't want them. They didn't make me feel the way she does," I say.

"Hey, I get it. You don't need to explain. I fell in love with my best friend's wife. There isn't anything shittier than that. We thought he was gone, and he wasn't. In your case, your brother has been gone a long time. Avery is a free woman," he says.

"And Jess is my niece. She is such a great kid. I never thought of having children, but with Jess, I just feel this strong need to protect her. To love her. To be a father figure to her," I say.

"I get it. I mean I came into Arabelle's life when she was a baby, but she always felt like my own daughter. I love her no less than I love Shane," he says.

A strong ache builds in my chest. I want everything with Avery. I want her to have my children.

"You there, Sheridan?"

His tone snaps me out of my daze. "Yeah . . . sorry. I just realized something," I say, reaching for my keys. "Got to go, Liam."

"What? Wait," he says.

"I can't." I end the call. I need to go to Avery. I swing my front door open and pause.

CHAPTER FIFTY

Avery

I wait a few moments at the entrance to Bennett's apartment door. The snow is falling and the temperature has dropped. A wide-eyed Bennett watches me like he's seeing an illusion.

"You're here," he says.

"Yes," I say as a cloud of my breath puffs in front of me.

"I was just coming back to your place," he says slowly.

"May I come in?" I ask, my teeth chattering.

"Yes . . . sorry." He takes a step back to let me inside. "You're freezing."

"I am." He seems hesitant and I don't blame him. He said he would stick by me no matter what, and he's kept true to his word. It's me who has faltered.

"I want to take you in my arms and warm you up," he says carefully.

"So take me, Bennett. I'm yours," I say.

"You're mine?" he asks.

"Yes. I was overwhelmed by . . . well, you know," I snicker. "What are the chances?"

"It's a lot to take in, but you do work with wounded vets. I'm not surprised my brother ended up enlisting. He probably didn't have money to go to college, and it's a respectable thing to do for someone who has nothing," he says, his face falling at the word nothing. His eyes look vacant.

I step up to him, wrap my arms around his lower back and press my head into his chest, taking in his heady scent.

He wraps me up in his arms, his body heat warming me. "It feels so good to hold you."

Oh, Bennett. The feeling is mutual.

He pulls his head back. "I hope this isn't weird, but would you tell me about him?"

"No, it isn't weird. Of course you'd want to know," I say.

Bennett guides me to his couch and uses the throw blanket to cover me. He says he's going to make me a hot cup of tea and while he goes off, I think. Do I tell him everything? Every gritty detail? Do I give him the hero version I've always told Jess?

He returns with my tea and I take it from him, wrapping my hands around the warm mug. "Thank you," I say.

He sits back beside me on the couch. "I've told you a little bit about how things were with Liam."

"Avery, I don't need you to sugarcoat. I met those people that raised him—they were bottom-feeders. He probably didn't have a better time than I did with complete strangers."

"He said they were okay. He went to school. Had lots of friends. Was popular," I say, thinking back to how I had this big crush on him. "He was the life of a party. Everyone wanted to be around him."

Bennett doesn't say a word as my memory drifts to the past. "I was this hollow version of myself. Drinking a lot at parties. I just wanted to feel something, anything. And Liam was a sweet talker. When I found out I was pregnant with Jess, I continued going to school, but once my stomach began to grow, I was shunned so I went to night school instead. I wasn't the only pregnant teen there," I say, thinking back to how tired I was and how hard it was to finish my degree.

"Liam went to school and worked in the local grocery shop. We lived with Aunt Bee and Uncle Jim. Then when he graduated, he said he wanted a better future for me and Jess, so he enlisted. I worked in a pharmacy as a cashier and he was off in bootcamp. I had Jess in daycare. Life was hard. I was basically a single mom from the start. Liam was good with her when he was there, but he had a hard time with his emotions. Like, they were locked inside him, and he got frustrated a lot. He didn't expect to get tied down at such a young age, but he didn't abandon us. He wanted to give us the best life he could. Then he was deployed. When he came back, he was even more withdrawn," I say.

"I can understand that. Some of the things we see . . . it's too much for anyone," Bennett says sadly.

"I figured that and so I never held it against him. We had this thing where we would say we were each other's family. He knew I had his back and he had mine. We weren't crazy in love or anything, but a friendship formed from the most unlikely circumstances and I knew I could count on him. I didn't have family of my own, so he became everything to me."

I place my tea on the coffee table and Bennett takes my hand and brings it to his lips. "I'm happy he had you and Jess," he says.

"I was happy, too. I mean, I always did dream of this romantic love affair with a man who would sweep me off my feet, but I knew what I had with Liam was stable and dependable. At least when he was around. For many years I lived on my own with Jess in a brownstone and then when Liam was killed, Aunt Bee and Uncle Jim said that I should come home to them. I was a mess and I worried how his death would affect Jess. Aunt Bee and Uncle Jim were okay when we first moved in. They weren't demanding of me at all. They gave us free boarding and I bought food but Aunt Bee cooked too," I explain.

"So, what happened? When did things change?" Bennett asks.

I interlace my fingers, feeling uncomfortable and a little stupid for staying in a bad situation for so long.

"It was slow. Aunt Bee would ask me questions about money

that Liam left behind. What type of payout we got from the navy. Stuff like that. I was naïve. I truly thought she was concerned for mine and Jess's future but then slowly, she began to ask about private life-insurance policies. Liam and I had never discussed it. Aunt Bee suggested I hire someone to look into it and they did in fact find a policy."

Bennett hisses. "Why do I not like the sound of this?"

I give him a sympathetic look. "I told myself that they weren't interested in the money. Around the same time, I told Aunt Bee I wanted to go college. She said she'd help me take care of Jess and that felt like such a relief. I was always worried. Kids get sick a lot, and I had no clue what I was doing. Having Aunt Bee around at the beginning was helpful in the sense that I didn't feel so alone," I say. "Now, looking back on it, I see she was like a crutch for me. I leaned on her, but I didn't need her. She didn't even give me any real help, but it was the thought of having someone there for me that eased my anxiety," I say and look at Bennett. I shake my head. "I'm probably not making sense."

"You're making perfect sense, sweetheart. Go on," he says softly.

"Anyway, I went back to school. Life was super busy between studying and raising Jess. Any money that I got from Liam's death I put into a trust for Jess. When Aunt Bee found out, she slowly changed. I'm not a complete idiot," I huff. "I suddenly understood Aunt Bee and Uncle Jim didn't have good intentions, but I was busy, and the thought of moving and having no one didn't sit well with me. Somehow, the years passed, and I found myself stuck in a cycle I didn't know how to break. I got my degree. Began to make good money, and then I told myself I should save to buy a house and in the process, my baby girl grew up and I didn't move forward."

"It's easy to get stuck, Avery. Trust me I've been there. Yeah, I had the navy and the SEALs I worked with are my brothers, but I missed out on so much, too. I think I was scared to find the right woman because that meant commitment. The word alone sent my blood pressure sky-rocketing," he says.

I laugh.

"Commitment meant marriage, which would mean kids. I didn't think I deserved that. I told myself I wouldn't be a good father or husband. Listening to how my brother struggled makes the argument in my head that much stronger," he says.

I sit up and look into his eyes. "Bennett, you've been an amazing boyfriend and you are so good with Jess."

"You didn't let me finish." His lips tilt up in the slightest of smiles that completely melts my heart.

"Sorry." I grin. "You were saying?"

"Before the explosion, I never dreamed I would have what I have with you, but now I can't imagine my life without you and Jessy. It makes me feel guilty that I am getting what was once my brother's, but I feel honored, too. Do you know what I mean?"

Tears fill my vision. "I do. You've been perfect."

"You're my perfect match. That's why. There is no effort involved in loving you. I just feel and act in a way that my heart tells me too. And I hope I can make you happy," he says.

"You make me so, so happy. Always follow your heart, Bennett. I love you," I say, reaching up and pressing my lips to his.

"I love you too, sweetheart." He kisses me back with every fiber of his being. This time when we make love, it isn't rushed. It's two bodies moving together; it's two hearts entwined. After Bennett comes inside me, he falls to my side and gathers me up in his arms.

"We are home, baby," he says.

"I know."

EPILOGUE

Avery

One year and a half later

Bennett and I recently moved to Virginia Beach. It was the right choice for Bennett, Jess and me. Jess and I had nothing holding us back in Jersey, once she graduated high school. Jess is starting at Duke University this fall. She had gotten into Yale but said that she felt like it was more my dream than hers. I never wanted to get in the way of my baby's dreams. She had her heart set on Duke and it's only a three-and-a-half-hour drive so when I'm missing my baby, I can hop in a car and see her and vice versa.

"Mom, you look stunning," Jess says, standing behind me as I look in the mirror.

I take a deep breath. "I seriously thought this day would never come," I say, palming my cheeks.

"Don't do that," Nat says, swatting my hands away. "You'll mess up your makeup."

I place my hands in my lap, feeling so calm and serene. Bennett and I decided to follow tradition and get married at Quinn's grandmother' beach house in Corolla. This place holds special memories for us and this time of year, the view is breathtaking.

There's a light knock on the bedroom door. Catherine, Ashton, Nat and Charlie are all in here with me. They are my bridesmaids while Jess is the maid of honor.

"I'll get it," Charlie says.

The men are downstairs watching the kids, so it must be one of them asking for help.

Charlie opens the door. "You shouldn't be here," she tells Mark.

She begins to close the door, but Mark stops her. "Wait. Avery . . . can we talk?" he asks, his tone serious.

"Um . . . okay," I say, watching him carefully since I know he's a jokester.

"Avery," he begins. "I know you and Bennett are highly against having me officiate the ceremony . . ."

"Oh, for crying out loud," Charlie says, placing each of her hands on her hips. "You need to get over it."

All of us in the room try to hide our smiles. "Thanks, Mark, but Bennett and I have chosen a minister. Is he not here?" My tone rises.

"Geez. What are you doing?" Quinn walks into the room and looks to Mark.

"He's being a troublemaker," Charlie says.

"Is the minister here?" I ask Quinn.

"He is. We are all ready," he says.

Ashton walks up to him and gives him a kiss. Then he takes Mark by the lapel of his suit and drags him from the room.

"No, please . . ." Mark shouts. "It would be a dream come true."

I roll my eyes and Charlie does the same. "I swear he's normal most of the time," she says.

"Okay, let's get this wedding started." Nat claps and orders us all downstairs.

The sun shines across a cerulean sky as I walk down the aisle, barefoot. Quinn is giving me away. It made sense, since him and Bennett are like brothers and Ashton and I have become so close. She is the one who found me my new job working in physical therapy at the local hospital. I love my job, and I can't believe this is my life.

As I walk barefoot in the warm sand toward my soul mate, I truly feel like I belong with these people who have become my family. Jess stands at the altar, waiting for me. Her beautiful blond hair blows in the wind and there's a slight smile on her face. Bennett looks to her and smiles, and then he looks at me and my heart melts. I hold his gaze as I walk toward him. This man completely upturned my life in the best way possible. I wasn't truly living until I met him. I reach him and I notice that his mouth is slightly open. He looks in awe as he takes me in . . .

Bennett

Never in my wildest dreams did I think I would have this life. To find the woman of my dreams and be a father to her child. Being a part of their world has made me feel grounded and wanted. It is now that I know I belong to them and them to me. I was a wanderer before I met them but now, I have a family. We love and cherish each other. We are there for each other, and we know we will never be alone.

The minister begins to officiate the ceremony. I'm in awe. Avery looks like a fairy-tale princess, her hair running down her back in ringlets. Her wide brown eyes are filled with so much love that I'm brought to my knees. Last month, she told me we are expecting. It was the best damn news of my life. I'm going to have a baby.

A warm breeze brushes across my face. I think of Liam Montgomery, my brother. He was taken from this life too soon. I want to believe that he would be honored I am here to care of his family. I want to make sure his memory isn't forgotten.

Avery and I exchange vows, and I thank the powers that be for saving me from the IED explosion, and for giving me a second chance at life and my only chance at love. Avery is it for me, and I plan to make her happy till the end of our days.

After I exchange vows with Avery, I turn to Jess. "I know you are eighteen and an adult already, but I like to think of myself as your dad, and I would love it if you would consider me the same way. So I'm wondering if you'd like to go through an adult adoption?"

"Really?" Her eyes turn so bright that my heart races with love for this kid.

I nod.

"I would love that. I knew something was special about you from the first time Mom brought you over for dinner, but since then, you have been so good to and supportive of me. I'd be honored to be your daughter," she says.

I pull a necklace I bought out of my pocket, and Jess smiles while tears run down Avery's face. I place the necklace around Jess's neck and place a kiss on her cheek. Then I look back to Avery.

"You may kiss the bride," the minister says.

I kiss my bride with everything that I am. I pour my love, my heart and my soul into the kiss. Our friends and their kids cheer in the background.

"I love you," I say to Avery. "You are my forever."

"Forever, baby," Avery says, taking my hand in hers.

"Let's party," Jess shouts, and our guests head back to the house where we have set up a tent with tables, chairs, lots of food and a DJ.

"Toast," Mark shouts two hours later, clinking a fork on his glass.

I turn to everyone. "We're having a baby." The announcement isn't planned but feels right.

Avery slaps my shoulder, then rolls her eyes playfully. Everyone congratulates us, and I look around to see my friends and their children surrounding us with hearts filled with joy and love. I look up to the sky. How did I get so lucky?

THE END

THE SALVATION SOCIETY

Thank you for reading, we hope you enjoyed this Salvation Society novel. Clink on the link below to become a member of the Society and keep up with your beloved SEALs.

Join the Society:

https://www.subscribepage.com/SSsignup

Check out these books in the Salvation Society available now!

Irresistible by R.C. Stephens

Kindred by Kristin Vayden

Legacy by Rachel Robinson

Mended by Gabrielle G.

Reclimation by Evie Graham

Want to see what else is coming from The Salvation Society? Click below for a complete list of titles:

https://www.thesalvationsociety.com/all-books/

BOOKS BY R.C. STEPHENS

Dick: A Bad Boys Novel

Halo: A Military Romance

Mr. All Wrong: A Billionaire Romance

Mr. So Wrong: A Billionaire Romance

Big Stick: A Hockey Rom Com

Butt Ending: A Hockey Rom Com

Dirty Swedish Player: A Hockey Rom Com

The Truth About Us: A Brother's Best Friend Standalone

Deceit: A Small Town Friend's to Lovers Romance

ABOUT THE AUTHOR

R.C. Stephens is a top 100 Amazon bestselling author. She has written ten romance novels and plans to continue to write many more.

When she isn't in her writing cave she is raising three lovely children with her adoring husband.

Her books are filled with humor, heartbreak, emotion and true love.

Born and raised in Toronto, she loves the winter, but Spring and Fall are her favorite seasons.

Keep up with R.C. by signing up to her newsletter-http://rcstephens.com/newsletter/

Made in the USA
Las Vegas, NV
04 November 2020